DOOM RIDER

DAVID GATWARD

Hodder
Children's
Books

A division of Hachette Children's Books

ISBN: 978 1 444 90769 8

Typeset in ITC Officinia Sans by Avon DataSet Ltd,
Bidford on Avon, Warwickshire

Printed and bound in Great Britain by
CPI Group (UK) Ltd, Croydon, CR0 4YY

The paper and board used in this paperback by Hodder Children's Books
are natural recyclable products made from wood grown in
sustainable forests. The manufacturing processes conform to the
environmental regulations of the country of origin.

Hodder Children's Books
a division of Hachette Children's Books
338 Euston Road, London NW1 3BH
An Hachette UK company
www.hachette.co.uk

For Su, Elijah and Gabriel. Just because . . .

'And I saw, and behold a white horse:
and he that sat on him had a bow;
and a crown was given unto him:
and he went forth conquering,
and to conquer.'

Revelations 6:2, King James Bible

'If the Apocalypse comes, beep me.'

Buffy the Vampire Slayer

PROLOGUE

Thirty-two years ago . . .

IN EXACTLY THREE MINUTES the boy would be dead.

'Who are you?' he stuttered, desperately looking for a way to escape, whipping his head round like a trapped animal. 'I don't understand! What do you want?'

It was a dark night, the kind where blackness oozes across the world like oil. The boy was soaked to the skin and couldn't stop shivering.

He was caught down a stinking, dark alleyway between a derelict apartment block and a row of tumbledown garages. It reeked of stale urine. Only one garage still retained its metal door. Hanging by its hinges, it creaked and groaned in the wind like it was in pain. The air smelled

 1

of muck and wet concrete, as rain pounded it into submission, sending up tiny crowns of dirt.

The boy yelled out again, but the dark silhouettes in front and behind didn't budge. They just stood there, two thick slabs of dark like great man-shaped holes hollowed out of the stormy night.

He couldn't even see their faces. Not just because of the night and the storm and the rain seeping from his hair into his eyes, but because they were all masked. Little more than a patchwork of stitched leather, all that was visible was their eyes staring through jagged holes, their mouths just a rough slash.

A sound like a poker being pulled out of a blacksmith's fire made the boy snap round to face two more shadows. Both were holding long and heavy swords. Against one shadow, he might have stood a chance at slipping away like a fox into the night, finding somewhere to hide until morning. Two would have made it difficult. But four made it impossible.

The clouds shifted a little and a shard of moonlight fell to the ground. Before it shattered into a thousand raindrops, it caught the blades of the men's swords, and the boy stumbled at the sight. These were nasty things with edges serrated like a shark's smile, designed to rip and tear as well as slash and slice. They were more like saws than swords.

Voiceless, the shadows closed in.

Panic squeezed the boy's heart. Blood thumped round his body, banged in his ears. One final, desperate yell tore from his throat like a wolf's howl, and he gave up on escape and went on the attack. He grabbed a broken brick, threw it with everything he had inside him – every moment of every day he'd ever lived – and watched it soar through the air . . . only to be swatted to the ground like a fly. The boy dropped to his knees and tore into the dirt to find another brick – anything to use as a weapon – but a gloved hand squeezed the back of his neck. It picked him up like a wounded rabbit.

The boy fought against the hand as it lifted him, his toes scraping at the ground only to find air. The hand held him high for the four dark figures to see.

A figure stepped forward. It pulled to one side its long, brown cloak, revealing a chest plate. With a gloved hand it unclipped two clasps welded over the heart. Two small stones fell from behind the clasps into the shadow's hand.

'Please . . .' mumbled the boy.

Another of the figures stepped forward, took the stones, and raised them into the air in a clenched fist. It muttered words. The boy didn't understand them.

The figure lowered the hand, opened it, nodded. All the boy could see was that the stones were smooth and had odd markings scratched into them: a strange black mark, like an ancient tribal tattoo, pierced right through with an arrow. The figure then leaned in so close to the boy that he could smell the mask it was wearing and see the black pupils in its eyes like dark, still pools in a cave.

'I . . . I ain't done nothing wrong!' said the boy, his voice cracked and broken. 'Not to no one! I promise!'

'But you will, boy,' the figure said, its voice calm, collected. 'And like the others, you must die.'

But the boy wasn't listening any more. He'd spotted something in the distance. For a moment he was sure he could see, like a phantom momentarily solid in the sad light of the moon, an emotionless face watching him. Then it was gone and a flutter of movement showed him a lonesome raven sitting on a beaten, broken road sign.

For a split second, the boy knew he'd caught its eye, that he and the bird were one. Then, as the shadows lifted their blades high above his neck, the raven let out a single caw, took to the wing.

And was gone.

I

SETH'S POCKET BUZZED AND he pulled out his mobile phone. It was the daily quote from the Bible. A few words of wisdom sent out to the population by The Way.

'And I will rid the world of prophets who pollute the air with their ill words . . .'

Religion was everywhere, thought Seth with a sigh. Even in his jeans.

Seth deleted the message and was half tempted to slam-dunk the thing into the nearest bin. But a shout snared him to a stop. He shoved the phone back into his pocket. In the distance music rumbled from the festival main stage.

'Hey, freak-en-stein!'

Seth didn't rise to it because he'd heard it all before.

Like they can talk, he thought, staring at the group now laughing at him from the safety of the shadows, dancing about like fashion-conscious clowns in their patchwork clothing and bodypaint and dreads. He could hear the dull ringing of the charms hanging round their necks and wrists. The moon was high tonight, the sky clear.

'What's with the cape?'

Something glanced off Seth's shoulder and thumped down at his feet. An empty beer bottle. Automatically, he raised his hand to his ear, rubbed its ragged edge between finger and thumb, and remembered the pain, the blood. This time he'd been lucky. Other times, not so. His torn ear was only one of the scars he bore. And it wasn't the worst.

Seth gritted his teeth and kept walking, his hand burning now from the soup he'd just bought from a food stall selling everything from samosas to hotdogs. The cup itself was hideously adorned with a picture of a man smiling. It was a face Seth, and indeed everyone, recognized because it was impossible to go anywhere without seeing it on a sticker or a billboard or during the adverts on television. Seth was sure he'd even seen it on fruit boxes. It was The Protector, the head of The Way, and he was everywhere. To Seth the smile looked sneaky, like The Protector was trying to hide something, perhaps even while the photograph had been taken. Well, he'd enjoy crushing the cup when he'd finished the soup.

Glastonbury was the biggest festival of them all, and

the ground shook with the rhythmic dancing of the masses. Thousands were gathered here in search of enlightenment and salvation. It was the music that drew them, but God that they came to find, or at least their version of it.

All life is here, thought Seth and more than anything he wanted to be in the thick of it: close to the bands, close enough to have the music rattle his bones, right in amongst the sweat and the mud and the tattoos and the girls . . .

But he'd never got close. Not even once. Of that his parents had made sure. And as for the girls? As soon as they found out what he did, what his family had always done here and at every other festival, they were out of there – like he wasn't just diseased but contagious. The cape was just another nail in an already well-sealed coffin.

Another shout, but it quickly crumbled into giggles and was gone. At least no more bottles had been thrown at him, thought Seth as he walked off, his hands clasping the soup close to help keep him warm against the chill wind.

The festival was a fantasy world of religious searching and celebration, of music and fashion and dance, and Seth did his best to ignore it as he made his way forward. But it was almost impossible to move five paces without bumping into someone pushing a new pathway to enlightenment, giving out free copies of *The Book*, preaching from a soap box, trying to save your soul through the magic of music. Or avoid The Protector, his face fluttering high above the festival on vast prayer flags as he mediated for the masses with God.

Seth eventually managed to escape the main crowds and was back out in the festival fringe amongst the many sideshows he'd grown up around. It was colder here, like the icy blast from an open freezer. Finishing his soup, Seth crushed the cup, smiling as the face of The Protector crumpled as if it was in a vice, and threw the cup into a bin. It bounced off the bin's edge and landed on the ground. Seth couldn't be bothered to pick it up and made to head off.

A figure glided out of the dark shadows and slunk from between a mismatched collection of tents, all leaning against each other like happy drunks.

'Excuse me . . .'

Seth stopped. He clocked a gleam of silver, caught in the light cast by a fire burning close by. The figure, a man, was wearing large silver bracelets on his wrists. He was wiping something from his hands.

Brilliant, a cleric, thought Seth. *Just what I need*.

The man finished wiping his hands and held up Seth's discarded cup.

'A little careless, don't you think?' said the cleric, stepping forward.

Seth was good at avoiding the fully paid-up members of The Way. Not just normal followers, the clerics were twenty-four/seven disciples. They were everywhere, trying to save souls – and spying, not that they'd ever admit to it.

'My fault,' said Seth. He didn't want any trouble and walked over to take the cup. He noticed that the cleric's hands weren't completely clean, despite the wiping. Though he couldn't be completely sure in the light, Seth had a horrible sense that it was blood.

The man kept hold of the cup and slowly uncrumpled it. 'You know who this is?'

Seth glanced at the cup despite knowing exactly what the cleric was referring to. He heard a whimpering from where the man had come from. What exactly had he been doing back there?

'The Protector,' said Seth, then added, 'May he always keep us safe.'

It wasn't the law to use the phrase, but Seth knew as well as anyone that to not do so in the presence of a cleric simply made them suspicious.

The cleric nodded. 'Then you are a believer in The Way?'

'Who isn't?' Seth answered cryptically.

The cleric smiled, glancing back from where he'd appeared moments earlier. 'All can be persuaded,' he said.

The smile, thought Seth, *would've better suited the scaly face of a snake*.

The cleric stepped closer and handed him the cup. Seth caught sight of his hands again. Definitely blood.

'Can I assume you are not as careless with your beliefs as you are with your detritus?'

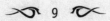

9

Seth nodded, taking the cup. But the cleric didn't let go.

'The Protector watches over us,' he said. 'His are the eyes of God.'

Seth nodded once more. This cleric was creeping him out now. It was his job, Seth knew that, but over a cup? He was taking his role way too seriously.

'I'll be more careful,' said Seth.

The cleric's smile grew just a little, curling up at the corners. To Seth it looked like he was sizing him up for a bite.

'Yes,' said the cleric, 'I know you will.'

And with that, the cleric nodded, turned, and slipped back into the shadows. Seth heard the whimpering again, then silence.

He spent a few moments gathering himself. Seth knew the clerics were everywhere, like biological CCTV cameras for The Way, always watching, but he'd never run into one at a festival before. It struck him as odd, but thinking about it would get him nowhere but more paranoid. He had more important things on his mind. He placed the soup cup in the bin, double-checked the cleric had gone, and continued on his way.

Dressed all in black, his jeans ripped and ragged, Seth looked like a splinter of night out on the prowl. Down his back hung the idiotic and threadbare cape that had drawn the insults, the hood pulled up over his head to hide his face in shadow. The oily smell of stage make-up clung to his nostrils like the reek of fish on the worn hands of a trawler man.

Seth was standing in the wings of a makeshift stage that was little more than a few collapsible wooden boxes pushed up against the side of the caravan he'd called home his whole life. Hidden in shadow, Seth watched for what seemed like the millionth time the travelling prophecy show that made what his parents laughably called their living. Barely had it ever been able to put enough food on the table.

Doom Night – it made his skin crawl to witness it yet again, like ants weren't just on his skin, but burrowing beneath it and setting up home.

Seth had decided long ago that life with a travelling family freak show of fortune-tellers was no life at all. And about as cool as socks and sandals. Which was why, in less than an hour's time, he was out of here. He was doing a runner with the money he'd managed to save, a bag of spare clothes and a sleeping bag he'd stashed out of sight backstage, and no goodbyes for his parents or sister.

He couldn't wait.

Not that he had a plan of where to go or for how long. But he needed to get away and find his own direction, or at least give himself a bit of breathing space to find out what he wanted to do with the rest of his life. The show, with its shabby costumes and even shabbier stage, was all he'd ever known, and he needed to leave it far behind. The festival circuit was as wide and as deep as the ocean, and Seth guessed he could swim in it for a while safe and anonymous, drift unnoticed like flotsam on the waves. His parents would worry for a while (Beth, not so much) but he'd get word to them that he was fine and would see them around sooner or later. It wasn't much of a plan, but it was better than his current every-night's-a-performance life. It had to be.

A figure brushed past in the gloom: Beth. At fifteen Seth's sister was three years his senior. She was all but hidden behind jet-black hair so long it swung to her hips like curtains draped across a stage. When she got angry, it would hang over her face like iron railings round a graveyard. Her ice-white dress, gathered round her in ill-fitting folds and matching her pale skin, made her look like a spectre.

'Watch it!' she hissed.

'Watch what? You're the one in a rush!'

Beth paused to look daggers at her brother.

Seth said nothing. Most times, he and Beth got on all right, but when it came to the show, they were like cat and dog.

'You can't just go wandering off!' said Beth. 'If Dad finds out, he'll kill you! Your trouble is you like risk, don't you? That little bit of danger in your life, right? Well, if you ask me, it's stupid.'

Seth didn't respond. She had a point though about the danger. What was life if there wasn't a little bit of risk to make it interesting?

'It wouldn't hurt you to take this seriously.'

'Who says I don't?'

'I do!' whispered Beth, leaning in closer, her eyes widening. 'And don't go thinking that I haven't noticed that you're up to something. And when I find out what it is, I'll—'

'You'll what?' Seth snapped Beth's sentence in two like bone-dry kindling. 'Not give me a birthday present? The last one was rubbish anyway.'

Seth hoped Beth hadn't worked out what he was actually planning. If she was suspicious, his parents might well have noticed something too. And that would be bad. 'Anyway, I'm not afraid of you! Or Mum! Or Dad!'

'You should be!' barked Beth, eyes wide like huge cat's-eyes glinting in the headlights of a car racing through the dark. 'And as for your impending birthday, well, if that's the way you feel about it then I won't even bother!' She went to say something else but her attention was caught by her dad on stage.

'Best hurry up,' said Seth jabbing a finger to point behind her. 'The fun's about to start.'

Beth spun on her heels and hurried off, the long dress billowing out around her like the sails of a ship. Part of Seth wished that they didn't have to argue so much. But that's just what brothers and sisters did. And they were good at it.

Seth caught the aroma of meat cooking on a grill drifting in from somewhere out on the festival field. It mingled with the strange smells of the night, of animals and diesel and tobacco smoke and booze, the reek of a world he'd soon leave behind – for good or bad he didn't care, he just had to get out.

Around him in the dark, scattered along the outskirts of the festival, Seth glanced at the other caravans presenting their own shows, punters milling around them like tired bees hovering by the hive. Most were pulled by vans or trucks, though a few were hauled by horse. Seth almost felt sorry for them as he stared at their custom paint jobs, all of them covered in lurid displays of religious imagery and mashed-up advertising.

Seth read a giant bumper sticker on a large four-wheel drive: *If going to church makes you a believer does going to a garage make you a car?* When he drew closer to the vehicle he spotted, hanging inside the truck's cabin, a large plastic fob with the picture of The Protector's face grinning out into the world.

The truck was towing a caravan that looked like it had survived numerous crashes. The small stage set up alongside it was covered in less than tactful placards and billboards, all promising that no matter what you were doing, God probably really hated it, and that you were in serious trouble unless you confessed to your sins *right now*. Seth noticed that those holding the placards were also asking for donations. Redemption was as much a commodity as anything else these days.

When it came down to it most were nothing but religious freak shows and Seth had no urge to go and waste his time seeing any of their acts. Fire-eaters and acrobats and herbalists and tattooists and sages and seers and preachers and teachers . . .

Occasionally, a roar from a crowd would rumble across and Seth would wonder what had impressed them this time. Another vision? A prophecy? A miracle even? But he'd seen and heard them all a thousand times over. Nothing was going to change his mind about any of it.

Then he heard the gasp of the crowd gathered round his father's makeshift stage.

Seth rolled his eyes and checked his watch.

Yep, right on time . . .

2

SETH WATCHED HIS DAD have another one of his spiritual fits as smoke started to spill and tumble across the stage from a small machine controlled by Beth. Oh sure, he claimed they were real. Even the tears and the screaming and the weird voices. To Seth it was little more than the well-rehearsed theatrics of a seasoned performer.

Yet for the crowds it was all convincing stuff. They loved it, particularly his dad's groupies, who always pushed to the front, their eyes wide in wonder. The ones who'd attend every show they could, read about him in the papers and leave notes for him under the caravan door to thank him for helping to keep the end of the world at bay.

The End of the World . . .

Seth shook his head. That anyone believed the end of

the world could be foretold, even prevented, made no sense. That it was pretty much a national pastime made it even worse. Which was why he kept his views to himself. If you didn't believe, you didn't belong. Seth remembered the cleric he'd met earlier, the blood on his hands, the sound of broken whimpering in the dark.

Seth breathed deep and his stomach tightened. This was the moment he'd been waiting for. With Beth and his dad occupied on stage and his mum reading someone's future inside the caravan, he could grab his stuff and disappear. He'd even sabotaged the truck his dad managed to keep going to pull the caravan, so his dad couldn't come after him.

Seth slipped away from the side of the stage, hidden by the thick, cheap, red velvet curtains, which hung like a huge spill of blood frozen in time. His mum, a woman famous for her divination skills with anything from cards to candle wax, had made them. The tacky gold tassels and the strange symbols that decorated the material were her attempt to give the show a little pizzazz. The frayed edges rested like thin, skeletal fingers across the stage as though reaching out for the audience. On the stage itself, Seth could still see his father and the wooden lectern, carved to look like someone stooping forward and carrying a vast, flat stone upon their back. On this stone, as always, rested *The Book*.

The Book . . .

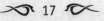

Seth had read it, not that he'd had much choice. Despite being home-schooled, his parents had made sure he didn't miss out on what every other kid was learning at school. They'd gone that extra mile though, made sure he'd committed most of it to memory, could quote it automatically. But then in his parents' minds, it had been all the education he'd needed. Seth disagreed and had done his best to learn other stuff in secret and discover the world. His parents had found out and given him a hiding more than once. It had done no good.

Edging around the caravan and now in almost total darkness Seth dropped to his knees and reached under the stage, expecting to find the bag he'd packed straight away.

He didn't.

Panic seized him as his hand scrambled left and right. Nothing. Where was it?

Had Beth found him out after all? It was like a kick to the stomach. And he'd been on the receiving end of his dad's temper enough times to know that if his father got wind of this, there'd be hell to pay.

'Seth?'

He froze. 'Mum?'

What was she doing here? Why wasn't she in the caravan?

'What are you doing, love?'

Seth's voice stuck in his throat. She'd called him *love*: he was in trouble.

'Dropped something,' he said, his hand still searching.

'You mean you weren't looking for this?'

Seth went cold like iced water had been thrown over him. His mum was holding his bag.

'Look, Mum—' he began, rushing to his feet, desperately trying to think of a decent excuse and coming up blank.

'Clothes, sleeping bag,' said his mum, interrupting. 'If I was to think the worst, Seth, I'd say you were planning on going somewhere.'

'It's not what you think . . .'

But it was, wasn't it?

'Then what is it, love?'

That word again! Only this time she sounded like she was trying to spit a bad taste from her mouth.

Seth didn't know what to do next. All that planning for nothing! Anger bubbled inside him, twisting his stomach even tighter.

A shocked scream burst from the crowd. Through a crack in the curtains Seth saw his father grab at his shirt, rip it open and then, with a blood-curdling yell, throw himself backwards to stumble off the stage.

But it didn't take his father more than a moment to get back on his feet and turn round to face him.

'Come here, Seth.'

Seth stayed put. Dad knew too? Oh God . . .

'Don't make me fetch you like a dog!'

Reluctantly, and scared now, Seth edged forward. His

mum backed away to stand by his dad, handing over Seth's bag.

'You've some explaining to do, lad.'

'Look, Dad—' began Seth, but a thick hand caught him sharp across the side of his head.

'Don't you dare "Look, Dad" me!'

Seth gagged at his dad's stale breath, a result of too much coffee and not enough toothpaste.

'We'll talk about this later, but for now, this is what I think of whatever it was you were planning . . .'

Seth watched helplessly as his dad ripped the bag open, tipped out the contents, and ground them into the dirt. Then, with a nod to Seth's mum, he pulled himself back into character, stumbled up on to the stage, and collapsed dramatically to the stage floor with a thud, like a felled tree.

His mum grabbed Seth's arm like he was a naughty child who couldn't be trusted. On stage, his dad was now writhing around as if he was wrestling with some great and invisible python. Of all the ways to make a living, this one had always seemed to Seth to be so utterly undignified and wrong. But it hadn't been forced on his dad; he'd chosen it. Or, as he'd often said, *it* had chosen *him*. Seth, though, had never been able to understand how this could ever be classed as a calling, something ordained by God.

Beth walked on to the stage, knelt down, and mopped

her father's brow with the care of a seasoned nurse. Once he was calm, she stood up and backed off stage like a spectre.

The audience rippled with excitement. Then, as Seth's father rose to his feet, the prophesying began . . .

Seth blocked out his dad's voice, closing his mind to it, like a door slammed shut. It soon became nothing more than background noise, the dull rumble of thunder over a far-off hill.

In a few minutes, it would be the highlight of the show, the bit everyone came to see, the bit Seth had hoped to be on his way before.

The stage shuddered and Seth glanced over to see his dad flat on his back again, his clothes so utterly drenched in sweat that they'd left a damp patch on the wooden boards. Beth, as she did every night, dashed out to check on him, lifting him gently up for the audience to see. To the sound of uproarious applause his father then stood up, clasped his hands together against his chest and, with tears falling, mouthed thank you to the crowd as Beth led him carefully from the stage as though afraid he would collapse once more. Seth, of course, knew that he wouldn't.

Seth caught his dad's eyes.

'Good show, Dad.'

'Shut it, son!' his dad snapped back, the act killed the moment he'd stepped off the stage into the dark safety behind the curtains. 'You're still in trouble, you hear? So get out there and make it up to me!'

Seth bit his lip and made to leave for the stage, but his father's hand caught his shoulder and spun him back round. Seth almost lost his balance with the force of it.

'Don't go giving any of those warm, cuddly visions, neither! They don't draw the crowd. People want a show!' his dad growled, jabbing his chest with the end of a hard finger as if he was trying to punch a hole. 'Give 'em what they want! The end of the world! Hell and damnation! Now, get out there and finish this proper!'

Seth wasn't given a chance to answer as his dad's thick hand, like a great slab of meat, caught him round the back of the head and sent him half tripping on to the stage.

Seth stared out from the thick, musty darkness of his hood. People were pointing at him, nodding towards the stage, their eyes wide with anticipation for what they would hear. The air was filled with hushed whispers.

Slowly, Seth slipped his hood from his head. His hair, cropped short and the colour of dark chocolate, brushed against his hands as he let the hood fall across his shoulders. Out of the corner of his eye, he caught sight of his mum, dad and Beth in the wings. They were all holding hands. And watching.

Raising his eyes to the crowd Seth caught the excitement in their eyes, could almost sense it burning the air around him, lighting him up like a spiritual firework. He grinned like a cat with a mouse snared under its paw. Then, with his voice as loud and clear as a church bell calling the faithful, he called out, 'I am the Apocalypse Boy!'

3

THE ONLY THING LILY remembered about her family was the placards. And she wasn't really sure that she truly remembered them at all.

Pushing through the festival crowds, Lily's feet splashed through the muddy ruts and dips and holes that littered the fields like traps. With the air of someone trained to ignore the temptation of junk food and palm readers and trinkets and psychics and souvenirs and everything else bombarding her senses that night, she tried to think back to her life before she'd been given away at the age of four by her parents; that moment when they'd driven her to an airport somewhere in the US and handed her over to two strangers, a man and a woman. They'd walked out of her life for good and not even waved goodbye. (Oddly, that was the one thing she really did remember.) Their faces and voices did not feature in her memory at all, but something deep down told her that they'd viewed her with distaste. She had a sense they had been desperate to be rid of her.

Those early years were a blank page in Lily's mind. According to the pictures she'd seen, she had proudly carried huge sheets of card emblazoned with words of fire and brimstone and judgement on anyone and everyone not following The Way as her parents had preached it. But all she could find in her mind was a torn scrapbook of fading photographs. And each time she opened it, she recognized fewer of them.

Ten years was a long, long time. Her memories had become all jumbled up with the pictures and the newsreels and what people had told her. It was hard to untangle what she really recalled from the strands of what she actually thought she did.

A shout jolted Lily, and she woke to reality as if it were an alien world. Her surroundings shot into focus, making her dizzy. Caught off guard, Lily did what she always did to refocus her mind on what she was really here to do, and reached up to her left shoulder to scratch it, though over time it had become more of a habit than a necessity.

The source of the shout was a preacher standing a head and shoulders above the crowd thanks to a battered, wooden box under his feet. It was covered in tourist stickers of places far off. A flimsy board was nailed to a pole to hang over the preacher's head. On it the words *R U Gonna Spend Eternity Smoking or Non-Smoking?* did their best to grab the attention of passers-by.

The sight of the preacher reminded Lily of why she was here, what she was searching for – or to use the term that had been drilled into her over the years: *tracking*.

The preacher was dressed like so many others she had seen, met, spoken to and followed, wearing weather-worn clothes that would be better off lining an old dog's kennel than covering a man's back. A cross was hung round his neck. But then so were half a dozen other faith and belief emblems, all tangled together in an impossible knot like they'd met at a convention and all got on a little too well.

There was no doubting the preacher's belief in each and every word he was expressing. And that was something Lily could at least understand, she thought. To some degree anyway. They weren't so different, the preacher and her, both following a cause. As to which was the right one (perhaps they each were in some way), well, that was the trillion-dollar question, wasn't it?

Lily made to turn from the preacher, but he'd already spotted her.

'So who do you think rules the world, kid?'

Lily said nothing. The preacher's accent was like something out of a blender. It was a colourful mix of dialects and tones picked up from a life obviously spent on the road. She recognized some of them, though at their heart was one that reminded her of home, a faint Yankee drawl that almost made her warm to him. Almost.

'Tough question, ain't it? Or is it that you just don't know the answer?'

Still Lily was silent. The preacher was clearly someone used to getting his point across by attacking, riling people up into responding. Part of her wondered if it was a con; The Way had a habit of employing good actors to play the field as followers of many religions. It helped them track what was going on at a grass roots level. And it creeped out Lily more than a little. But anyway, her task was to observe. Opening her mouth had consequences. Now was not the time. Not yet.

The preacher wasn't giving up. Behind him, a dozen people passed by, all chanting, all carrying dreamcatchers. They looked happy at least, thought Lily, wondering if those things in their hands, like elaborate spiders' webs, worked at all, catching the nightmares and allowing only the good dreams through.

'This world's burning, not blooming, right? Only have to check out the news to realize how things have gone from bad to worse to a full-on storm of death and destruction and despair!' A wild grin. 'Like that!'

The preacher clicked his fingers and a burst of flame exploded from his hand, reflected in his wild eyes like a fire in a window. Lily noticed some of the people round her stop at this, stare a little. She didn't react. She had seen it all before. Nothing but a cheap conjuror's trick. Effective though, she had to admit.

The preacher didn't give Lily a chance to respond, even if she'd wanted to. And now with a few others listening in, he kicked it up a gear. It was time for faith in the fast lane.

'Earthquakes, right? Tsunamis? Famine? You all know what I'm talking about, don't you? Don't you!'

A few nods and mutters of approval served as dry wood to the preacher's hungry evangelical fire.

'Poverty? Financial meltdown? People striving and striving – and for what? A better car that's gonna get repossessed? A future for their children when there ain't one to be had? What's the point?'

More people were listening now. Tree-hugging hippies with half-asleep children strapped to their chest. Followers of The Invisible Good, all wearing as little as possible and carrying baskets of pocket-sized first-aid kits to give away. Born-agains with their cool-to-be-religious T-shirts and *What Would Jesus Do?* wristbands. Gaia's groupies, decked in clothes of sewn bark and leaves to become more at one with the true spirit of Mother Earth. The orthodox and unorthodox, the fundamentalists and not-so-sures. If it could be believed in, followed or prayed to, evidence of it was here, thought Lily, and she liked that, despite her own personal reasons for being there. It was always fun to hear where an argument was going, what crazed back alley it was about to stumble down, drunk on its own peculiar blend of ignorance and arrogance.

The preacher was still shouting.

'No wonder we've got riots, people looting to get what others already have, communities breaking down, blood on the streets!'

From the few gathered round came calls of 'Hell, yeah!' and 'You got that right, brother!'

'The world needs cleansing, people! And it's all leading up to that final conflagration! A great flood of destruction that'll wipe this planet clean of its filth!'

Even more agreement now. Lily had to work hard to not just shake her head and walk off. The preacher had a point though; the world really was in a mess, or at least it seemed to be. But hadn't it always been? Was it not just a case of more people, less space, and one great, big, fat game of Chinese whispers gone nuts on digital technology and the World Wide Web?

It didn't matter. People were grasping at anything to give them a sense of hope. Which again was something The Way exploited. And it worked.

'Who here knows even just a little of what I'm talking about?' the preacher yelled, sweat flying from him as his excitement boiled over like a kettle left on the hob too long. 'Who here knows of the truth about Naribu?'

And there it was, smiled Lily. One of the classics.

The great and mysterious Planet X supposedly on a collision course with Earth. It almost needed its own corny theme tune.

Lily had heard enough. She'd read the Sumerian texts. She knew pretty much all there was to know about every single apocalyptic, end-of-the-world, Armageddon-loving prophecy, theory, or story that had ever been thought up by humanity during its brief time of existence. She had to admit that Naribu had always been one of her favourites, but she had other things on her mind now.

Lily turned from the preacher, still scratching her shoulder, and forced herself to focus. Her eyes strayed to one of the giant prayer flags high above the crowds, and to the face of The Protector. Unlike most at the festival, Lily had met him. And she knew very well that he didn't always smile like that.

The phantom itch was covered by her clothing. It was a mark in black ink that had brought tears to her eyes when it had been etched into her skin. The pain had been unbearable, like a red-hot scalpel cutting deep. But she'd endured it because she'd believed – unquestioningly at the time – that taking the mark was the right thing to do. It was a divine calling to wear it. A black tattoo pierced by an arrow, representing the barriers in life the wearer had broken through to achieve true enlightenment and communion with God. The mark of The Way.

Lily closed her eyes against the tingle of the cold north

wind on her cheeks. It sent a shiver through her and pulled at the hairs on the back of her neck like a thousand angry tweezers. The air itself was flavoured with so much humanity that she could almost put out her tongue and taste it.

All of life was here. A concoction of hotdogs and onions and burgers and chips, coffee and beer and smoke and fire, sweat and mud and soul.

It was time to get to work.

Lily had never been to the Glastonbury Festival before. She'd been sent out on plenty of other trips, spent days and weeks and months living the life of a human bloodhound, seen her fair share of the festivals where religions were on show and the music mixed with the prayers like a great, wondrous cocktail that, if you drank deep enough, would have you buzzing and spinning for eternity. But never to the one festival all the others were measured against. And it was here, she knew for certain, in this bizarre, alien, light-and-sound-and-sense-filled patch of green in the Somerset downs, that her life would at last have some true meaning.

Something caught her attention. It was right at the edge of her sense spectrum and anyone normal would've missed it. But she caught it, recognized it and followed it, like a radio finding a channel in a world of static.

With each step Lily checked her bearing. If the signal grew weak, she turned till it became strong again and walked another step. And with each footfall she drew ever closer to the very reason she was here. A reason that, if word got out, would give her so few hours to live she'd have trouble making it to the exit gates.

Ahead, a crowd had gathered. It was bigger than some of the others she'd seen, and she sensed anticipation in the air. It was as though the people were waiting for something they knew was worth it, something they had travelled for miles and miles to come and see.

Lily edged closer, her senses going crazy now as she slipped unnoticed into the fringes of the growing crowd. She started to make her way forward, like a tiger creeping through the grass towards its prey.

At the front of the crowd was a makeshift stage, fringed with red velvet curtains that she could see, even at this distance, had seen better days.

The man on the stage was ranting, but his words were clear and compelling and hooked his audience like a fishing pro. He was clearly building up to a big finale, and it was that which Lily now knew was what had drawn her here. The thought of it made her heart race. Usually, in these moments, the cold sense of dread would threaten to engulf her, the knowledge that death was only a few heartbeats away. But this time adrenalin was charging through her veins like fire in zero gravity. She was taking a deliberate step into the unknown. It thrilled her. And terrified her.

On the stage the man had tumbled on to his back and

was now being lifted up by a girl in a white dress with astonishingly long hair. The crowd erupted, arms were thrust into the air to applaud and wave. Then the man, hands together against his chest, was led carefully off the stage by the girl.

Of all the things Lily had ever known in her life, she knew more than anything that what faced her now was her moment, her chance to do something about everything that had come before.

This was it.

She'd lost count of the number of people, the number of *children*, she'd seen murdered for the supposed good of all. But that was all about to change. It had to. And it was all down to her.

From the darkness sitting in the wings a figure stepped on to the stage and slowly slipped back the hood hiding its face. The crowd hushed to whispers.

Lily breathed deep.

4

THE CROWD ERUPTED, SCREAMS and cheers and applause bubbling and boiling together like a witch's brew. Seth choked back a laugh with a cough to clear his throat. Not because he thought the people in front of him were foolish (even if many of them, in his opinion, were), but because there was no denying the thrill of putting on a good show.

The sound of someone muttering a prayer drew Seth's eyes and he spotted the individual. It was a beautiful girl, with hair so blonde that when it caught the light it shone like gold, her hand in the air as though throwing something towards him (the holy spirit probably). He waited for her to finish but as she did, a man at the front of the crowd cheered so loudly that his voice broke, turning a great lion-like roar into little more than a cross between a budgie's cheep-cheep and a smoker's hacking cough. But that didn't stop the man waving his hands like crazy and, in his high-pitched, ruined voice, trying to call for Seth's attention.

Seth stared at the man for a moment, nodded in his well-rehearsed, thoughtful way, and then turned his gaze elsewhere. He would come back to the man if he had to but something told him tonight was going to be special. He'd always been able to read a crowd with such accuracy that most times he could play them with the ease of a professional conductor. And tonight he would orchestrate such a symphony of doom and destruction that, if he did manage to escape as he'd planned, people would talk about him for the rest of their lives.

Seth couldn't remember exactly how the Apocalypse Boy had all begun, though he'd first started copying his father as soon as he'd learned to speak. With an above-average, active imagination and a young boy's fierce determination to win his father's approval, Seth had embellished a little, added stuff to his dad's visions and made them his own. Without realizing it, he'd developed a natural talent for cold reading, convincing those who came to hear him that he knew more about pretty much any subject given than was in any way possible. It was almost uncanny, to the point that Seth soon started to believe in it himself. What had started out as a fun way to impress his dad quickly became very, very serious – and his father had encouraged it. He'd told Seth it would make him a better prophet in the end, allow him to uncover the real and the unreal in mankind's future. And Seth had not only believed his dad, but quickly come to believe that he was special, that he could foretell people's future, that he could see things others could not.

Closing his eyes hard enough to see sparks flare in the comforting darkness inside his skull, Seth took a deep breath. Despite his ruined plans, this was still going to be his last night. He was going to make it one to remember.

Seth's first believer that night was as obvious to him as a banana on an apple tree. She was old, yet her wrinkled face radiated with such vibrancy and life it was as though she'd come to the decision to burn her remaining time more fiercely then she'd ever done before, like she was desperate not just to make the most of what she had left, but to have it count for something. Her eyes were bright and searching, like the single, sweeping orb of a lighthouse. Seth knew that the way to really get a show stoked up and blazing was to lay on some big hope for a little nobody. He also knew that when he asked for a volunteer, this old girl's hand would be up quick enough to snap off. And volunteers were good. They wanted to believe. Desperately.

Seth opened his eyes wide, allowed them to look a little wild, then called out the question they were all desperate to hear: 'Who of you will dare hear their end?'

And there was the hand!

Seth slipped slowly across the stage towards the old woman until he was facing out across a swaying mass of faces desperate for him to speak to them and tell them something of their own future (or lack of it in most cases). That was something that had always intrigued Seth: the fact that, despite giving out positive prophecies, what had made him his name was the dark twist he brought to what he did.

Making someone's future rosy and bright was one thing and easy as hell. But to fill it with a great and terrible and violent end that would shock even the most hardened horror-movie addict? Now, that was something worth talking about! And that's exactly what the people did.

It didn't take long for news of Seth the Apocalypse Boy to spread, a nickname he hadn't asked for, but it had stuck nonetheless. He'd even heard that some people were coming to hear him as a dare, pushed into it by their mates to see if they had the spine to face up to their own end. And hadn't he heard that someone else had started up a fan site on the Web? Seth had followers from all over the world. It was a fame he couldn't wait to leave behind for good. But there was still tonight to get through so he opened his eyes owl-wide and stared down at the woman. He crouched down (it always worked well to get down to the level of those who'd come to see him, a trick he'd learned from his dad). Raising his left hand, he beckoned her over. 'I'm Seth,' he said, but in such a way that he was also asking the woman to give him her name. Which gave him a chance to quickly check her for visual clues – anything that would tell him something about her.

'I'm Alice,' said the woman, beaming like a light had been flicked on behind her face. 'And I'm eighty-one years old tomorrow!'

The crowd cheered and as one fell into the palm of Seth's hand. He knew he'd struck gold.

Seth reached out and, without any resistance at all, Alice raised her hands to his. In those few moments, Seth quickly learned all he really needed to know about her. It wasn't difficult – well, not for him at least: practice makes perfect. He knew her age now and, from the moment he'd spotted her, could see that she was going all out to live it up in her twilight years. She looked fit, not just from her shape, which was more upright and muscled than a woman twenty or perhaps even thirty years younger, but from her footwear – expensive trainers that were clearly not just for show – and the health magazine poking its way out the top of her handbag. She was wearing a necklace from which dangled a beautifully crafted swirl of milky-white bone and he'd have happily bet everything he had on it being from New Zealand. It looked new, too, so she'd clearly been there only recently. He doubted very much that the necklace was a present. Alice was a woman wearing a new skin and anyone who knew her well enough to buy her a necklace would probably have been surprised by the choice of what she was now wearing. It was another assumption but Seth was used to making them and to getting them right. He had good instincts. Even his father said so.

'I've a feeling,' said Seth, staring right into Alice's eyes, 'no, a sense . . . that you've recently returned from a place that changed your life completely. Right, Alice?'

Alice's eyes lit up so brightly they almost burned like fireworks.

'Yes! You're right! Oh, you're so right!'

Holding Alice's hands and smiling, Seth noticed she had no wedding ring but that the finger which would have been wearing such a thing had a faint indentation, a physical memory of what had clearly been there for many, many years and had only recently been removed. It was another clue that he could use to his advantage.

'You have gone through a very hard and difficult decision,' said Seth, guessing that the ring had either been removed because Alice had left a husband of many years (perhaps a lifetime) to live a little at last, or because the old boy had died and she couldn't bear to have the physical memory of him around as well as the mental one. He gave a fleeting thought to the idea that Alice had bumped her husband off, but that just seemed too idiotic to consider, despite it being exceptionally amusing to think of her laying into him with a claw hammer after an argument over a ginger biscuit and a cup of tea.

Alice's eyes were agog with wonder and Seth knew he'd caught her now, like a fish mad and desperate enough to hook itself to any fishing line for a promised look at the sun.

Seth was about to say something more when a pain pierced right through his temples and into his brain with the ferocity of a pneumatic drill. He almost toppled forwards, letting go of Alice's hands and squeezing his eyes shut to combat the pain and the dizziness. The pain vanished as quickly as it arrived. Seth opened his eyes, rubbed them, then through a blurry film of tears caught sight of someone in the audience. It was a girl, staring at him, walking through the crowd towards the stage, and the look in her eyes, for a moment, made Seth think he recognized her. His head exploded with pain again, as though the girl was the cause, but he shook that thought away as the pain, once again, disappeared. He looked up again for the girl, but she was gone, swallowed by the crowd.

'Yes?' Alice's voice knocked him out of his stupor. 'What else do you see?'

It's nothing, Seth thought, *Just a headache. Get a grip!*

Seth yanked himself back into character. He reached out for Alice's hands, deleting the memory of the girl from his mind. But when his hands touched Alice's, he gasped. Something was wrong.

Deep breaths. Just take a few deep breaths . . .

'Everything all right, love?' asked Alice.

Seth glanced up into concerned eyes then scanned again for the girl. He saw a movement in the crowd, like a snake slipping through tall grass. He winced, half expecting pain again, but nothing came.

'Yes,' he ventured, forcing himself to hold it together. 'It's just that . . . your future . . .'

He had to recover, not least because if he didn't his dad would be down on him so hard he'd probably be picking mud out of his teeth for days.

'What did you see?' asked Alice. 'You let go of my hands. I thought something was—'

'Wrong?' said Seth, cutting in, shaking his head, forcing a wry smile. There was no movement in the crowd now. 'No, Alice. Just sometimes I see things so intense I . . .'

He was back in character. Brilliant! He'd take a painkiller for the headache after his turn on stage but for now it was on with the show.

Seth reached out for Alice's hands, confident he was back in control. Then his skull exploded with visions and pictures and sounds and voices and he *knew* what he was seeing was real and not just his slick act going into cruise control. All he could see, all he could smell and touch and feel was Alice's end. Her final breath etched into his brain with the burning permanence of acid.

Alice was older, but only by a couple of years, had done her best to live those last few days crazy and wild, give it her

*all, but it hadn't stopped the thing inside her reaching out
to kill her, the thing that no one had ever known – until it
was too late – was even there in the first place, the thing
that had ripped out her soul, chewed it up, then spat it back
out, old and tired and empty and lonely and there she was,
helpless at the end in a sad hospital bed, and so very lonely,
the thing clogging her up, growing at such a rate the radio
and chemo hadn't even touched it, and all Seth could hear
again and again and again and again was that last, warm,
moist trickle of air seep from Alice's lungs as they, like the
rest of her . . .*

Stopped.

Seth dropped Alice's hands as though he'd accidentally
grabbed hot coals. He backed away, scuttling across the
stage like a frightened crab.

Alice leaned in, desperation in her eyes. 'What did you
see?' she asked again, anticipation seasoning her every
word, her voice louder now, scaling an octave with the
ease of an opera singer. 'You must tell me! I have a right
to know! Tell me, please!'

The crowd cheered for Alice but even more so for Seth.
They'd all come here wanting to see the Apocalypse Boy in
action and that was exactly what they were getting. All
they needed now was for Seth's prophecy about Alice to be
just as nasty and horrible as they all secretly hoped it
would be.

Seth, eyes closed, raised a hand to calm the crowd. He

had to work to keep it from shaking. What he'd seen still had him in its clutches. Whatever he'd just experienced had never happened before. At least not as far as he could remember. He made this stuff up, right? Just read people, worked out what they wanted to hear, then gave 'em hell! Perhaps he was too tired for this tonight, too stressed? That would make sense, what with his escape having been discovered by the very people he was trying to escape from. It was enough for anyone to go a little crazy. No vision this, just a bad dream. A nightmare clawing at his mind, like a cat at a door, despite him being wide awake.

Seth raised his head then opened his eyes to glance down at Alice. The old woman's eyes were puppy-dog wide.

Then from behind her stepped the girl and the pain came again, not just in his head but this time right down his spine, like he'd just been plugged into the national grid. It held him rigid, a statue of agony and fear.

The girl pushed past Alice and reached for Seth. Her hands clamped on to his arms, almost as though they were trying to sink into his flesh.

And then what Seth saw made him scream.

5

THE WORLD WAS AFLAME.

For a moment, Seth was high above planet Earth watching it get torn apart by great ribbons of fire. Yet in that moment it seemed to him that he had been watching Earth for thousands of years, just waiting for this moment to arrive. As he drew closer, the flames, miles high and burning through the atmosphere like a welding torch cutting through plastic, raced across the Earth's surface. The continents buckled and split, seas boiled, mountains burst like septic boils. The ferocity of the Armageddon Seth was witnessing scorched itself into his mind, and closing his eyes made no difference; this vision wasn't one he could block out. It was everywhere, in everything and in every part of his being. Almost as though he were a part of it, and it him.

Then he fell down from his dark, cold heavenly heights into the very flames themselves, with such speed he thought he might shatter into a million tiny pieces.

Seth saw himself become a ball of fire, a flaming meteorite streaking across the sky. His hands burst into balls of fire, his skin lost to the heat, his blood boiling, his body little more than the fuel to feed the furnace below. He yelled out but his words were lost to the terrifying sounds of the terrible destruction, an increasing crescendo of rock crushing rock, countries smashed to pieces like brittle toffee under a hammer, giant volcanoes turning the seas to thick, broiling clouds of killer steam hot enough to scorch the surface of the moon.

A voice called to him. 'Hold on,' it said. 'You must see more. You *have* to see more.'

Seth tried to pull away. He knew that if he could just get himself out of the vice-like grip of the strange girl then this would all be over. But the vision had become more real to him than reality itself. He was no longer at Glastonbury. He was no longer the Apocalypse Boy. He was here at the Apocalypse itself, witnessing the end of all things – and from it there was no escape.

Seth was no longer aflame, but on land, standing on ground as still and silent as a winter's morning after a fresh fall of snow. Or a nuclear war. The world was quieter, yet no less awful. Seth had no idea whether it was before or after what he had just experienced, but he sensed the Earth was dying. It was like standing in a room with a person about to be taken off life support. The body was still there, but the soul had long departed, and it was now only a matter of time.

'Walk . . .'

That voice again. It had to be the girl's, thought Seth. It certainly wasn't Alice's.

Seth walked directionless into the featureless vista of dried ash, dead grass and the occasional sun-bleached bone. Then something broke the line of the horizon and immediately he was there, the world sweeping by in less time than it took him to catch his breath.

Seth knew what it was instantly.

The torch, despite being on its side, towered above Seth, its green copper surface shining out amidst the ruined world around him like a giant emerald on the surface of the moon. He recognized it immediately. Though where the rest of the Statue of Liberty was, he had no idea.

Again the horizon caught his attention and again Seth was swept towards it, only to find himself in front of another carcass of man's achievements; the remains of the Sydney Opera House, its great sail-like skin now little more than a moth-eaten coat. But no sooner had he identified his location than he was taken again to yet another landmark dying in an already dead world, the Taj Mahal, then to the Great Wall of China, the Tower of London, the

Eiffel Tower, the Leaning Tower of Pisa, the Coliseum, the Pyramids, Machu Picchu, the Great Wall of China, Stonehenge, Temple Mount, the Kremlin . . .

Seth's head spun as he tried to keep up and a wave of nausea crashed down on him without warning. He dropped to his knees, heaved, then saw beneath his hands tracks leading into the distance. What were they? Something had made them. He wasn't sure if a sign of life in a world so clearly dead was more terrifying than a sign of hope.

'Follow,' said the girl's voice.

'Why?'

No response.

'Tell me what's going on,' Seth demanded, almost choking on each word in the dry air that spun around him.

Still nothing.

'Who are you?'

Silence.

With little choice left, Seth pushed himself to his feet. Every movement he made ached, as if he'd just completed a double marathon. And he'd never been a big fan of exercise.

The tracks, Seth soon realized, despite being so scuffed and cut up, had been made by horses. He was no expert on horses but there was something a little unnerving about the markings, as if the horses they belonged to had been super-sized.

The land started to rise. Seth did his best to get some bearing on where he was but no clues could be found. Wherever the track was taking him, it seemed as though it had been blasted to nothing, ground down to dust and ash.

Ahead, something at last broke the monotony. A great peak rising, its pinnacle hidden by cloud. The shadow it cast was before Seth as if it was reaching for him, creeping across the land to drag him towards it.

Once more, everything about him swept by rapidly and Seth knew he was on the mountain he'd just spotted. And, impossibly, he was up above the clouds now. At his feet, the tracks were still visible and something in his stomach tightened, telling him that whatever caused them was now little more than a few steps away.

As the clouds danced and swirled, taking on shapes and forms he recognized before changing once again, it was as if he was staring into the last moments of a dream. Then the clouds cleared, and Seth saw what had caused the tracks. His blood froze.

The horses were unlike anything he'd ever seen in his life: four great towering beasts, black silhouettes against the blinding sky, almost as though they'd been cut out of it like stencils. But the horses had nothing on the riders.

A power seeped from them that made Seth feel like he'd just walked in front of an open smelting kiln. It was heavy and hot and impenetrable and thick with an acrid, metallic stink, like a thousand matches had been lit, and he knew that to be here at all was to have the very air in his lungs burned away.

Seth coughed and choked and stared. These riders were more than just a part of all he had seen, they were the cause, and he could see their hand in each and every bit of it. They had walked the Earth and they had witnessed its end and now they were surveying the destruction, before leaving it to its final fiery farewell as the sky fell and all things burned.

Seth screamed out. This couldn't be real. Had the girl done something to make him see things? It had to be a trick . . .

And then he was back on stage. The girl was staring at him, her hands still stuck to his arms. Alice was wide-eyed, the crowd was silent.

'What . . .' Alice spoke. 'What you saw,' she said, her voice trembling, tears in her eyes. 'Is it true? Will it happen?'

'I . . . I don't understand,' Seth stuttered. 'I haven't said anything.'

Another voice, from deeper in the crowd, joined in.

'Is that how it will end? Everything burning up like that?'

Seth was speechless.

'How soon?' asked Alice. 'How much time have we got? We have to know! We have to! Tell us!'

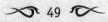

The girl's hands squeezed Seth's arms and he whipped round ready to tear into her and demand answers. But all he saw in her eyes was the deepest of sorrows.

'I'm sorry,' she said, and Seth knew that she meant it. 'But there is something else that you must see as well.'

Seth began to protest, but it was already too late.

He was running for his life. The road was little more than a dirt track, lined with mud huts covered by roofs constructed of leaves and bark. Then he was beyond the borders of the village, legs pumping, heart thumping, the long grass whipping at his legs as he made for the thicker jungle ahead. Then a great shadow stepped in front and Seth skidded, tumbled, crashed to the ground, cutting his legs open, grazing his hands, his arms. He looked up and saw a flash of metal driving down at him . . .

. . . he was no longer in the jungle, but wading through snow in the wild north, but this time he wasn't hunting; he was being hunted. He had no weapon, no warm clothes and something was closing in on him. Snarls were echoing in the wind, snapping at his heels. He looked back, saw shadows flicker between the trees. If he could just get to the river, to the raft, he'd have a chance, but then something whipped through the air, caught round his legs and sent him tumbling. Hot, foul breath was on him and he looked up into the jaws of death . . .

. . . only to then be racing through a city on fire. The buildings were wooden, leaning against each other as though trying to prop each other up after a boozy night out. The blaze was jumping from rooftop to rooftop, but he hadn't the time to think about that, he just had to get away from whatever had come for him in the night. But the road ahead was blocked, the buildings left and right were alight, then something smacked into his back and Seth looked down to see the dark, damp shape of a spear head jutting from his chest, dripping with his own hot blood . . .

The visions didn't stop. They rained down on him like hailstones the size of golf balls, each one ending violently. Thousands of lifetimes, spanning millennia, spanning the globe, and each lifetime his own. Just like this one right now.

Seth snapped his eyes open. The girl was gone. Alice was pale. He pushed himself slowly to his feet, his body aching as if he'd just left a boxing ring, and the crowd backed away. He saw fear in their faces. Seth edged away from them, until at last the darkness at the side of the stage took him in its arms.

'Seth . . .'

His father was standing in front of him, his mother and sister at his side. They looked astonished and afraid.

'Don't . . . speak to me,' Seth said, pushing past. 'Please, just don't.'

'But, son,' said his dad, his hand brushing against Seth's shoulder as he went past, 'those things you saw, what you spoke of . . . Where did it come from? I've never seen anything like that. Not once, you hear me?'

'Neither have I, Dad,' said Seth, not stopping for the conversation.

'But, Seth—'

Seth snapped round, a shaking finger pointing like a pistol at his father's face. 'Leave it, Dad! Just leave it!'

He whipped round to the front of their caravan and pushed through the door, slamming it behind him, barely holding on to the contents of his stomach, or his sanity. The framed picture of The Protector on the back of the door jumped from the nail it was attached to and fell to the floor, the glass smashing like ice on a pond. Seth went to clear it up then stopped as if he'd walked into a tree.

The girl was sitting waiting for him.

6

SETH SWEPT BACK ROUND to the door, but the girl was already there, blocking his way, one hand outstretched to stop him.

'If you don't do exactly as I say,' the girl stated, her voice calm and clear, sounding like someone speaking in an acoustically perfect church, 'I guarantee that you will be dead within the hour.'

'Is that a threat?'

'The truth often is,' said the girl and then fell silent.

Seth ripped off his cape and stared at her for a moment, looking for clues, falling back on the skills that had become his profession. But this girl was almost impossible to read. Her hair was black, cropped close to her head, but not boyish, just easy to care for. She was wearing denims, a black fleece jacket, and Dr Marten boots. Seth could see no jewellery, no scarring or birthmarks. If anything, it was her seeming lack of uniqueness that made her unique. She was hiding something, but what? The girl was dressed to blend in, to go unnoticed in a crowd. As for her age? Well, she was a few fingers taller than him and had an air of confidence about her that made her seem older than Seth guessed she was, though he reckoned she still had at least a year on him. Whoever she was, Seth thought, she was remarkably unremarkable. It was unnerving.

'Then how about this,' Seth growled, walking up to the girl till her hand was almost touching his chest. 'If you don't get the hell out of my life, you'll be dead in five seconds!'

He'd have stepped closer but was wary of her touch. It had already done too much and whether it was drugs or hypnotism or whatever, he wasn't keen to experience it again. Instead, he looked round the caravan for a weapon, found a magazine and rolled it up.

The girl dropped her head a little to one side and laughed, though there was no humour in it. 'You're going to swat me like a fly?'

Seth slapped it against his open hand. 'No, but I'll definitely give you a killer of a headache! Now—'

A knock rap-rap-rapped at the door.

The girl flinched.

'Seth? Everything OK? You got someone in there?'

The last thing Seth needed now was his dad interfering. He'd never been a big fan of his son having friends over, particularly girls. Said they were too distracting. Mind you, it would almost be worth it, thought Seth, if only to see the look on his dad's face.

The girl shook her head, widened her eyes pleadingly, fearful.

'I'm fine, Dad,' Seth called out. 'Just a headache, that's all.'

The door rattled, but the girl was up against it, blocking it from being opened.

'Why won't you let me in? Look, Seth, I'm sorry about earlier . . .'

'Dad . . .'

But the door stopped rattling and footsteps sounded as his dad slouched away, muttering something Seth couldn't make out.

There was a moment's silence, filled with nothing but Seth and the girl staring each other down.

The girl went to speak as Seth opened his mouth and their words tumbled clumsily into each other. The girl motioned for Seth to start.

'I was just going to say,' said Seth, taking the cue, 'you've got five minutes, that's all. If you're an Activist, then you may as well just get out right now. But whatever you did to me, I want to know how and why, and who put you up to it.'

'It's not like that,' said the girl, moving away from the door to sit down at a table, leaning her head in her hands for a moment to calm down. 'What you saw . . . it's complicated. *We're* complicated. And I'm not an Activist.'

Seth wasn't a big fan of riddles, but he wasn't a big fan of Activists either. He'd met a few here and there: environmentalists who wanted humanity wiped off the face of the Earth, save for a few on a little island growing organic veg and playing crap tunes on their guitars; capitalists who wanted to secularize everything, ban all spirituality and focus on the just-as-unreliable god of materialism; anarchists who seemed to have little interest in anything other than a good fight and whatever stuff they could loot from a broken window. And that was the trouble with the whole movement; one label to slap on an ever-growing bunch of crazies, all of whom were as busy fighting each other as they were trying to bring any perceived power to its knees.

As yet, they'd had no such luck with The Way. Seth doubted anyone would. The Protector was everywhere and in everything and The Way was a new world order that had been growing for decades. It wasn't about to go any time soon. The Way seemed to have a *way* of managing things like Activists.

'Just get to the point,' snarled Seth. 'And seeing as you know my name now, thanks to my gobby dad, why don't you at least be polite and tell me yours?'

'Lily,' said the girl, sitting up. 'Hi.'

A smile attempted to slip across her face, but it seemed nervous to be there too long and vanished just as quickly.

'Nice to meet you,' Seth replied coldly. 'But don't let me interrupt. You were going to tell me how you made me see all that stuff, remember?'

Lily leaned back in her chair. She'd always known this was going to be difficult but she hadn't bargained for Seth being quite so stubborn and headstrong. Still, she wasn't about to give up – when it came to stubborn streaks, hers was long enough to reach the moon and back.

'I didn't make you see any of it,' she said.

Seth noted a weariness in Lily's voice that certainly didn't sound as if she'd come out here just to make him look like an idiot.

'What you saw, it's inside you, Seth. I know, because I've done this to you before. I find you, confirm who you are . . . and then it happens. All I did this time was open a door and give you a peek.'

Seth barked out a sharp laugh.

'What do you take me for? I've never even seen you before in my life!'

'I don't take you for anything,' said Lily, remaining calm. 'But I know who you are and what you could become. Finding you is my job. It's what I've always done.'

Seth's confusion spun out of control like a racing car on an oil slick.

'You've got me confused with someone else,' he said. 'Trust me, I never forget a face, even one as normal as yours.'

'And what's that supposed to mean?'

Lily looked injured, almost, realized Seth, as though his words had grazed her a little.

'You're hiding something,' he said, looking for another reaction, spotting a flicker in her grey eyes. *And don't go trying to tell me you're not . . .*

'We all are,' replied Lily enigmatically, not wanting to give too much away. 'Some more so than others.'

'That's not what I mean – and you know it!' said Seth, frustrated with Lily's cryptic approach to answering questions. 'You're all confident and filled with purpose, right? But that doesn't go with how you're dressed. Nothing about what you're wearing tells me who Lily actually is – and that's just the point, isn't it?'

Lily tilted her head to one side slightly.

'You should sit down.'

'I prefer to stand.'

'Are you always this argumentative?'

'Are you?'

Lily took a deep breath and tried to start with something simple. 'What do you know about The Way?'

Seth sat down, shaking his head as though at last

seeing something that had been staring him hard in the face all this time. If there was one thing he could rant about it was The Way. And he was more than a little disappointed to discover that Lily was clearly just another religious nutjob. Though it made sense that someone from The Way would want to freak him out a bit. He remembered the cleric he'd met earlier. It had struck him as odd that the man had questioned him over a discarded soup cup. Perhaps they were watching him, but for what reason? Seth wasn't a big fan of paranoia. But then neither was he a big fan of strangers turning up and giving him freak-out nightmares and headaches from hell. The thing was, though, Seth couldn't help but think that it was a pity Lily was associated with them. She was clearly a pain in the butt, but there was something about her that he figured he could learn to at least like. Even if that was just the look in her face when she got all angry and riled up.

'Not a fan?'

'What's not to love?' replied Seth, pulling out his mobile to flick his finger across the screen. 'I've always wanted to live in a world where I'm ruled by a party that texts me a regular quote from *The Book* twice a day, haven't you?'

Seth turned the screen to Lily.

'*"In the mouth of the foolish is a rod for his back,*' he recited as Lily read the text, having already committed the verse to memory earlier that day, '*"but the lips of the wise protect them.*" Seriously, what does that mean, and why the hell should I actually care?'

He watched another smile venture on to Lily's face and this time it hung around for a while. It suited her, thought Seth. Made her look more approachable.

'They love humanity,' said Lily, understanding in her voice, but sadness, too, as though she was speaking about a friend she'd at some time fallen out with and never made up. 'In their own way. Everything they do is out of love. To protect us.'

'From what?' argued Seth, slipping his mobile back into a pocket. 'The world's still a mess. Or don't you watch the news?'

'Impossible not to,' Lily replied. 'War, disease, famine, natural disasters. Same old, same old. No wonder so many think the world's on the brink of self-destruction. All it needs is a spark and that fuse'll go up like stink.' She narrowed her eyes, as though trying to peer into Seth's skull to read his thoughts. 'Isn't that why people come to see you? The Way is the reason you have an audience, Seth. And if you don't believe that, then you're even more blind than the sheep flocking together outside this rusty shed of a caravan you call home!'

Seth wasn't about to take the bait, though he agreed with Lily's description of the people outside enjoying the festival. 'They're no different to any other group, if you ask me; no different to the Activists! Just more powerful and better at bullying and brainwashing. Oh, and they clearly have a dress code.'

Lily remained quiet.

'So what has The Way got to do with you messing up my show?' asked Seth, more annoyed now than anything. He wanted to know how Lily had made him have such convincing hallucinations, if only so he could do something to prevent it ever happening again. 'A cleric cornered me earlier. Anything to do with you? And those visions you gave me; was it something on your hands that got into my bloodstream as soon as you touched me? Is that how it works?'

The smile fell from Lily's face and all colour drained from her. This was the moment she'd been waiting for, where it all either went smoothly, or ended up like a train wreck. She ignored the nausea snaking its way through her stomach.

'The cleric had nothing to do with me,' she said. 'But I know this: The Way are coming for you. The Chosen have your scent and when they find you, they will kill you.'

'Tell me when I'm supposed to take this seriously.'

Lily continued, despite Seth's clear and present uninterest. 'You have to leave with me! Now!'

Seth didn't budge. Then leaned back, his arms outstretched along the back of the sofa.

'You're kidding me, right?' he said, rolling his eyes. 'Is this still all part of what you did earlier? Another little bit of trickery to really make me look an idiot? And you seriously think I'm going to believe that The Chosen are going to show any interest in some kid who cold-reads the gullible and wears a crap cape like Batman on benefits?'

Lily went to speak but Seth cut her off and wagged a finger at her knowingly.

'You *are* an Activist, aren't you? Just admit it! But what type? I mean, they're all completely mental, it's just that I'd like to know what kind of mental I'm dealing with right now.'

Lily shook her head, then grabbed Seth by the scruff of his neck, hauling him to his feet as if she was pulling in a heavy net stuffed with fish. Seth was again amazed by her strength.

'I'm serious!' she barked at him, leaning in close, giving him a violent little shake. 'You actually want to die? Is that it? I'm giving you a chance here! Come with me, Seth, and—'

Seth ripped Lily's hand from his clothes then pushed her back down in her seat. She was strong, that was more than obvious, but no more than his equal.

'Here's the thing,' he said, again holding a finger out to Lily, though this time jabbing it at her like a sword to keep her quiet as he spoke. 'I'm leaving anyway. It's just fortuitous that you happened to turn up on the night I'd planned to go.'

'Then what's the harm in coming along with me?' asked Lily, working hard to stop her frustration boiling over.

'You've got nothing to lose but your life.'

Seth raised an eyebrow.

'What, hook up with a strange girl who drugged me to give me visions? Yeah, as if!'

Infuriated now, Lily raised her hands high into the air as if she was calling on God to help her out. 'I did not drug you!' she yelled, each word coming out like a bullet. She dropped her hands to her hips. 'What you saw . . . Look, I can't explain it all, but—'

Seth didn't give her a chance to finish. That his parents had found all the stuff he'd prepared for his escape wasn't about to stop him going ahead with it. Grabbing what he could from his few scant belongings, including an old sleeping bag from under his bed, he stuffed it all into a military surplus holdall, then went to grab his dad's wallet from a drawer in his parents' room. But when he pulled it out, something came out with it; an envelope clearly containing a card, sealed and with his name on it. They'd remembered . . . Not wanting to waste any more time, he emptied the wallet, put the cash into the bag and the card in his back pocket, then heaved himself into his old, ankle-length waxed mac, the kind of thing an Australian farmer would wear out on a ranch. It was ripped in places, worn in others, but it was waterproof and, thanks to the fleece lining, seriously warm.

Lily appeared, tried to pull him round to face her, but Seth didn't budge.

'Where are you going?'

'Anywhere,' said Seth. 'Because wherever it is, it'll be better than here, right?'

He then walked through to the back of the caravan and opened a window.

'They'll kill you,' said Lily. 'They will find you and you won't be able to do anything about it and just before you're dead you'll think: Crap, that Lily chick was right!'

'When they find out I've gone it'll be too late,' replied Seth.

'I'm not talking about your parents.'

Lily's words were already dead in the air as Seth slipped out through the window, hitched the bag on to his shoulder and ran off into the dark.

It swallowed him whole.

7

SETH WASN'T A GREAT runner at the best of times but in the dark, and with a heavy bag bouncing around on his shoulder, he was having trouble not tripping over his own feet. What made it worse was that he had no idea where to run to – just anywhere to get away from Lily and her crazy talk. He nearly lost his footing twice – down a hole, then in a puddle, diving head first into the milling crowds he'd usually try to leave behind. Seth was amazed to have not at least once slipped on to his backside, when out of nowhere stepped a man in an enormous and idiotic hat, who was selling 'genuine' wooden wands as used by the druids. He was wearing a T-shirt with a picture of Stonehenge on it. Nothing Seth could do would have stopped his collision and he and the man crashed to the ground, causing the wands to spill everywhere.

'My wands!' exclaimed the man, desperately trying to pick them up before they became too dirty.

'I'm sorry,' Seth apologized, climbing quickly back on to his feet.

'You know what you've done, don't you? You've confused their auras! Everything's all mixed up! How can I sell them now? You idiot!'

Seth had nothing to say to that. He just apologized again, handed the man a wand that had somehow found its way inside his coat and walked away – realizing too late that another had also made its way there. He decided to keep it as a souvenir.

Getting his bearings, Seth headed for the main exit gate. That way, he'd have a good chance at slipping out anonymously with the crowds. Upping his pace, and focusing hard to stay on his feet and not crash into anyone else, Seth pushed on. It seemed everyone else was going in the other direction, and it was like swimming upstream, but Seth just kept his head down and pushed through.

A few minutes later, having successfully navigated his way through the crowds to a point where he could now see the tall, orange flags that fluttered over the main gate, Seth realized where he was, and it was exactly where he didn't want to be; back close to his parents' caravan. Hunching his shoulders, and doing everything he could to not draw attention to himself, Seth strode on purposefully. And with each step that took him closer to his exit out of the festival he drew ever nearer to the ones he was trying to leave.

Seth passed a large and expensive-looking caravan, the kind he'd always dreamed of living in, the kind his parents had never been able to afford. Down its side, bursting out of an exploding fizzy drink can, he read the airbrushed words *God is it!* He was impressed with the artwork but the slogan itself was a common one and still made him thirsty every time he saw it. Which was probably the point, so that eventually, every time he bought a can of cola, he'd think of the Protector, too. It was frightening. Insidious. The owner was asleep in the cab of the truck. He was wearing a T-shirt with the slogan *Read The Book – it will scare the hell out of you!*

You got that right, thought Seth, as he spotted a small group of people dressed as aliens, handing out leaflets to come to a UFO Calling Night somewhere in the Brecon Beacons.

The exit was close now. Freedom. Space to become who he wanted to be, rather than what his parents had always tried to mould him into becoming. Beth had given in easily, but then Seth knew just how persuasive his dad could be. And Beth had always been more afraid to question their parents and their beliefs and lifestyle. It was as though she believed that the very weight of a question was something you struggled with. To Seth, questions had always been the things that freed him. The more you ask, the more you know. Or something like that.

Knowledge wasn't the enemy, ignorance was. And twice as dangerous.

Seth wish he'd parted with Beth on better terms. Yes, they bickered and snapped at each other, but he still cared for her deeply, if anything more than he did for his mum and dad. If he spotted her, and if his parents weren't around, he'd risk saying goodbye properly, perhaps even give her the chance to come with him. He knew it was crazy, but she was his sister and at that moment, as the caravan swung into view ahead, Seth realized that it meant something to him.

The explosion that a heartbeat later shredded the caravan into a thousand ribbons of flame and glass and twisted metal dropped him to the ground as if he'd been hit by a bull. Heat flooded across him, leaving him gasping for air and then the world was filled with the smell of smoke and burning.

Seth coughed and rolled over, unable to comprehend what had just happened. The star-shaped burst of damage seemed to stretch its long fingers out far into the festival crowds. Pushing himself to his knees, he caught sight through the rolling smoke of dozens of other people, other bodies, lying about him on the ground. Some were unconscious, others dazed, and those too close to the explosion were undoubtedly either already dead, or soon would be. The sickly-sweet smell of burning flesh was in the air and Seth, standing now, covered his mouth and nose with his jacket sleeve then stumbled forwards, towards the smoking remains of the only home he'd ever known.

The caravan had, to all intents and purposes, vanished. The chassis was still there, but looked more like the skeletal remains of a shipwrecked boat than something that had carried his family for longer than Seth could remember. Everything else was gone, obliterated in an instant.

Seth refused to think the worst as he searched through the crowds, as much looking for the dead as the living.

'Dad! Mum! Beth!'

He called out again and again, but no answer came, just the awful sound of roaring flames and the pained, frightened moans from the injured and the dying.

'Activists!' shouted someone nearby. Despite the smoke, Seth saw that it was a cleric, the one he'd met earlier. And there were others in the crowd, all rushing towards the confusion like vultures to a fallen deer.

Panic spread. People were screaming, half running, half tripping in their desperation to escape. Those on the ground were trampled and kicked and crunched, but their screams made no difference. If Activists were the cause, thought Seth, then they'd be talking about tonight for years.

It was then that he noticed other figures in the crowd. Wearing long grey jackets they moved among the fallen like dark sentinels. These were not clerics. These followed a higher calling.

The Chosen . . .

He'd only ever caught glimpses of them before, jumping into cars to race between important spiritual appointments, observing the weekly Sunday worships from afar that filled football stadiums, arresting Activists, guarding The Protector. With the smoke and confusion all around, it was impossible to make out their faces, but he could see what they were doing. They were searching through the bodies, using a torch to check faces, kicking over the bodies, rolling them on to their backs to get a proper look. It was sinister and chilling and he could hear Lily's voice in his ear repeating her warning, again and again and again.

Something inside Seth told him he had better get out of there fast but, as he whipped round to get his bearings again and make for an exit, he stopped dead. Not ten metres away were his parents, or what was left of them. They were lying on the ground like smashed dolls, their limbs busted and twisted and wrong. And studying their faces was one of the grey-coated Chosen.

Vomit rushed to Seth's mouth and he heaved, dropping to the ground in shock. Wiping his mouth, he pulled himself to his feet, turned to run, but tripped over a body.

He managed to catch himself before his face crunched into the ground, but pain still jolted up his arms. Gritting his teeth, he tried again to stand, but a bubbling, wet moan from the person he'd fallen over stalled him.

'Beth . . .'

She was lying on her back, breathing and fading in and out of consciousness. Her once white dress was wet and sticky with mud and blood. Her hair, her one true pride and joy, was matted and scorched. The hairs of her eyebrows were little more than tiny melted balls of carbon.

Panic seized Seth. He'd never had to deal with anything like this, had no first-aid training, didn't have the faintest idea what to do, what to look for, how to save his sister's life. Forgetting everything else for a moment he desperately checked his sister, to find something broken, anything that would give him an indication of what was wrong, but the more he did it, the worse he felt and soon tears were streaming down his face. He tried to wipe them away, but all that served to do was smear his face with Beth's warm blood.

Beth coughed and her eyes flickered briefly.

'Beth!' Seth yelled, grabbing his sister by the shoulders to shake her.

His helplessness washed over him with such force he thought he might drown. He did his best to make her comfortable and brushed her hair away from her face. Her skin was cold, as if she'd just been out in the snow. For the first time in his life he realized she was beautiful.

'Seth?'

Surprised at the mention of his name, Seth looked down to see his sister staring up at him. He pulled her in close, holding her to him, willing her to survive.

'Beth – it's me! I'm here! What happened? How . . .'

Beth reached a hand up to Seth's face, and with her thumb, wiped weakly at the blood and grime that covered it.

Then she smiled, closed her eyes . . .

And was gone.

Seth willed time to rewind, screamed at it to do the exact opposite of what it was doing now, taking his sister away and to a place he wasn't even sure existed any more. He didn't want to let go and leave her still body on the festival field, because if he did, that would be it and he would be alone. No family. No friends. Nothing.

Movement.

It was the figure, one of The Chosen who had stood over his parents. And it was staring at him.

Fighting against every instinct in him to stay with Beth, to hold her and to never ever let go, Seth stood up. Then he spotted something round Beth's neck; it was the silver chain she'd worn since a child and from it hung a small silver shell. Quickly, Seth dropped to the ground, unclipped it, pocketed it, then with a final kiss to his sister's forehead, scrambled back to his feet.

The figure over by his parents was pointing at him now, then something swept past his head and a gunshot cracked the night.

The figure wasn't pointing. It was taking aim.

8

SETH COULD HARDLY BREATHE.

After the second shot, he hadn't looked back, not at the still-smouldering remains of the caravan, not at the bodies of his parents and, hardest of all, not at Beth. He could still feel the sensation of her body resting in his arms as she died, the weight of it, as he drove on, his legs pumping like steam pistons.

Seth had no idea if The Chosen chasing after him were any closer, but he figured he'd only really find that out if a bullet thumped into his back and then it would be too late anyway. So he just kept on running, past crowds staring in shock at the explosion, through tents of dancers oblivious to the outside world, and onwards until something caught him and dragged him into the shadows and clamped a hand over his mouth.

Seth went to lash out at whoever had hold of him when he recognized Lily's face in front of him.

'Stay quiet and stay here,' she whispered. 'Got it?'

Seth nodded. Lily's face was stern and her eyes had a predatory glint in them. How had she managed to find him again in all the confusion?

'Promise?'

Seth nodded again.

'I'll be back in two minutes.'

With that, Lily let go of him and sprang into the dark like a panther. Seth was about to call after her when, at the far end of the row of Portaloos, one of the grey-coated figures appeared.

Seth froze. It couldn't see him, could it? Not in this gloom. Then he saw a flash of light appear at the hand of the figure and a tiny red dot chase along the ground until it rested on his chest. Just as Seth realized he was being targeted by the laser of a pistol, the figure crumpled to the ground like a puppet whose strings had been cut. And Lily raced towards him. How had she done that?

'I'm truly sorry about your family,' she said, pulling him to his feet, 'but you'll have time to grieve later. The only way for you to survive this now is to trust me. And you have to survive, do you understand?'

No, thought Seth, *I don't understand*, but this time he

wasn't about to argue. If Lily could get him away from here safely then that, for the moment at least, was good enough for him.

Lily shook Seth. She hadn't time for him to go soft on her, not now. Things hadn't just hotted up; if they stayed around much longer, they'd both burn.

'I asked you a question!' she hissed. 'So answer me!'

'OK, I understand!' Seth hissed back, snatching Lily's hands away from him. 'And sorry if I'm not quite with it yet! My family—'

He wasn't given time to finish as Lily dragged him away from their hiding place towards the nearest exit. But as they drew closer, Seth became increasingly aware that he was starting to pull her back.

'Come on! Move it!' Lily shouted, sounding more frustrated and scared by the minute. 'We have to get out of here!'

'I know that!' Seth shouted back. 'But the guards at the exit – they'll recognize me! The Chosen will be there waiting. We'll have to try something else!'

'No time,' said Lily. 'So just follow my lead. Do as I do, OK?'

Seth nodded as Lily switched her hand from gripping his wrist to holding him round the waist.

'I said follow my lead!' she whispered into his ear, her mouth close enough to bite. 'Put your arm round me, you idiot!'

Too astonished to argue, Seth did as he was told and, as he did, Lily pulled him in tighter.

Seth looked at the exit gate. It was only a few steps away now. Whatever Lily was planning on doing to get them through without him being recognized, he needed her to get to it sharpish.

Then, just as Seth was sure the guards were going to glance up and see exactly who was approaching, Lily twisted against his hips, flung her other arm round his neck and kissed him.

Seth instinctively pulled away, but Lily had hold of him and wasn't about to let go. That it was the first time in his life any girl had kissed him didn't escape his thoughts. He was dazed and confused.

Lily leaned back a little as a few wolf whistles jumped around them.

'Don't look up, stay close and just keep kissing me, right?' she said. Then with a wink, she added, 'And don't worry, you're not as bad at this as you think you are.'

Seth nodded, then he was half stumbling, half kissing his way through the exit gate, and finally outside the fence.

'Quickly!' said Lily, pulling him once again by the wrist, away from the festival and towards some thick bushes. 'We're still not out of it yet!'

At the bushes, Lily disappeared, only to reappear pushing a battered scooter. She jumped on and, despite its appearance, the scooter started first time.

'Here,' said Lily, handing Seth a pale-blue helmet. 'Put this on. Ever ridden pillion before?'

The look on Seth's face said it all.

'Just lean with me,' Lily explained as Seth climbed on to the seat behind her. 'Don't fight what I'm doing, OK? Just go with it. And hold on!'

'To what?'

'Me!'

Lily accelerated and with a sharp spin of the rear wheel pulled the scooter out into the road. It wasn't the quickest mode of transport, but it was all she had and it would just have to do. Next time, if there *was* a next time, she'd make sure she stole something a little faster.

As Lily slowed for a junction, Seth caught sight of a helicopter coming down to land close to where his parents' caravan had been. And when he saw four shadows emerge from it, like crows falling from the blackened husk of a tree, something told him that meeting them would've been very bad indeed.

Seth's hands were so numb that he had no idea how he was holding on at all. The lack of sensation was also moving slowly up his arms and he was beginning to get seriously afraid that if Lily didn't pull over and stop soon then he'd probably just topple off the back. He was freezing, too, despite his jacket, and the weight of the bag across his shoulders was doing its best to drag him off as the wind whipped round them.

· But that wasn't the main problem. Alone on the back of the scooter, Seth's world had come crashing down on him. He tried to block it out and focus on just holding on to Lily, but it wasn't enough. If anything, it made it worse.

The fact that he'd been planning to run away from his family made everything so much worse. They were gone. That was it. He'd never have a chance to talk to them again, see their faces, say sorry for what he'd done. Yes, they'd had their disagreements and Seth still stood by his reasons for having wanted to escape in the first place, but it was all such a mess inside him now that he had no coping mechanism. He had no home. No parents. Nothing.

Then there was Beth.

Seth, as best he could, attempted to push the memory of her from his mind, to block it out, wall it up, shut it away. But nothing worked. Whatever he thought about, it would just come crashing down and there he would be, once again holding Beth, willing her to live, watching her die.

Seth was about to attempt to get Lily's attention, persuade her somehow to pull over, when she did just that, slipping the rattling scooter into the open mouth of a leafy farm track heavy with so many trees leaning over it that it looked more like a dark, green tunnel than a road.

Lily put the kickstand down and slipped off the seat.

'We can't hang around.' Her voice was brusque, but then she changed tone almost immediately and said, 'Seth . . . I really am sorry. I hope you know that.'

She knew Seth was probably coming apart at the seams. And she wasn't being hard on him for no good reason; she had to keep him alive, and that meant keeping him moving. But they needed a short break.

Seth nodded, but he wasn't really listening. He couldn't think straight. His nerves seemed on fire. His brain was in full-on meltdown.

They're dead . . . they're all dead . . . They're dead . . . they're all dead . . .

Seth bolted.

'Seth!' yelled Lily, seeing him leap off down the lane. 'Don't be an idiot!'

All Seth was aware of was his feet thumping into the ground, his legs driving him forward. Perhaps, if he kept running, he'd never have to think again. He just had to keep moving, never stop, never give himself enough time to settle down, to think, to deal with it.

Something drove into Seth's side and he tumbled to the ground with a yelp.

'Running away won't solve anything!' yelled Lily, now sitting on Seth, slapping away his badly aimed punches. 'It never does! And trust me, I know!'

'They're dead, Lily!' Seth screamed back. 'My family! I saw

them! My parents! God, my sister died in my arms! I held her!'

'I know,' Lily answered, her voice loud and commanding, rather than harsh and angry. 'It's awful and terrible and wrong and it'll haunt you for ever, but you have to hold it together, you got me? You have to!'

Seth held his hands up for Lily to see, his skin stained a faint reddish-brown. 'It's her blood! It's all over me! I couldn't stop it! I didn't know what to do! Then she touched my cheek just here –' Seth pointed to where Beth's thumb had brushed against him in that last, impossible moment '– and then she died! I couldn't stop her dying, Lily! I'm her brother and I couldn't stop any of it and I was running away and leaving them and now they're dead and—'

The slap came out of nowhere and stung like a bee on steroids. Shocked, and angry now, Seth roared and launched his retaliation. But it was utterly futile. Against Lily he didn't stand a chance. Every punch he threw, she blocked. Every time he struggled to get free, she pinned him tighter to the ground. And eventually he gave up, as much from exhaustion as disgust at himself for being so weak that even a girl could have him whipped.

'You brought this to me,' Seth said, his breaths coming short and fast as he tried to calm down, his voice breaking like the sea against rocks. 'It's your fault. All of it.'

'If I hadn't come to you,' said Lily, 'you'd be lying with your family, just as dead.'

'If you knew The Way wanted us dead—'

'No, Seth,' said Lily. 'They wanted *you* dead, that's all I was aware of. I had no idea they would do what they did to get to you. Killing is what they do, but that . . .' She paused, drew breath. 'They've done everything to get to you before, but never gone so far.'

Seth caught that last comment and threw it back.

'What do you mean, *before*? You're talking about the stuff I saw, aren't you? Where I was being chased and killed but not here, more like I was someone else or . . .'

The truth crunched into him.

'If everything I saw is true,' Seth said, pushing himself up on to his hands as Lily shuffled off his chest to sit next to him on the road, 'then that was me, wasn't it? I wasn't seeing things at all, I was *remembering* them! But how? Past lives . . . I don't believe in any of that!'

Lily slumped forwards, at last displaying some degree of fatigue. But she was exhausted, physically and mentally. Helping Seth escape was the biggest, most dangerous decision she'd ever made. And at any point from now on everything could all go horribly wrong. And then where would all this have got her? Dead, that's where.

'I don't understand it too well myself,' she said. 'But I know someone who does. And that's where I'm taking you now. Assuming you're finished with the whole running away thing.'

Seth shook his head, not just in disbelief but also in the

hope it would dislodge all the pain he'd just experienced. It didn't work.

'Reckon you'd catch me anyway,' he said.

'You bet your saggy butt I would,' replied Lily, lifting herself to her feet then offering Seth her hand. 'Coming?'

Five minutes later a small rusting scooter, with two young passengers, was racing its way through what was left of the night. And not even a buckled rear wheel and nearly one hundred thousand miles on the clock was going to stop it.

9

SETH HAD NEVER BEEN on a train in his life.

'You OK?'

Lily reached over and rested a hand on his arm, shook it a little, smiled.

Seth nodded unconvincingly.

Once they'd reached the station and hidden the scooter, they'd had little choice but to find somewhere to huddle down before catching the next train. And as it wasn't going to be turning up till the early morning, they'd had just over five hours to get through. Thankfully, the waiting room had been left open. Small, cold and decorated with little more than a few posters promoting the benefits of rail travel, and one very large poster with a quote from *The Book*, it had at least got them out of the wind. They'd managed to clean Seth up a little in possibly the most unhygienic, reeking toilets this side of hell's own sewage system. After that, neither of them could sleep, and Lily was for ever getting up to check the door to make sure no one else was out there coming for them. But eventually she settled down and, hunched up together with Seth in a corner on a floor, they had both fallen asleep.

The train had departed at just after six in the morning and, despite the little bit of uncomfortable sleep they'd managed and the wash Seth had grumbled through to get rid of as much of the grime, blood and stage make-up as possible, he looked paler than ever. He needed to eat, Lily realized. And so did she.

'I need to get us some food,' Lily said, slipping out of her seat. 'What do you want?'

'What's available?'

Lily tapped her cheek, as though in serious thought, then said, with a knowing finger in the air, 'Well, if the chef's the one I requested, then I'm sure he'll be able to whip us up a decent rib-eye steak each, medium rare, with triple-fried chips and garlic mayonnaise, followed by . . . ooh, I know, how do you fancy—'

Seth cut her off with little more than a look.

'Yeah, I'm lying,' sighed Lily. 'I'll bring you what I can, OK? But don't expect too much. In fact, expect to eat badly flavoured cardboard and if it's an improvement on that, then we're laughing.'

Lily walked towards the food kiosk carriage, swinging herself from chair to chair down the centre aisle in rhythm with the sway of the train. With nothing to do Seth flicked through the onboard magazine. Discovering that it was funded by The Way, and was little more than one big advert for them, he put it back where he'd found it and stared out through the window. Seth's phone buzzed in his pocket. Pulling it out to stare at it through tired eyes, he saw that it was another quote sent by The Way. He deleted the message. The world outside was a hypnotic blur of colours and shapes bleeding into each other like paint spilled in a puddle.

By the time Lily had returned, Seth had fallen asleep. Clearly the rest on the waiting-room floor hadn't been enough. She was pleased then that she'd decided against getting whatever sorry excuse for a burger the man at the kiosk had tried to persuade her to buy, and instead gone for sandwiches, crisps, Coke and a bottle of water.

Lily peeled open the cellophane to get to her sandwiches, snapped open the bottle of water and looked over at Seth. He didn't look peaceful and she knew it was a fitful sleep, no doubt filled with the nightmare of the past few hours, but it was better than nothing so she let him sleep on. For a moment, she remembered the kiss and smiled. That it had worked at all amazed her.

A couple of minutes later, Lily was asleep herself, her half-finished sandwich still clasped in her weary hand.

Seth woke with a cry.

The images in his mind refused to stop playing over and over and over. Death and bullets and blood. His parents lying in a grave. Shaking Beth, unable to wake her up. More blood. An explosion. His whole life going up in flames. But there were other things in there, too. Glimpses of what he'd seen when Lily had touched him that first time. And he couldn't break his mind free of any of it.

Lily reached over and shook him gently.

'Seth? It's OK, you're safe. It's just a dream, that's all.'

Shaking his head, Seth rubbed his eyes, pushing the heels of his hands hard into the sockets till he saw stars explode.

'I wish,' he muttered, then more clearly, 'Where are we?'

'Coming into London,' Lily replied with a yawn. 'We'll be pulling into Paddington in about five minutes. You've been asleep for two hours.'

Seth sat up, stretched. The train had slowed and now the window was a cinema screen of London. They rolled past expensive flats and high-rise office buildings seemingly built out of little more than steel and reflections. Other older buildings did their best to stand proud, but many wore spray-can graffiti like tattoos and could do nothing to hide them. In places huge billboards were pinned to walls. The words on one caught Seth's eye: *You're on this planet for a purpose. Find it!* Another had a huge picture of a man smiling down on London like a benevolent king. It was the same picture of The Protector that appeared on the soup cup, only much, much larger. He turned back to Lily.

'You look pretty tired yourself.'

Lily shrugged and showed Seth the sandwich still in her hand. 'At least you didn't fall asleep while eating.'

Seth reached over for a sandwich yet, despite having not eating for hours now, didn't feel very hungry. But he downed his drink in a few gulps.

'Better?'

'Oh, I love the taste of Coke in the morning,' Seth said, burping halfway through his sentence.

'Nice.'

'Thank you.'

People in the carriage were standing, preparing to leave once the train had arrived.

'We'll wait till everyone else is off,' said Lily. 'That way we won't get crushed.'

Paddington Station was packed. It was like waking from a deep sleep and finding yourself in a giant ants' nest. Streams of people were flowing into and out of each other, everyone determined to get to their destination no matter who or what got in their way. And wherever Seth looked, slogans glared back at him. Not just the banners above the little kiosks run by The Way saying things like *Free Trip to*

Heaven. Details inside! but on the clothes people were wearing, the bracelets on their wrists, the chains round their necks. A man walked passed with a slogan on the back of his T-shirt: *When down in the mouth, remember Jonah. He came out all right!* Seth smiled. His personal favourite, and one he used to have on an old key fob, was: *To err is human, to arrrrrr is pirate!* It made him chuckle just to think about it.

Seth was utterly bemused. That people existed like this was something he'd always been aware of, but his life had always been on the road, travelling from religious festival to religious festival. And festivals were busy places, the roads leading to them often packed with pilgrims searching for another glimmer of enlightenment, but it was never like this.

They passed a wide exit on their right, filled with people queuing up for ticket machines, beyond which more people were queuing up for taxis. Two clerics walked past, people moving out of their way unasked. Then someone shoved a leaflet into his hand. She was wearing a T-shirt daubed with the words *When you see only one set of footprints, it was then that I carried you*. The leaflet, Seth discovered, was a quick questionnaire about life, which, when you turned it over, told you that the only way to find the one true answer was to follow The Way and that the best way to do that was to get to church and get praying. Seth screwed it up and threw it in a bin as Lily pulled him on and then came up sharp at a telephone booth.

'Stand there and don't move,' she ordered, searching for some change in a pocket.

'Who are you calling?'

'Someone who changed my life,' replied Lily, 'and helped to save yours.'

Lily punched in the number. When whoever it was on the other end picked up, Seth leaned in to try and hear what they were talking about, but the conversation was over almost as soon as it had started, and Lily hung up.

'Right,' she said, 'I don't know about you but I could do with a decent cooked breakfast. American style!'

Seth stared at the plate in front of him. Never before had he seen so much food. It was like staring at an unscalable mountain of calories.

'Don't let it scare you,' said Lily, her eyes wide with lustful hunger. 'Trust me, you eat this and you'll be fine for a week at least!'

'But pancakes?' said Seth, bemused. 'With syrup and bacon?'

'Too much?' asked Lily. 'Never! You don't have to eat it all, you know, but it's worth trying, surely!'

'Well, that would've been enough on its own, but does it really have to come with two fried eggs and two hash browns?'

'Yes,' said Lily. 'It does. And even though I've never been back and really can't remember it, this reminds me of

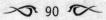

America, the place I was born – and I love it. So eat!'

'And I have to have it with an extra-large chocolate milkshake?'

'With ice-cream floater and extra cream? You betcha!'

Seth stared at Lily's plate, which contained a smoked salmon and cream cheese bagel, and a glass of water.

'Sure you don't want some?'

Lily held up a hand, shook her head.

'How did you find out about this place?'

'It's in my blood,' said Lily, swallowing some of her bagel. 'If you listen, most of the customers here are American. It's that kind of place, you know?'

Seth charged into the pancakes with abandon. The wounds of the night before were more than raw, but focusing on getting some good, sustaining food inside him helped take his mind off it all a little. Though he still had to occasionally shake away the urge to let tears form in his eyes.

With half the food gone, Seth decided to take a rest, picked up his milkshake and drank. There wasn't much left but he didn't care, and it was soon gone.

'Want another?'

'You're joking, right?'

Lily shook her head. 'Refills are half price! Anyway, we've ages yet. We're not due to meet Colin till mid-afternoon.'

'My life was saved by a man called Colin?' said Seth, raising his eyebrows. 'Doesn't he have a more heroic name?'

'Like what?'

Seth shrugged. 'Brett?'

'And that's heroic?'

'Best I could do with little warning,' said Seth. 'So how did Mr Hero – Colin – help save me?'

Lily tapped her head. 'Helped me unravel what was locked in here,' she said mysteriously. 'So tell me about yourself, Seth. What does the Doomsday Kid do when he's not on stage scaring people?'

Seth wasn't sure how to begin, or where. He couldn't recall the last time anyone had been interested in him for who he was, rather than what he did, and he was stumped. Then he remembered something.

'For a start, it's Apocalypse Boy,' he corrected, although he kind of liked Lily's version more. 'And it's my birthday tomorrow. Not that we've ever really done birthdays as a family, so it's not like it's a big celebration. Just a cake and a small present and that's it really.'

The words suddenly hit him and he remembered the card he'd found by his dad's wallet. Not only had they never really done birthday parties or anything, they'd never do them again would they? From now on, his birthdays would be alone.

A great, bottomless hole opened up inside Seth, and he choked back tears as he stared into it, teetering on the edge of oblivion.

'I'm sorry,' said Lily. 'I didn't mean to pry.'

'I know,' said Seth. 'And I know it's not your fault.'

Lily saw a dark shadow fall across Seth, dragging the colour from his face, and it scared her a little. Up to now, she'd seen a terrified boy, confused and ruined by what had happened to him and drowning in sorrow. Now she saw something else. A force in those eyes that unnerved her, and for a second she wondered just how sensible her plan was. But she pushed those thoughts away; she'd come too far now to change them.

'Do you think many people have funerals on their birthday?' Seth asked. 'Not that I'll be having one, but do you think they do? Because it should be me burying my family, but I can't because someone's trying to kill me – and that kind of sucks.'

Lily knew Seth was trying to be flippant, but it wasn't really working.

'How were you going to mark turning thirteen then?' she asked, but the look Seth shot across the table made her immediately aware of her error.

'I never said I was going to be thirteen. How did you know?'

Lily hesitated just that bit too long.

'Lucky guess?'

Seth didn't respond.

'Listen, I can't explain here,' said Lily. 'You'll find out everything you need to later on, just like I promised.'

'But why my birthday? Why's that important?'

'It just is,' said Lily and then noticed something hanging from one of Seth's pockets. Thankful for the distraction she quickly asked with a nod, 'What's that?'

Seth looked down.

'It's Beth's necklace,' he said, pulling it out of the pocket. 'I'd have killed myself if I'd lost that. Thanks for spotting it.'

Lily took the necklace from him for a closer look.

'It's beautiful,' she said. 'You should wear it.'

Seth shook his head. It was a girl's necklace and he wasn't one for jewellery. And, at that moment, being that close to something physical that had been a part of his sister just didn't feel right. Perhaps even a little creepy.

'I don't think so,' he said with a shake of his head. 'It wouldn't suit me.'

'Well, if you stuff it in a pocket again it'll just get lost,' said Lily and, before Seth could react, she'd leaned over and clipped it round his neck. 'There,' she said, 'it suits you. And Beth would like you to wear it, don't you think?'

Seth looked down at the small silver shell now hanging round his neck. He didn't want to admit it, but maybe Lily was right.

'So what about you?' asked Seth. 'Seems like you know enough about me as it is, but you're still little more than a stranger I'm having breakfast with.'

'You'd be surprised,' replied Lily, pulling what looked like a pen out of a belt pouch hidden under her top. Then, as Seth watched, she flipped off the lid and stabbed it into her leg.

'Diabetic,' Lily explained. 'Insulin injection.'

Seth realized then why she hadn't had the breakfast.

'I come here for the smells as much as anything,' she said, putting the insulin pen away again. 'I can't eat most of it, but I can close my eyes in here and in a heartbeat I'm back there, you know?'

'Do you miss it?'

'Never knew it to miss it,' said Lily. 'I was four when my parents gave me up and I came to England.'

'No way.'

'Way.' Lily nodded. 'But enough about me,' she said, cutting the conversation short. 'Ready to get moving?'

Seth, taken aback by the sudden change of tack, nodded and followed Lily out of the diner.

'You don't like trains, do you?' she asked.

Seth shook his head.

'Then you're going to just love the Underground . . .'

10

'YOU WERE RIGHT.'

Lily looked across at Seth.

'About what?'

'The Underground. I loved it almost as much as being shot at.'

Seth was following Lily through London and hoping to any god that happened to be listening that they didn't get split up. It was already the most time he'd ever spent in a city.

'It takes some getting used to,' said Lily, 'but the Underground's all right really. Just got to pick your times right if you can. Rush hour is nothing but armpits and bags being shoved in your face.'

'Where are you taking me?' asked Seth, trying his best

to not look like an alien just landed on a new planet. 'Not that it'll make any difference, but it'd be nice to know.'

Lily pointed through the bustling crowds to a gap on the far side of the square they were crossing. A man was standing on a pavement corner wearing a placard foretelling the end of the world and demanding that people repent. He was handing out leaflets, not that anyone was taking the blindest bit of notice. Seth caught one as it got whipped up in the wind.

'Planet X again,' laughed Lily, looking over Seth's shoulder at the picture of a huge planetoid smashing into Earth. 'People will believe anything, right?'

'I guess so,' said Seth, and pocketed the leaflet. Since the encounter with the cleric, he'd been a bit more careful about disposing of his rubbish.

'That way,' she said. 'Take a left and then we're there, so you'll find out soon enough.'

Seth asked no more questions and focused on keeping up. And, just as Lily had said, he did indeed find out soon enough.

It was past two in the afternoon when they arrived at the destination Lily had promised yet never described. After the first experience, Lily had decided taking Seth on the Underground again would be both a bad idea and a little unfair.

'So it's a church,' he said. 'And there was me thinking

that I might be able to escape religion for once.' He sighed. 'More fool me, huh?'

The building was squeezed into a row of small Victorian terraced houses. It looked awkward and a little ashamed, thought Seth, probably because it was so run down. The windows were covered in wire mesh and the walls were the colour of soot. Against the sandblasted stone of the rest of the street, it made the church look like a rotten tooth in an otherwise perfect set of teeth. The steps leading up to the front door were stained and cracked and, standing on them, with his hands in his pockets was a man, and at his heels a large, well-fed dog that looked part wolf, part every other dog that had ever been bred. Its tail was wagging so furiously it was having to work hard to stay on all-fours.

'That's Colin,' said Lily.

'Funny name for a dog,' said Seth.

Lily laughed.

'The dog's called Snuggles,' she said. 'And he belongs to me.'

Seth baulked. 'Snuggles? You're kidding me, right? But it's built like a bear!'

'*It* is a *he* and he's a real softy,' smiled Lily as she then whistled and the dog, as if the effort was almost too much, got off its backside and sauntered over to her to roll over on to its back for a good belly scratch. Lily looked up to Seth and nodded to the man still on the steps of the church. 'Colin is the one who can help you.'

Colin waved and Lily returned the gesture. He was in his forties, thought Seth, but it was difficult to tell what age exactly thanks to the beard and straggly hair. He was wearing brown corduroy trousers and a checked shirt. Thankfully though, he wasn't wearing socks and sandals, which would have really set the outfit off just right. Seth smiled to himself.

Colin came down to meet them.

'It's really good to meet you, Seth,' he said, and held out his hand.

Seth shook it and immediately noticed the silver glint of the bracelets on Colin's wrist, the sign of a cleric of The Way. The handshake was firm, but at no point did Colin try to crush his hand, a habit Seth had never been able to get his dad to break, despite years of complaining.

'You too,' said Seth. 'Lily never mentioned that you were a cleric.'

Colin said nothing and stepped back to allow Lily, Snuggles and Seth to walk up to the church in front of him. Inside, the place was more of a community centre than the place of worship Seth had been expecting, with posters on the wall, a children's soft play area, another area for teenagers with a pool table. Colin led them to a café, where a number of other people were gathered.

'I thought you said we were just meeting one person?' said Seth, and he could do little to disguise the nervousness now creeping through him, made all the worse thanks to the silver bracelets on Colin's wrists.

'I said I knew someone who could help,' replied Lily. 'Colin can. And his help involves everyone here. So chill, OK?'

Seth sat down on a deep, soft sofa with a high back, and cushions so large it was as though, at any moment, they could join forces and swallow him up whole. He dumped his bag on the floor with a yawn and was brought a mug of hot chocolate by a woman with grey hair and a big smile.

'This'll warm you up, love,' she said. 'I'm Jan. If you need anything, just shout.'

Seth took the drink. It was heaven in a mug and with each sip his eyes grew heavier. But he didn't want to fall asleep. So he pulled them open and looked around.

Lily was standing, speaking to Colin quietly away from everyone else. Snuggles had found a spot on the floor and, after a few circles, simply flopped into it and started snoring. The others seemed intrigued by his presence as if they knew him already.

Seth trained himself back on Lily and Colin, but couldn't make out what they were talking about. He drained his mug of chocolate, the thick sweet liquid slipping down easily. Too easily. Exhaustion fell on him like a tidal wave. Within minutes Seth had drifted into darkness.

When Seth awoke, with a yawn powerful enough to suck in a swarm of bees, he had no idea of the time or where he was. His brain, fuzzy from the sleep, eventually sparked into life, like the spluttering engine of a classic car. He looked around, taking in the details bit by bit. Then, as the faces around him came into focus, he remembered everything.

Colin walked over, hands in pockets, smiling.

Seth remembered Colin, remembered that he was a cleric. And as though his dreams had worked as a sorter of information, carefully ordering all he'd seen since arriving at the church, he worked it all out.

'You're Activists, aren't you?'

'And what makes you say that?' Colin replied with no twitch of emotion.

'I'm used to reading people,' said Seth. 'It's what I do. And I'm good at it. The best. The church as a community centre is a good cover, but there's something more to all this.'

Colin sat back.

'Then tell me, Seth,' he said, 'what is it you can see that other people cannot?'

'That expensive watch you're wearing for a start,' said Seth. 'It looks plain, like what you're wearing, but it's not, is it? It's worth at least a couple of grand. So I'd say that you run this place part time and have another job, one that pays well and allows you the flexibility to be here as often as you can.'

Colin nodded thoughtfully rather than to confirm

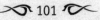

whether Seth was correct or not. 'What else?'

'The bracelets,' continued Seth, 'they say you're a cleric, I say you're not. Just a hunch.'

Colin offered nothing.

'And the church looks tired and badly maintained,' said Seth, 'but you've got security cameras everywhere. Not huge obvious ones, but sneaky little ones, like that one behind you tucked inside the window.'

'Minor details,' shrugged Colin coolly.

'On their own, yes,' agreed Seth, 'but together, they don't add up. And there's much more. The pool table I saw, that looks hardly played on. The posters are up, but they're all a little bit too new, a little bit too neat and tidy. A proper community place like this would be more of a mess, you know, worn in. I could go on . . .'

Colin leaned forward, folded his hands.

'I have no doubt about that,' he said. 'So what do you want to do, Seth?'

At this, Seth was confused. 'How do you mean?'

'Well, you've come all this way, found out who we are. You could hand us in if we really are who you think we are. After all, pretending to be a cleric is a crime, isn't it? You could just walk away. Or not. It's up to you entirely.'

'Really?'

'Look . . .' said Colin, dropping his head and closing his eyes before looking back up at Seth. He slipped the silver bracelets from his wrists and put them in a pocket. 'The

Way isn't as strong as it wants us all to believe, Seth. Powerful, yes, but not as invincible as The Protector would like it to be. Groups are breaking away everywhere. And that's all we're trying to do.'

'You forgot to say "may he always keep us safe",' noticed Seth, 'which means you are Activists, doesn't it? So why don't you just cut to the chase and admit it?'

'The Way uses that phrase to cover everyone and anyone who tries to upset the order they've created,' said Colin.

'So what are you then if you're not Activists?'

'We're just a cell,' said Jan, taking over from Colin. 'A freedom cell, if you will. We grow, we split to become two cells, then four, then eight.'

'I'm not here for a biology lesson,' said Seth.

'Oh, but it's just like biology, you see!' said Jan, warming to her audience and clapping excitedly for a second. 'There are cells everywhere, all across the country, the world even. And their purpose is to grow.'

'Wake me when this gets interesting,' said Seth, rolling his eyes.

Jan wasn't listening and just continued. 'Each cell has a critical mass, the maximum number of members it can have before it splits in half to become two cells. And so on. It's quite simple really.'

'Is it?' said Seth.

Jan nodded enthusiastically. 'It stops any one cell becoming all fat and bloated and huge. And it means our

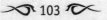

movement is always growing rather than stagnating by just staying in one place. Each new cell has to find new premises, somewhere to grow.'

'Oh, right,' said Seth, beginning to understand what Jan was on about. And it did make some sense. Though still not so sure about Colin yet, Seth already liked Jan. She had an open, honest face, which was a rare thing. Jan wasn't hiding anything, or if she was, when you found it you'd probably wonder why you'd bothered looking in the first place.

Seth nodded, but when Jan had finished he said, 'To be honest, I don't care who you are, what you believe, or why you're doing what you're doing. I'm here because my family are dead and Lily saved my life. So now what? Are you going to help me do something about that?'

'Unlike The Way and their all-powerful Protector, you can trust us,' said Colin, opening his arms to include all the other people in the room with them. Seth had counted nine, and got the measure of most of them already. 'I know better than most what The Way is about and what the true nature of The Protector is. And I truly am sorry for your loss, Seth. It is awful that such a thing can happen.'

'Lose the faith?' asked Seth. 'You talk like you were once as much a believer as anyone else.'

Colin's eyes flickered as though spying a memory far off. 'Yes, long ago. The bracelets are a reminder. But I have family still in the fold, as it were,' said Colin. 'And I hear things.'

Lily sat down next to Seth.

'This all begins and ends with you and me, Seth,' she said. 'But let's start with me, right?'

Two years ago . . .

HUDDLED DOWN A BACK alley, a twelve-year-old girl shivered against a foul wind, laced with rain, doing its best to pick up every ounce of city stink as it gusted past her. She scratched her left arm, the four-year-old tattoo on her shoulder itching like mites burrowing a nest under her flesh.

A sound made her jump and when the cool wet nose of a huge dog nudged her hand she stayed absolutely still. It nudged again, snuggled in. The warmth of its body quickly seeped into the girl and she relaxed. They were both lost and alone. A little bit of company was something they both needed.

In the fitful blackness of sleep, the girl's mind strayed down a thousand other alleyways. The longest led home, back to a time before she'd left her family. The rest, though, always led back to the house as if it was stalking her.

She remembered a bathroom, a patch of grass outside surrounded by a mesh cage, like a giant kennel – for humans, not animals. Food and fresh clothes were delivered through a door hatch. A tutor at the house taught her to read *The Book* and commit it to memory. The rest of her time she learned about world religions, the many paths that existed, all leading to the one true road, the only way to salvation: The Way. She learned about prophecy and the economy and the family unit and charity. She learned about evolution and creationism and the history of moral law. She learned about health and survival and Armageddon and death.

Soon these things shaped the visions that came to her unrequested when she closed her eyes. The girl could not remember when the dreams or visions had started except that her parents had recorded them, prayed about them, then handed her over to those better able to interpret.

As she grew older the visions intensified, became darker and more real and the girl dreaded them. They were no longer adventures into the unknown, but things she'd done before, *lives* she'd lived before.

Something in her visions, a thorn buried deep in her mind, was pulling at her, dragging her towards the realization that she had to get out and find it and remove it or else she would go mad. So when, for the first time in all those years, the door of her room was left open, the girl ran.

But the running had brought her to this alley and no further. The searching for the thorn had led to this.

Another sound stirred the girl and, opening her eyes, she saw two large boots. The dog, clearly sensing a threat, growled. To be protected by something that hardly knew her made the girl reach out with her arm and hug the animal tight.

The boots creaked and the wearer, after kicking the dog hard down the alley, crouched down, a long, grey coat brushing the damp, dirty ground. The girl watched a hand pour something from a bottle into a white rag in another hand. Then the rag was over her mouth and nose and she breathed in such a reek of chemicals that she nearly gagged, but the surprise kept her awake, and the dog had crawled back now and was barking, but her arms were growing weak and she couldn't hold on to the animal much longer – the only friend she'd ever had – and she was tired, oh, so tired, all she wanted to do was let her eyes fall shut . . . when in that moment's hesitation the figure slumped into her and something warm and wet splashed against her face. Too dazed to understand what was happening, the girl watched, as though in a dream, as giant hands pulled her from the ground and held her like a baby and carried her. And then sleep did take her at last . . . and when she awoke the dog was with her and she saw a face she'd never seen before, a friendly face, and that was enough.

'She was delivered to our door two years ago,' said Colin, his eyes resting for a moment on Lily with fatherly affection. 'Unconscious. A mess. Being out on the street had nearly killed her. Snuggles probably saved her from freezing to death that night.'

'You didn't take her to hospital?'

'She was in safer hands than you would believe.'

'I was in bed for two weeks,' said Lily.

'Who drugged you? And what about the person who saved you and brought you here?'

'We took her in, asked no questions,' said Colin. 'She was talking in her sleep when she arrived. At first we thought it was the drugs making her hallucinate. But it soon became clear that it wasn't.'

One of the group, a man in jeans and a threadbare jacket who wore the kind of face you only get by working the roads and digging holes and fuelled by a diet of sausage rolls and strong, sweet tea, tossed a pile of notebooks on to the table. 'She was talking about stuff she could never have known of,' he said. 'We cross-referenced it to historical records from across the world. Everything's in there if you've a spare few hours. Though days would be better, if only to give yourself enough time to get your head round it.'

Seth was finding it hard to keep up. He reached out for the books, flicked through one, didn't really take any of it in, the words just a blur, like newspaper clippings spilled across the floor.

'So that's what this is about? You came and saved my life because of Lily's dreams?'

'Visions,' corrected Colin, a single finger raised slightly on his left hand. 'Past lives, Lord knows how many of them, told with an accuracy that could only come from having been there in the first place. But that wasn't the worst of it . . .'

Lily reached out for Seth's hand and held it gently.

'We don't know how many lives I've lived,' she said, deadly serious, 'but it's thousands. And in each one of them, my sole purpose has been to find you, Seth.'

At that, Seth's blood ran cold. He shivered, tried to pull away. 'Why?'

'To have you killed before you turn thirteen,' said Lily.

12

SETH SNATCHED HIS HAND from Lily and stood up, kicking the chair out from behind him to clatter to the floor.

'You brought me all the way here to kill me?' he stuttered, acutely aware that he had no way of escape; the door was at the other end of the café, and between him and it was what looked now like a sea of tables and chairs. 'It doesn't make sense! You saved me, remember? If you hadn't found me, I'd be dead in the caravan with Beth! With Mum and Dad!'

Colin, as though now dealing with a cornered animal, slowly held up his hands and leaned back in his chair.

'You have to listen to us, Seth,' he said. 'Please, just listen. That's all I ask.'

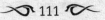

'You're mental!' replied Seth, his voice shaking just like the rest of him now. 'All of you! Why save me only to kill me here? What sick stuff are you into? Am I a sacrifice? Is that it?'

He'd have laughed if he'd not been so scared, his eyes now darting about, searching for a sacrificial knife hidden behind someone's back.

A laptop computer was placed on the table between Colin and Seth. Colin flipped it open, tapped a few keys, swung it round so Seth could see what was on the screen.

'Know what this is, Seth?'

Seth hadn't the faintest idea – a map of the world, lots of data; at that moment in time, he didn't give a stuff. He just wanted out.

'This is Prophet,' said Colin, his kind demeanour replaced by an altogether more calculated one. 'Believe it or not, The Way has been working on it since the mid-nineties, since the advent of the Internet.'

The screen displayed a highly detailed world map. Pinpoints of varying colours could be seen appearing and disappearing like tiny fireworks. A data feed was continuously updating itself down the right of the screen. On the left was a menu.

'So what is it?' asked Seth. 'And why should I in any way care?'

Colin clicked on the menu and another box of data appeared. Some of the information was related to specific events in an area deep inside China. The rest of it was cross-referenced to numerous prophecies and predictions, covering all known beliefs, religions, prophets and seers, from Nostradamus to Zoroastrianism, the Mayan calendar's supposed prediction of the end of the world to the Bible.

'The how is not important,' said Colin. 'Not to us anyway. But that it exists at all is enough.'

'But what does it do?' asked Seth. 'Or are you just going to sit there not getting to the point?'

'In simple terms,' replied Colin, his voice still calm despite Seth's obvious impatience, 'it tracks world events to predict the end of the world. And it is able to identify, with a high degree of accuracy, those who may be a threat not simply to The Way, but the world itself. Thus the name, Prophet.'

Seth let out a short, sharp laugh. 'But that's impossible!' he sneered. 'It's just guesswork. And believe me, I know a little about supposedly seeing into the future.'

Colin clicked another item on the menu. And there, in front of them as clear as day, was a stream of data showing the connection between a volcanic eruption that had recently destroyed an island, killing hundreds and forcing thousands to flee, a little-known text from a fragment of the Dead Sea Scrolls, a prediction by Nostradamus and finally the rise of evil that brought about the last world war.

'Proves nothing,' said Seth, shaking his head, but just

as he was about to say something else derogatory about the whole idea of Prophet, he noticed something: a date in the top right-hand corner and, next to it, a clock counting down. It was tomorrow, his birthday.

'What's that?' he asked, jabbing a finger at the screen. 'What's the countdown for?'

Colin ignored him.

'Software such as this is up there with the kind of advanced stuff only the world's top military and intelligence departments get their hands on. Does it strike you as odd that a religious organization supposedly run for the good of all and with our salvation at heart would have something like this so easily to hand?'

'I asked a question,' reminded Seth.

'And I shall answer it,' said Colin patiently. 'Prophet is an advanced data analysis program. It tracks all Internet traffic across the globe, cross-referencing this with the data it has already collected since it was made live a few years ago.'

'Is this going anywhere? Because if not, I am,' said Seth.

'Prophet,' said Colin, 'takes this information, compares it to every possible prophecy from whatever source you can think of and then uses it to identify signs that point to the end of the world.'

Seth said, 'What, this is a map to Armageddon or something? But that's—'

'Impossible? No,' said Colin, shutting Seth down.

'Until now, The Way has depended on the likes of Lily to help them – people born with a gift to see things; seers, if you will. Or Finders, as they are sometimes called. And that's how it's been for a thousand years at least, maybe more.'

Seth was back in his chair.

'So are you going to tell me why this huge piece of software has a countdown to my birthday or what?'

'The Way believes in the end times, Seth,' said Lily. 'Full-on fire and brimstone stuff.'

'Everyone does, or hadn't you noticed?' Seth replied. 'How do you think I got to be so successful?'

At that, he laughed. Successful? Yeah, whatever.

'And the reason everyone believes,' said Colin, 'is because The Way has encouraged it, nurtured it like a flower in a greenhouse. Only now that flower no longer needs any care – it's big enough to look after itself.' Colin took a calming breath. 'The difference now is that The Way has taken it a step further, Seth. It believes its purpose is not just to save humanity through spiritual guidance, but to prevent the end times ever happening in the first place.'

'That's impossible,' said Seth.

'Is it?' said Colin. 'The Protector doesn't think so. He doesn't just want to bring people to God. He wants to play at *being* God.'

Silence.

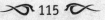

Colin then asked, 'How well do you know *The Book*, Seth?'

'Well enough,' Seth replied. 'Going to test me on it? Dad always did. I was an A-star student.'

'Then allow me to paraphrase: *And I saw in the right hand of him that sat on the throne a book with seven seals.*'

'Revelation.' Seth shrugged. 'So what?'

'Remember what happens?'

'I guess,' said Seth. 'The world ends, right? But it's all OK because it was God's idea.'

Colin bowed his head, clasped his hands, then spoke as if praying. '*And I saw, and behold a white horse: and he that sat on him had a bow; and a crown was given unto him: and he went forth conquering, and to conquer.*'

Seth knew the verse Colin had recited. If he'd wanted, he could have continued where Colin had stopped, probably made it all the way to the end of *The Book* without so much as putting a single word wrong. Like he'd said, an A-star student.

'The first of the four Riders,' said Seth. But then, just as he was about to deride Colin's very obvious fear of little more than a few words, he remembered what he'd seen when Lily had touched him, the vision of a scorched Earth, and the hellish silhouettes of four riders staring down from a mountain. Realization exploded in his brain like a grenade.

'You're kidding me,' he said, voice quiet, as if he was

whispering at a funeral. 'The Way thinks I'm the first Rider?'

The words were awkward in his mouth, as though he was attempting to communicate in a foreign language for the first time. They stuck between his teeth like toffee.

'But that's impossible!' said Seth, keenly aware that he'd already overused that word in the past few minutes. 'I mean, it's not just impossible, it's stupid! Only an idiot would believe anything so nuts!'

'Not so,' said Colin.

'Thanks to me, you've never before lived to reach thirteen,' said Lily. 'The Way believes that you, or anyone it thinks has the potential to become the first Rider, will achieve their destiny when they turn thirteen years old.'

'Which is why they're now probably scouring the country looking for you,' added Colin. 'Tomorrow, it won't be just your birthday, Seth. To The Way, it's Doomsday. And you, Seth, are its harbinger.'

Seth let out a long breath.

'And you actually believe this?'

'We believe that it is wrong for any organization to achieve its ends through calculated, premeditated murder. That it involves the killing of children makes it barbaric and evil in the extreme.'

'So saving me is a way of sticking two fingers up at The Way, yeah?'

Colin, at last, smiled.

'Something like that, yes.'

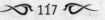

'You realize this is insane.'

'It doesn't matter if you think my dreams are just that and not visions,' said Lily, 'or that this whole Prophet thing is crazy. In fact, you don't have to believe any of it; you'd probably be better off if you didn't. But the truth of the matter is that The Way tried to kill you because *it* believes it. That in itself is pretty terrifying, right?'

Seth stared into the middle distance. Outside the day was turning to evening now, a dusting of grey to the sky that signified darkness was coming. You had to really look to see it, but it was there.

'I need to take a wazz,' said Seth.

Colin at first looked confused then said, 'The toilets are back the way we came in, first door on the left.'

Seth nodded a thanks as he got up from the table, stepping over his bag on the way.

'We don't mean you any harm,' Colin told Seth as he made to leave the café. 'You have to believe us.'

Seth didn't respond, just kept on walking. When he came to the toilets, a dizziness took over and he leaned against the cool wall to regain his composure.

In the past twenty-four hours he'd had visions of the end of the world, seen his family murdered, been shot at, kissed a girl, and had now discovered that the people who wanted him dead did so because they believed he was the first Rider of the Apocalypse.

He rested his head back, but all that did was make him

feel worse and, as he brought it forward again, his world spun once more – only this time it was worse and a wave of nausea crashed down on him with the force of a tsunami. He threw up, reaching the toilet just in time.

Seth flushed away the vomit then washed his hands and splashed water over his face, leaning on the basin to let the water drip from his nose and down into the plughole. Whether it was information overload, or exhaustion, or both he didn't know, but he was overheating and the water seemed to steam against his skin. His reflection stared back at him from a small mirror pinned to the wall. Seth hardly recognized himself. It was like staring into the eyes of a total stranger.

Seth imagined being able to swap places with his reflection, let another version of himself take over where he'd left off. Then he imagined it reaching out of the mirror to wrap its fingers around his neck and squeeze the life out of him.

Seth left the toilet and made to go back towards the café, towards Lily and Colin and Jan and Snuggles and the others, when the front door of the church caught his attention. It was open. He wasn't thinking about running, but if he could just get out there and have some time alone, perhaps this would all make a little more sense. Well, it couldn't make any less sense, could it?

Quietly, Seth turned on his heels and started towards the door. He had an inkling that Colin would get suspicious and come looking soon, so he had to get safely outside before he was found out. But sprinting out through the door would make too much noise, so he stuck with creeping out like a thief in the night.

As he reached for the door, Seth heard a voice call out behind him.

'They'll find you.'

'They don't even know I'm here, Lily,' Seth replied, stepping through the door. 'No one does.'

'Don't . . .' said Lily.

But it was too late.

Seth raced out into the late-afternoon sun.

13

SETH HEARD LILY'S VOICE again as he pelted round a corner in the road and spotted some parkland ahead. All he wanted was a bit of space. Just some time to sort out his head without being stared at by a bunch of people he'd never met before. Was that too much to ask? Clearly, it was.

He kept going, gulping air, amazed at the amount of running he'd had to do since yesterday, wondering why anyone would ever do it for fun.

Dodging a couple of angry-beeping cars, their drivers spitting verbal filth out of their windows along with cigarette butts, Seth made it across road after road and was soon lost.

He walked and walked – for minutes or hours, he wasn't

sure. The world went by like a spill of paint on water, mixing and swirling into a thousand different colours. Buildings merging into pavements into roads into people.

Seth found a park. He was getting hungry, too, and rummaging through his pockets found some change. The last time he'd bought anything was the soup back at Glastonbury. A lot had happened since then. Too much.

With enough cash to buy a hot chocolate and a warm and greasy cheese-and-ham-stuffed croissant, which leaked delicious fat down his chin to stain his clothes, Seth slipped off into the trees of the park, and hopefully out of sight of anyone walking by. Leafy shade spilled over him and he no longer felt like he was in the city at all, but some odd, green oasis of calm and quiet.

Out of nowhere, Seth cramped up and he almost dropped to the ground. He'd heard or read somewhere that it was always best to run through a stitch rather than stop, but he didn't believe any of it and slumped down against the trunk of a huge oak tree.

A buzz from Seth's pocket jarred him and he pulled out his phone. Another quote from *The Book*, but this time with the added joy of a picture of The Protector. Seth resisted the urge to throw his phone hard and lose it for ever. Knowing his luck, another cleric would turn up and start hitting him with questions. Or worse.

For a few minutes, Seth was jittery. Every sound, every movement, every change of shadow, would have him thinking either Lily had found him or, worse, that figure with the gun from the night before. But eventually he calmed down and accepted that he was, for a while at least, alone.

It felt good.

Seth rested his head back against the tree and stared up into its branches, the sky slipping now from late afternoon to early evening. Something crumpled in his trousers and he remembered the card he'd shoved into his back pocket. Reaching round, he pulled it out. It was an envelope with his name on it. With a quick rip, he tore through to the card inside. It was handmade, no doubt by his mum. She'd had a habit of taking up odd craft hobbies, he thought, then stopped when he realized he was thinking about her in the past tense. That alone was enough to tip his world into chaos and disorder. And, right now, he had plenty of both.

The picture on the front of the card was of an unopened book, next to it a pen. Some metaphor about his future being the book for him to write or something, he guessed. Inside, they'd all signed it: Mum, Dad and Beth. No money, no gift, just their love, always.

Always . . .

They'd not known how little time they'd had left, had they? What use to him was their always-and-for ever now that he was alone? Rage bubbled inside him and he screwed up the card and with a roar launched it into the sky, closing his eyes as tears and pain and sorrow took over.

Something wet nudged his hand. Seth opened his eyes to find himself staring into the enormous jaws of a huge dog. In its mouth was the card, still balled up.

'Get lost!' said Seth, pushing at the dog. 'Go on – get!'

The dog stayed put. Stared at Seth. Wagged its tail. Then dropped the soggy ball of card on to his lap.

Seth reached down to throw the card away once more when he realized he recognized the dog.

'Snuggles?'

The dog wagged its tail. It hit the ground like a thick cable whacking a mattress.

'He likes you.'

The voice had come from above. Seth looked up to find Lily looking down.

'You suck at hiding by the way. I mean *really* suck.'

Lily swung down from the tree and dropped in next to Seth. Snuggles nuzzled her then flopped on to his belly, his head falling into her lap.

'You coming back now? It's gone seven, you know. And it'll get cold soon. Wouldn't want to be out here when it's all dark and creepy and you've nowhere to put your head down except under a bush.'

Seth shook his head, his eyes half closed.

'Doesn't make sense yet, up here,' he said, tapping his skull. 'Not sure it ever will.'

'Never said it would,' said Lily. 'Or that it ever should.'

After everything Seth had gone through, Lily was surprised Seth wasn't a gibbering mess. She was impressed with his grit. And she also found it impossible to imagine him as anything like what her visions had shown her he could become. Saving his life was her good deed. She'd never really considered the consequences. Now, sitting with him under that tree, and with Snuggles by her side, the evening in full swing, the consequences didn't seem to matter. Seth was just a boy, nothing more, and she'd stopped some warped fools murdering him. That was it. Job done.

Snuggles jerked his head up, ears pricked.

'Stupid dog,' said Seth. 'Jumps at anything. What's he seen, a hotdog stand?'

Lily wasn't so dismissive.

'We have to go,' she ordered. 'Like right now.'

She sprang to her feet. Snuggles was growling, the hair on his back up like a porcupine's spines.

'I'm not going anywhere,' said Seth. 'You said no one knew I was here, right?'

'No one *did*,' said Lily. 'Past tense. This is now. Get up!'

Seth had no choice but to comply as Lily heaved him off the floor, again displaying a strength not generally associated with someone of her size.

'We need to get back to Colin,' said Lily. 'He'll know what to do.'

'You're serious, aren't you?' said Seth. 'You really think

that your stupid dog there has sensed something?'

Lily didn't answer. She was already running, Snuggles by her side.

Seth caught up as they rounded the corner on to the road where Colin's church sat hunched and tired. They bounded up the steps. Colin was waiting for them.

'What's wrong?'

'Snuggles,' said Lily. 'Something put the wind up him. Didn't want to take any chances.'

As they followed Colin into the church a phone rang. Colin pulled out his mobile and answered. The conversation was short and when he hung up he was wearing the face of a soldier about to go into combat.

'Colin?'

'No time, Lily,' he said, his complexion growing paler by the second. 'Keep Seth safe. No matter what. Understand?'

Seth was about to comment on the unnecessary drama when something smashed through a window. Smoke poured out of a grey canister now spinning on the carpet.

'Colin . . .'

'No arguing, Lily!' Colin snapped. 'Now, move!'

Seth almost fell backwards as Lily grabbed him and flipped him round to run through the church. As he found his feet, terror once again tearing its claws into his back, he saw the church door blast open and a figure walk in and knock Colin to the ground. Even through the smoke and dust, Seth recognized what this person was just from the clothes it was wearing: it was one of The Chosen.

Seth went to yell out but a shout from the direction they were running in caught him and he turned to see another of The Chosen knocking Lily to the floor as though she were little more than a fly. Seth was about to cry out to her but Lily was on her feet in a second, Snuggles at her side. And her eyes were fierce, burning.

The figure laughed as Lily made ready to fight, then it raised a pistol to take aim. But Lily was into the figure faster than the trigger could be pulled. With the advantage of surprise on her side, she grabbed the hand holding the gun and swung it down into the stomach of the intruder. She then went in with a flurry of punches and Seth was astonished to see the pistol fall to the floor. Snuggles bounded over and stole the weapon as Lily regained her posture, breathing deep to suck oxygen into her lungs.

The figure was on its knees and Seth thought they had a chance. But then two more of The Chosen appeared and, before Seth was able to react, one had grabbed him round his neck and was dragging him towards the front door, and the other had Lily's hands behind her back and tied with a plastic tag. Seth saw that whoever was dragging him had their pistol drawn.

Screaming and kicking and yelling and scratching – none of it did any good. The figure just kept on dragging Seth towards the church entrance. He saw Colin being pushed through a door. He was putting up a fight, but it was doing no good. The door slammed shut and the next sound he heard was gunshots. Two of them, short and sharp.

Lily screamed. Seth was numb. At the church door, a shadow unrolled itself across the entrance. It was a man in a black suit carrying what looked to Seth like a body bag. The man dropped it to the floor and Seth noticed the weapon at the man's side. It looked capable of blasting a hole through a bank vault. Then Seth did a double take. Round the man's neck was a white dog collar: he was a priest.

Seth didn't even pray. No time. No point.

With fearsome speed and ferocity the man launched himself at the figure holding Seth. He wrenched the gun from its hand in a snapping move which, judging by the yell, broke every finger. Immediately after came two shots in rapid succession and the arms that had held him fell away. Seth looked down into the blank eyes of a woman with two neat holes in her forehead. The back of her head was a mess of blood and gore dripping on to the floor.

The priest dipped to the ground, holstered his own pistol and armed himself again with the pistol that had been only a moment ago clasped in the dead woman's hands.

Seth backed off. The Chosen were scary enough, but this man of God was a lot more unsettling. Not least because, as he checked the pistol's magazine, then pulled back the sliding mechanism to chamber a round, he was crying.

'Keep down,' the priest said, glancing at Seth through wet eyes. His voice was quiet, almost caring. It didn't quite fit with the act of fierce violence he'd just committed. He wiped his tears with a cuff then added, 'I'm here to take you somewhere safe. Understand?'

Seth nodded sharply and noticed that the priest's hands were gloved.

The priest briefly rested a hand on Seth's shoulder, squeezed it, then stood up. A volley of gunshots rang out and Seth, backed up against a wall now, his hands over his ears against the sound, watched the other intruders fall, almost more surprised than he by the turn of events.

The priest went at it like he was in a computer game: *bang-bang-bang-bang-bang*. He then switched his aim to where Colin had been taken and called out a name, his voice clear, but shaking. The door snapped opened and the priest blasted two shots into the figure behind it, sending them sprawling back to the floor, dead. For a split second Seth had thought it was Colin, but then realized it wasn't. Because Colin was already dead somewhere beyond that door. He'd been the first to die.

Seth wasn't given time to think as the priest grabbed him and hurried him out of the church and down the steps.

'Into the car! Now!'

Seth, battered and bruised, looked up into the face of a

vehicle that looked as though its only mission in life was to scare other vehicles. What it was, he didn't know, but it was long and black and creepy: a four-door saloon built from the ground up out of shadows and the night. It was an odd car for a priest, he thought, but then again when was the last time he'd seen a priest with a gun, never mind kill anyone?

Lily sprinted out of the church with Snuggles hot on her heels. She leaped over Seth and slid across the bench seat in the front of the car.

'Get up, you idiot!' she yelled, Snuggles jumping up to sit on her lap. 'Get in!'

But Seth was now staring up at the church. The priest was at the door, his bag still in his hand. For a moment, he swept his eyes left to right, surveying the scene of destruction. He wiped his eyes with the back of the hand holding the pistol then unzipped the bag, rolled its heavy contents out into the church, about-faced and raced down the steps, tossing the pistol back into the church behind him.

Seth pushed himself to his feet and stumbled to the open door of the car. He went to climb in, then remembered his bag, the one containing the only possessions he had in this world, back in the café. He made to go back for them, but the priest didn't give him a chance to take one step back towards the church, pushing him unceremoniously down into the car, then sliding in after him. Seth sat squashed between Lily and Snuggles and the priest.

The priest slammed the door, checked his watch, stole a glance back at the church, then fired the engine. Seth noticed that the man was shaking and his pale face was clammy with perspiration, his eyes red.

Finally, and without a word spoken, the priest clipped in his seatbelt then punched the accelerator.

Seth didn't even have time to buckle up.

14

THE FORCE OF THE church exploding in a fireball of glass and brick and shattered prayers quickly caught up with the car. Seth ducked as the wave of dust, billowing out like the train of a wedding dress caught in a storm, rolled past. His ears popped and, for the next few minutes, the world was a technicolour silent movie of speed, rushed traffic lights, and terrified pedestrians.

Seth finally managed to clip in his seatbelt, and braced his feet hard against the floor to stop him sliding left and right into Lily or the priest. Just in time, too, as the priest then flicked the back end of the car round and sent the vehicle into a sideways slide, careering off in a new direction completely.

But it was the traffic lights that really caught Seth's

attention. As they raced through the first few sets on green he figured it was just good luck. And as far as he was concerned, he was overdue a little bit of that, to say the least. But when he noticed that the lights were changing to green *as they approached* it made him sit up and take notice. It was as if the city of London was clearing a way for them to get out, damming up the other traffic as best it could to allow them to race through the city's guts unhindered. Seth hadn't a clue as to their destination, but how was that any different to the past two days? Or indeed his whole life?

Seth's hearing exploded back into action as the priest pulled the car on to a sliproad and down on to a larger thoroughfare. He caught the words *North Circular* on a large sign and, for the first time since racing away from the death and destruction back at the church, they were in traffic. Horns blasted out as they cut between a lorry and an expensive BMW, the driver clearly doing his best to look like businessman of the year. Free of the smaller roads and all the junctions he'd had to negotiate, the priest dropped a gear, nailed the accelerator and heaved them forward at an even greater pace now, zigzagging in and out of the traffic like a needle mending a tear in cloth.

It was then, as all of Seth's senses came back online, almost as though they'd been waiting to check that the coast was clear, that he noticed Lily's hand gripping his leg. Her knuckles were white with the pressure of it and, even though she was pinching hard enough to make him wince, he did nothing about it. And that was because, when he looked up to ask her to stop, he saw the tears streaming down her face. He gently placed his own hand on hers and squeezed his fingers a little, in the hope of giving her at least some comfort. Seth remembered the look he'd seen in Colin's eyes as he'd gazed at Lily. It had been an affection few have for another unless they are the parent of a child in whom all their hopes and loves are contained. But Colin was dead now. Seth was beginning to believe death itself was following him. And perhaps it was.

It was late, the moon low and bright, staring out across the world with all the interest of a bored teenager. Clouds were quickly gathering, pulling their way across the sky like a great blanket of misery, for there was rain in them, great black sheets of the stuff, and the world already in their shadow was sodden.

The priest steered the vehicle up a sliproad as rain began to fall. Soon, with the clouds now fully overhead, and the moon blocked out completely, the rain was coming down like solid rods, exploding on the bonnet with a thunderous racket. They sped past a sign for the M11 then down on to a dual carriageway, which, Seth saw now, was completely clear of traffic.

'We'll be out of London soon,' the priest said, clearly fighting to keep his voice calm and level. But it was shaky at the edges and Seth saw how the knuckles of the man's hands as they gripped the steering wheel were white. He gave no explanation for what had happened. And no hint as to where he was taking them.

It wasn't enough for Seth. Escaping with Lily after the murder of his parents was one thing. But being raced away from a scene of untold violence by a priest was completely different. He *needed* answers. And immediately.

'Who are you?' he asked. 'Is that a disguise or are you actually a priest?'

Nothing.

'Where are you taking us?'

Still nothing.

'How did you know where to find us? Why did you have to—'

Seth flinched as the man reached inside his jacket. He half expected to see that huge pistol again and have the thing jammed under his chin to blow a great pink-and-red fountain of brains out from the top of his head. Instead, he saw a mobile phone.

'I'll explain everything when we're out of here and safe,' said the priest punching numbers on the phone, his eyes not leaving the road ahead. 'I promise. You just have to trust me. And believe me, after what just happened, I really do know how hard that must be for you.'

Lily squeezed her hand harder into Seth's leg.

'Hush!' she whispered, wiping away with the back of her other hand the now pretty much dried-up tears from her face. 'He saved our lives. And he's called Saul. That's all you need to know. He'll tell you more when he's ready. Got it?'

Seth made to argue but the look in Lily's eyes made him change his mind. The pain and loss there was clear. He'd trusted her this far, so why not a bit further? It wasn't as though he had anything to lose. Not any more.

Whoever the man had called answered. Seth couldn't make out the words, but tried to listen in anyway.

'The target is eliminated,' said Saul, his voice firmer now, more in control, but there was still a faint quiver to it, like a cry was waiting at the back of his throat to come out. 'All the evidence has been destroyed.'

A fuzzy, crackly response came down the phone. The car raced past a sliproad signposted to the M25 and Seth saw it pass beneath them, a river of traffic bumper-to-bumper and unmoving.

'I was just in time,' said the priest. 'It was exactly as I'd suspected: an Activist had infiltrated The Chosen. By the time I'd arrived, she had already killed the others—'

The voice on the end of the line interrupted. Saul rubbed his eyes with his right hand before replying.

'I got there as quickly as I could. She must've been there to take the boy.'

The boy? thought Seth, guessing that Saul was now talking about him. He'd known immediately on seeing them that the intruders, who were now all dead, were The

Chosen, but why was Saul saying they were trying to take him? As far as he could tell, they'd turned up with the express purpose of killing him! And hadn't Saul just pinned their deaths on the woman he'd shot first?

Another crackly response.

'Dead,' said Saul. 'It was the only option. I'll report in later.'

He hung up and Seth saw pain and remorse rake its way across the priest's face like the wound from an angry scythe.

The rain was still hammering down, as though trying to beat the world into submission. And still, inexplicably, the road ahead was absent of all other traffic. It was like driving along a road in a world empty of humanity, with only the concrete around them to serve as a reminder that they had ever existed at all. Seth considered the notion of pestering Saul with more questions but decided to go with Lily and keep quiet. With no reason yet to think she was doing anything but trying to look after him, he figured now was no different. And Saul was clearly a man with some power. And anyway, with the drone of the tyres on the road, and the relentless rain beating out a tattoo of drums on the car, his head was beginning to ache.

Seth flicked a glance over to Lily, wide awake next to him and staring ahead, unblinking almost, as London faded behind them.

The world ahead pulled them forward.

* * *

By the time they finally left the motorway the world was a different place. Instead of the empty, black lanes, the Morse code trail of cat's-eyes reflecting the car's bright headlights, and the occasional glimpse of housing and industrial estates fading into evening, the blackness of night was around them. The single carriageway was raised metres high on a great dyke. Down the left side ran a river. To the right, the land dropped away to a seemingly endless patchwork plain of fields as flat as a pool table, and when the car's headlights swung out to the horizon, like the line of a fishing rod cast out, Seth could see for miles.

Seth caught sight of a watch on Saul's wrist. It was gone midnight and one a.m. was fast approaching. It took Seth a few moments to realize exactly what this meant. And when he did he remembered the crumbled card in his pocket that Snuggles had returned to him back in the park.

'It's . . . my birthday,' he said, his voice quiet, as though sharing news born of sorrow. 'I'm thirteen.'

'I know,' Lily smiled weakly, as though such news was enough to scare. 'Happy birthday. Though I was expecting more, to be honest. You know, the sky turning black, perhaps an earthquake or two. But nothing.'

'Sorry,' said Seth. 'Must be a real disappointment to be sitting next to the first Rider of the Apocalypse and not to see even a horse.'

Seth wasn't entirely sure why they were joking about it.

Or how. But it was true that here he was, and a big fat zilch had occurred. Perhaps the world wasn't ending today after all. He looked across at Saul.

'So,' said Seth, folding his arms across his chest, 'seeing as you and Lily clearly know each other, how about you start to tell me who you are?'

15

'I AM A PRIEST,' said Saul, reaching up to rip the dog collar from his neck and toss it over his shoulder into the back of the car. 'I am also the head of The Chosen and, by default, the personal bodyguard of The Protector of The Way.'

Seth wasn't sure he wanted to hear any more. He was sitting between a girl dedicated to hunting him down to have him killed before his thirteenth birthday and a man who worked for the one running the organization that would have done the killing.

'It was not supposed to be this way,' said Saul with real hurt in his voice as the words choked on each other. 'I am so . . . sorry.'

Seth's mind started to work overtime. Things he'd seen

and heard were beginning to click into place like the hidden gears and locks in the door of a safe. Those old skills from his life as the Apocalypse Boy were back online and running white-hot.

'You phoned ahead to warn us,' he said, remembering Colin's short phone call before everything had then turned to hell back at the church. 'But it was too late and you only just turned up in time.'

'Colin is – I mean *was*,' said Saul, correcting himself, 'my brother.'

His voice broke on that last word, as though speaking it was enough to rip his heart out from his chest.

Seth's eyes opened at this and the words 'I'm sorry' fell from his mouth without him even having to think them.

'He knew this was dangerous,' said Saul, his hands clenching and unclenching on the steering wheel. 'We all did. *You* are dangerous, Seth, though by what you do or cause, or simply because of what you represent, none of us really knows. Not yet.'

A few more gears and locks slid smoothly together. At least he now understood how Saul knew Lily.

'It was a body you were carrying in that bag, wasn't it?'

Saul said nothing, just stared at the road ahead. They passed two cars lying down the side of the dyke, both on their roofs and on fire, wheels still spinning. It was a haunting scene and seemed utterly out of place with the quiet of the landscape around them. That it had happened recently, judging by the fire and that no police or fire engine were anywhere to be seen, struck Seth as equally odd.

As the crash site drifted by, Seth turned his attention back to Saul. 'Somehow you discovered that The Chosen had found us, didn't you?'

Saul nodded.

'And I don't want to know where you got the body,' continued Seth, 'but it's a double for me, right?'

Still, Saul said nothing, though Seth watched him clench his jaw like he was grinding ballbearings.

'You took the gun from the woman you first shot so that the rest of the killings would be traced to her instead of you. I noticed your gloves. No fingerprints, right? Then, with the church burned to the ground, thanks to whatever explosives or incendiary stuff you'd brought with you in that bag with my body double, the corpses would be discovered and The Way would find one they'd assume to be me.'

'It is as you have said,' nodded Saul. 'You're bright, Seth, I'll give you that. And as for the body? Well, let's just say that morgues are easier to steal from than people would ever want to know.' Saul then tapped a finger against his neck where the white dog collar had, just a minute or so ago, been. 'Particularly if you wear one of those.'

That he'd worked it out at all had Seth stumped for what to say next. He hadn't expected to get it so quickly. But he had and he was now left with the stark reality of what had happened. And it was all because of him, once again.

'When you killed them, it was like watching a machine or something,' he said. 'And you knew them, didn't you? And you still killed them to rescue me. It doesn't make sense. None of it does.'

'I've bought us some time,' said Saul, and Seth saw how, since starting to talk, the man seemed to have shrunk, almost as though the weight of what had happened was crushing him. 'The Way now believes you to be dead, Seth. As far as The Protector is concerned, he will now be thinking his mission in saving the world from an end it damned well deserves is complete. If you'll excuse the pun.'

The raw aggression in Saul's voice didn't go unnoticed to Seth, but he said nothing about it.

'So what happens now?' he asked. 'If I'm dead, and haven't got dozens of people scouring the country to find and execute me, what are we going to do next?'

'We will see what we shall see,' said Saul cryptically.

'Well, that's a lot of help,' said Seth. 'Thanks.'

And then a huge shape flashed in the headlights. Saul jammed his foot down hard on the brakes as though he was trying to kick a hole in the floor. The car slid forwards, wheels screeching, rubber melting into a thick oily smoke. Saul released the brakes, pumped them again, tried to heave the vehicle back online, get it facing down the road in the right direction again, but it was having none of it, momentum now taking full control and dragging the car into a dramatic sideways slide.

All Seth saw then was the world flip and spin as though he were trapped inside a giant washing machine. The horizon flew past twice before the car landed on its wheels, but that didn't stop the spinning. It rolled down the side of the dyke, eventually coming to a halt as it slammed hard into a tree. The ageing silver birch groaned under the impact, splintering halfway up its trunk to fall over the vehicle.

Seth snapped open his eyes. Fluttering in front of him was a small piece of paper, folded and creased. His vision was blurred but it quickly went back to normal and he recognized the piece of paper. It was the leaflet he'd picked up back at the station when he'd arrived in London, the one about Planet X. He figured there were no clerics nearby at that moment to chastise him for not picking up litter, and he closed his eyes again, ignoring it.

For a moment then, Seth moved nothing. Not a finger, not his head, just sat, waiting for the pain to hit. But it didn't and Seth realized he was not injured at all. Miraculously he'd survived a crash that had written off the car. But what about Lily and Saul?

Saul, Seth could see, was at least breathing. Across his forehead was a gash bleeding profusely down his face.

Whether he'd smashed it against the steering wheel or what, Seth was unsure, but there was nothing he could do, so he turned his attention to Lily.

Lily was slumped sideways in her chair like a rag doll. In her lap was Snuggles' great, drooling head. The dog whined anxiously. But like Seth it seemed unharmed.

Trapped between Lily and Saul, and with the roof crushed and the windows blown in, Seth almost lost himself to panic. But when he tried his seatbelt and heard it unclip, and then found that he could move and shuffle round in his seat, he figured they had a chance. All he had to do was get out.

He reached over past Saul, but the door was jammed and getting past the huge man would've been impossible. He tried the windows but cut his hands almost immediately and gave up. If he couldn't open Lily's door either, then he'd have to try climbing out through the back.

Seth leaned over, tugged at the handle. Nothing. He tried again, frustration making him roar. He then flipped himself round and, with a cry of rage and sorrow and confusion and desperation, he drove his feet into it. The door, clearly weakened by the crash, snapped off at the hinges, bounced on the ground then, for a few seconds, spun like a penny on its edge, before crashing to the ground. Snuggles jumped out, but didn't leave Lily's side. Seth clambered out after him, released Lily's seatbelt, then allowed her to fall across his shoulders to carry her out and on to the ground.

* * *

Lily woke to see a concerned Seth leaning over her, the wreck of the car like a broken dinosaur behind him, Snuggles at her side.

'I remember skidding,' she said. 'Something ran out in front of us. What the hell was it?'

'No idea,' said Seth. He'd seen something too, but what it was, or what he *thought* it was – well, that was just too stupid to even admit to. 'But don't move, OK? Just take it easy. I'm amazed any of us are alive after that.'

'Saul?'

'He's alive, I think, but he's cracked his head. Other than that, I don't know. The door's jammed. I couldn't get him out.'

'What about me?'

'I got angry,' said Seth. 'You wouldn't like to see me when I'm angry.'

Lily, despite the nausea and the throbbing headache, laughed. 'Do you turn green too?'

'Purple actually,' said Seth.

Snuggles nudged Lily's arm with his nose.

'Your dog seems OK,' said Seth and reached out to stroke the animal's head. But as he did so a sound from behind him in the dark stopped his heart.

'What the hell was that?' said Lily.

Snuggles made a low growl and it rumbled around in the dark as if it was searching for the source of the noise.

To Seth it had sounded like a beast the size of a rhino was breathing out through its nose, like it was readying itself to charge.

'I . . . I don't know,' he said. And he didn't want to find out either. He wanted to run, but it was as though his legs were no longer working. He couldn't move, was stuck fast. 'Probably just a fox or badger, right?'

Lily said nothing, just stared with Seth into a darkness as thick as treacle.

The sound came again, closer this time, and louder.

'Whatever it is, I don't like it,' said Lily.

When it came once more, they both saw what looked like two great blasts of dragon steam shoot out from the shadows. They were on their feet immediately and walking backwards.

'It's probably just a cow or something,' suggested Seth, trying to ignore what his mind was telling him he'd seen in the road moments before the crash. 'Must've escaped from a farm. Yeah, that's it – right?'

'Yeah, that's it totally,' Lily agreed. 'An escaped cow. Of course. What else could it possibly be? Probably caused that accident we passed earlier.'

It was then, as though sensing a break in the clouds, that for the first time that night the moon seemed to focus its brightness on just where Saul's car had come to a halt after the crash. A pale, eerie glow fell over that place, like a shroud blown from a corpse, and Lily and Seth at last beheld what was before them.

The horse wasn't just huge, it was colossal. The world seemed to bend around it to give it space. And, despite its size, it simply stood there, calm, peaceful almost, heaving great plumes of breath like kettle steam from out of its nose. It towered over them, a prehistoric beast inexplicably shot forward in time to stare at them, defiant and impossible. Its hair and mane were so white it was as though it were clad in freshly fallen snow. It neighed then, and the sound was surprisingly gentle. The animal was clearly not at all threatened by the presence of Seth or Lily or Snuggles.

'What the hell is it?' asked Lily, her voice barely a whisper. 'And if you say *horse* . . .'

But Seth couldn't answer. Something about this horse, despite its beauty and its quietness, was more terrifying than he could find the words to express. He was frozen to the ground now, utterly unable to move. And he knew that what he'd seen that split second before the crash was now standing right in front of them.

The beast stamped one of its great feet, the silver shoe pinned to it catching a stone and setting off a flash of sparks that fizzed and spat in the air like fire crackers. The earth beneath their feet shook. When Seth looked at it again, the creature was slowly, gracefully, lowering itself to the ground.

The horse was magnificent. A king amongst kings. A

perfect specimen of just how wondrous a thing creation and life could be.

And for Seth, everything that had happened in the past few days fled from his mind. All he could see now was the beauty of this impossible creature before him, a vision of such heavenly splendour that all he really wanted to do was go over there and touch it, stroke its hair, sit on it . . . because it was his, had come for him now, hadn't it? And it was just waiting for him to go over and then things would really start to happen, big things, terrible things, scariest-stuff-you-ever-did-see things . . .

'Seth,' gasped Lily, seeing him step forward as though drawn by an invisible thread. 'Don't . . .'

But Seth couldn't hear Lily, couldn't hear anything. All that mattered was the horse. *His* horse. And as he approached, the creature lowered its gigantic head and whinnied like it was welcoming him home after a long, long time away.

Seth stopped centimetres short of the creature. Then, with the wide-eyed fascination of a four-year-old child on his first visit to the zoo, reached his hand out to stroke it.

16

IT WASN'T THUNDER OR lightning that split the air, but a voice that seemed as if it were that of the Earth itself speaking, the sound seeping up from the ground, squeezing itself though the particles of dirt and grit and stone, the branches of the trees, the grass. It was neither loud not quiet, just there for all to hear it if they were listening. And in resonance to its words the world trembled . . .

> **'And I saw, and behold a white horse:**
> **and he that sat on him had a bow;**
> **and a crown was given unto him:**
> **and he went forth conquering, and to conquer.'**

Seth was no longer at the bottom of the dyke standing next to a crippled car, a man with mass murder on his hands and a girl with a dog. He was sitting astride the great white horse and behind him three other Riders sat quiet and still. He could not see them, but he knew they were there, sensed their presence like the burning heat of a vast wave of flame about to come crashing down.

They were on a mountaintop, staring down through cloud that danced and spun like fresh candyfloss at the fair, at a world utterly erased from existence. And as he stared, the very path to the world's destruction burned brightly behind his eyes. Of vast armies in great violent clashes of mass destruction, battlefields piled high with the rotting dead and the rusting weapons they used down to the very last man. Of villages and towns rising up against each other, home against home, families at war. Of disease and war and death and turmoil and the world breaking and groaning and eventually swallowing up the cause of its pain, having wiped itself clean of the disease of humanity it had put up with for so very long. And still he looked upon it and saw that it was good.

A yell tore itself from Seth's throat like it was trying to drag his lungs out behind it. He snapped open his eyes and hadn't even realized they were closed in the first place. Lily was staring up at him, which struck him almost immediately as odd, but then he realized why. He was, as he had imagined only seconds earlier, astride the great horse, and its height made him tower over her like a prince surveying a penitent subject.

'Seth . . .' gasped Lily, eyes wide in both terrible fright and awesome wonder. From the moment she had decided to change what she remembered doing so many, many times before, and to allow Seth to live, rather than to watch him die, she had puzzled about what would actually happen on the day the boy turned thirteen. Well, now she knew, didn't she? For here he was, standing in front of her, sorrow in his eyes, and confusion, but in his hands – indeed in his very *soul* – the power to bring the world to its knees and then crush it completely. She was too scared to regret what she had done. Too in awe.

'I am the first Rider . . .' breathed Seth, but his voice was different. 'I can feel it!'

It was like listening to someone speaking in a well – there was a damp, echoing resonance to his words. The voice was creepy and haunting and not just from another place, but another time, another existence.

'Feel what?'

'This!' replied Seth, sweeping his arms out. 'All of it! The world, the sky . . .' He stared then at Lily. 'Your heartbeat, Lily . . .'

Lily went cold.

'Come down,' she said, ignoring the awful distant echo of Seth's voice, pushing from her mind the shadows falling behind his eyes like a million bodies thrown over a cliff. 'Get down and come to me. You don't know what you're doing.'

'I do, you know,' said Seth knowingly. 'I know *exactly* what I'm doing. And the very reasons as to why I am here!'

A shout burst from the cabin of the car. Ignored, it came again, and Seth and Lily turned to see Saul dragging himself across the seat to try to climb out.

Then, as Saul drew closer to the door, his pistol in his hand, Seth noticed that he himself was holding something. Bringing his hands up, Seth came face-to-face with a bow of silvery, almost alien metal. He expected it to weigh his arm down, yet it was feather light, more an extension of himself than an object now clasped in his hand. The bow's limbs were arched back sharply only to hook out again at the end in a fierce curve. It was strung with a white line of twisted thread that was waxy to the touch. Seth wondered where the arrows were and immediately he noticed the presence of something against his back. Reaching over his right shoulder he drew one forth. The fletchings were grey goose feathers, the arrow itself a dark material he couldn't place, ending in a lethal triple-bladed arrowhead the colour of brass. As he clipped the notch at the end of the arrow to the string, Seth noticed something else; a plain crown of gold, twisted like rope, and hung from a thick plait of the horse's mane, looped back on itself.

Saul called out again. He was on Lily's seat now, the pistol still in his hand.

Seth was too awestruck to hear what Saul was shouting. Raging through every single fibre of his body was a power only the collapsing of stars and creation of universes could have any hope of understanding.

The boy just stared at the man on the ground, flexing the limbs of the bow as he drew the string back just enough to sense the power in the simple, beautiful weapon should he unleash it. And he really wanted to. It was the kind of sensation he guessed he'd feel if he were sat unexpectedly in the driving seat of a sports car. That tingling in his fingertips of the power in his hands and what he could do with it.

Lily's voice cracked his concentration like an ice pick.

'Whatever it is you're thinking about doing, don't do it!' she yelled. 'I broke my destiny, didn't I? Smashed it full open so I could save your life this time, and not have you dead! You can break yours, too. I know you can! And you have to! It's why I saved you, Seth!'

Seth wasn't sure what Lily was talking about. Sitting on that horse seemed to him as natural as breathing. Why would he therefore want to do anything else? Such thoughts were madness. And of no importance.

'Don't you dare ignore me!' Lily shouted again. She had to get his attention, make him see what he was doing. If she didn't then she would be responsible for everything that happened thereafter. Everything. It was too horrifying to imagine, but imagine it she could. She'd always had the visions, seen what was possible. And now it was made flesh before her. If she hadn't been so desperately scared, she'd have thrown up and passed out.

Lily dropped to the ground, grabbed a stick and hurled it. The wood, damp and sticky to the touch, flew past Seth, right past his face. He didn't even flinch.

'But I belong here, Lily,' said Seth, his voice calm and measured. 'The horse came for me. It is mine. And I shall ride it. Can you not see that now?'

'You'll do no such thing!' Lily snapped back, going for another stick, a bigger one this time. 'You'll come right down this minute before you go any further, you hear? Seth? Listen to me! You have to!'

'You can't stop it,' Saul called out and Lily spun round to face him. 'You can't stop him. No one can. Not now. Not now . . .'

That wasn't good enough for Lily. You could always do something. Checkmate was something that belonged only in the world of chess, not in the here and now of the reality of life and death.

'Well, we have to do something!' she yelled as Seth's horse stomped the ground restlessly, almost as though it was excited about what it had been brought here to do with its new owner. 'This wasn't supposed to happen! Visions aren't meant to come true! They're not!'

'I said we can't stop him,' said Saul. 'I didn't say we couldn't do something else!' Saul then raised his voice to Seth, calling out. 'Find the other Riders, Seth! Find them before The Way finds them!'

Lily stared at Saul, aghast. 'Are you crazy?'

One Rider was bad enough. The four together was Armageddon.

Saul shook his head. 'It's a race now,' he said. 'Seth's thirteen. Once The Way realize he isn't dead they will know he's changed and they'll be out looking for the other Riders. Prophet will be their eyes and ears, though they will still be looking for you in the hope that they can persuade you to help them again.'

Lily didn't like how Saul said *persuade*. It had an air of terror and promised violence about it that knotted her stomach like cables hidden behind a television.

'I'm finished with them,' she snapped back. 'I still don't know how they never found out it was you who took me from the streets to Colin.'

Saul scratched his forehead through the blood with the barrel of his pistol. 'They never suspected me,' said Saul. 'And they still don't. They have no idea I have been working to bring them down, no idea at all. And we can still win this. We can still change the world!'

'I'm not sure I want to,' replied Lily and looked at Seth, who was still toying with his bow. 'And what's the point now, anyway?'

Saul let out an exhausted breath.

'You have to persuade him,' he said. 'You're the only one who can get through to him. He trusts you. Make him understand.'

'Understand what?'

'That he has to find the three remaining Riders before The Way gets to them! He has to!'

'But why? I was wrong, Saul! Seth should be dead!'

Saul breathed deep and slow to calm his voice. 'Seth has the power to change everything. Think what he and the other Riders could do! The Way wouldn't stand a chance.'

'You're gambling the world – the whole of *creation* – on the idea that Seth can hold it together enough to convince the other Riders not to pull the world apart? Is that really it?'

'Yes,' said Saul. 'That really is it. That's exactly what I'm doing.'

Lily went to say something but saw a look of horror fall across Saul's eyes as he held up a hand as though shielding himself from the sun. When she looked round, Seth had his bow drawn and aimed directly at him.

Lily screamed.

'Seth, no! Don't do it! Don't!'

Seth heard Lily, but what he heard more was the sound of war he sensed inside Saul, a vision of everything the man was. He had no idea how he sensed it, but he could, and it was enough. Because despite Saul's act in rescuing them, there was a deep and harrowing darkness inside him. And hiding behind a priest's garb wasn't enough. Seth could smell it, taste it even. And as he stared into Saul's very soul it was like downloading videos off the Internet, except these were the kind you shouldn't even lay eyes on, not even for a moment. In the blinking of an eye, Seth saw it all. Everything Saul had ever done, the damage he'd caused, the people he'd hurt, and the numerous ones he'd either killed himself or sentenced to death. The ones he could've helped, but had turned his back on. There was too much decay and disease inside Saul. He was little more than a tree with a trunk rotted away so badly that it needs to be felled before it becomes dangerous. The glint of the diamonds blinked out.

Seth loosed the arrow and it flew from him to Saul with the sound of wind rushing through a tunnel, and drew a line of fire in the air like a burning spray of oil. The heat of it turned the leaves of the trees immediately black and, when it slammed into where Saul had been lying, the car exploded, a fat mushroom cloud of flame shooting skyward as though it was trying to escape.

The force of the explosion pushed Lily to the ground, landing on Snuggles, who yelped in pain. When she looked up, sure to see Saul dead and his corpse broken and burning, she was amazed to see him rolling on the ground to put out the fire scorching his clothes, smoke forming round him like a magic carpet.

Lily wrenched herself off the ground to face down Seth, ready to tear into him. She didn't care that he now had the power to blast her off the face of the planet without a second's thought. But when she found him gazing down at her, his hand held out to help her to climb up and sit next to him, she was astonished.

She stepped back, shaking her head.

'No, I can't. I won't. I've gone far enough with this. Too far by far!'

Seth said nothing, just kept his hand held out, then, with a nudge of his heels, somehow told the horse to drop low enough to allow Lily to climb on up behind him.

'Go.'

It was Saul.

'I can't,' she said. 'I . . .'

Saul said nothing more. Just nodded at Seth's outstretched hand.

Snuggles, as if understanding what was happening, stood up and went over to Saul's side, licked his face, then turned to stare at Lily.

Lily had never been so scared. With a final look at Saul and her dog, she whipped round and strode up to Seth, forcing herself to take each step with purpose. She did not want him to see her afraid and she stared him in the eye as she took his outstretched hand and jumped up on to the horse behind him. The beast seemed even larger now she was sitting on it, and when it rose into the air it was as though a great chunk of the world itself had come free and they were riding it.

Seth took one last look at Saul, wondered at the man's survival, but knew there was more important work

ahead, work he'd been destined to do since the dawn of all things. And with the power to crush mountains coursing through him, he'd let himself go to wherever the horse wanted to lead.

And they were gone.

17

THAT SCHOOL WAS OVER for another day was no bad thing. Not that Kelly didn't enjoy it. She was one of those kids who actually got a kick out of learning and most days would race out of the house excited about what she was going to be doing and learning and discovering. But today had been bad. From the moment she'd woken up (at midnight, which was a whole car crash of hours too early and should've been her first warning something was up) Kelly had felt not ill exactly, but *off*, as though she'd become a little bit detached from everything going on around her. It was as though the invisible stitching holding her in place had somehow come loose – she wasn't sure where exactly. She had just figured the strange feeling would go away, but it had set her off kilter and was rather irritable by the time she got downstairs for breakfast.

So Kelly went to school despite something deep inside telling her that she wasn't quite right. And, as the day wore on, the detachment grew, and a few more stitches fell loose.

By midday, Kelly had already excused herself from her studies four times, on each occasion rushing to the toilets to be sick, only to do little more than dry heave. It brought her out in a sweat, and when the end of school came she raced out of the building, down the steps, and didn't stop till she crashed through the front door at home and slammed it hard behind her, drinking in the atmosphere of an empty house.

By now, the feeling of detachment and the overwhelming urge to vomit had intensified to such a degree that Kelly considered bypassing calling her parents and going straight for an ambulance. But what could she tell them other than that she was feeling a little bit queasy? She hadn't actually even been sick and the nurse at school had checked her temperature and come up blank. The whole unstitched thing would sound plain crazy, because it was. Then, of course, there was the tune . . .

It had started about halfway through her first class. To begin with, Kelly had thought someone had earphones on and was listening to music in secret. But after a quick sweep with her eyes she found this wasn't the case. Where was the tune coming from? The realization that it was not actually coming from anywhere at all, but from inside her head, caused Kelly to start to freak out . . .

The tune was growing clearer by the hour, was so strong now that at times she found herself whistling it unintentionally, and was the most skin-crawling blend of discord she'd ever heard in her life. And Kelly could do nothing but try to ignore it.

Now home alone in the quiet stillness of the house, the tune quickly became deafening. Kelly dumped her schoolbag on the hall floor and rushed through to the kitchen, poured a glass of water and downed it, hoping it would help.

Kelly, unsteady on her feet now, placed the glass on the counter, only to watch it slide off and smash all over the floor, a broken splatter of stars racing across the tiles like meteorites burning up in the atmosphere. She shuffled through the glass shards, back down the hallway, and headed upstairs.

She held her head, trying to stop it exploding from the pressure inside, thinking that perhaps lying down in a dark room would help.

Kelly collapsed through her bedroom door and landed on all-fours. She had to get rid of the tune, do something to pull it out of her skull, or stop it completely. She closed the curtains, lay down on the bed, and shut her eyes. But all that did was make it worse. In the darkness behind her eyelids it was as though the tune had taken on a whole new life, and it exploded in a great symphony of disharmony and crescendo. And Kelly – the usually calm, collected Kelly, who knew where she was and what she was doing and where she was going, thank you ever so very much – lost it completely and screamed and screamed and screamed and screamed and screamed.

And still the tune was there.

Kelly leaped out of bed, pulled at her hair, clapped her hands over her ears, rolled on the floor and cracked her head hard against something standing in the corner of her room – her electric piano.

Close to passing out now, Kelly dragged herself from off the floor, on to her knees, and then climbed on to the stool and sat in front of the piano. What force controlled her hands, she had no idea, but she was too weak to argue and fight it and no sooner had she sat down than they had slipped the headphones over her ears and were on the keyboard, racing up and down the notes like scampering mice chasing after the tune as if it was a tasty piece of cheese on a string. When her fingers finally found it, Kelly started weeping with relief.

The tears streamed down her face unhindered and the music played on and on and on . . .

18

THE SOUND OF THE horse's hooves galloping onwards was that of the Earth's crust splitting, and when Seth glanced down he saw the ground not just quake as they raced ahead, but crumble. It was as though they were riding across a vast skin of rock, and it was falling away from them, tumbling below into an endless void of eternal emptiness.

Seth was aware of Lily's arms wrapped tightly round his stomach like steel rope. She was holding on for her very life, her head pressed against his back like she was hiding from the reality of where they now were and what they were now doing.

For Seth, though, there was no hiding. It was right before him and inside him and all around as though every part of his being had changed to something new. The way ahead was a world of fog – colours bleeding like ink on wet paper, eerie and transparent like a chalk picture on a pavement being slowly washed away. His destination was still unknown but it didn't seem to matter. The ride was the focus of everything. He could sense the power within him, and the connection with the great horse underneath him, as though he were feeding off it somehow and drawing strength from it.

Seth closed his eyes. The horse didn't need him as guide; it knew where it was going and why it was here. In Seth's own darkness now, the sense of what he had become flowed through him like rich wine, intoxicating him in moments. The rhythmic gallop of the horse was hypnotic. Seth allowed himself to slip deeper into his new self. And what he saw was such a rich riot of darkness and destruction, all of it his own making. He wanted to fall into it and swim in it and wallow in it. He could see the world in his mind's eye, but it wasn't a planet of greens and blues and life and creation, but of waste and destruction. A gift freely given by whatever power had given it, but a gift misused, abused, destroyed.

Seth sensed then a rage unlike any he'd ever experienced before. The world was screaming to be torn apart, put out of its misery once and for all. And it was calling to him! As Seth stared, he was sure that in amongst the vision of a crumbling Earth, a figure was beckoning to him. It seemed to shift whenever he stared at it directly, as though it was only truly comfortable to be seen from the corner of Seth's eye, but it was definitely there. It was as though the world's tired soul was begging him to end its suffering.

Was he really experiencing the Earth's darkness calling out to him? Seth turned towards the figure, but it slid from view. He turned again. Yes, there it was! Its arms were outstretched, its hands clawing for him. If he could just reach out to it then he could do as it asked. It was closer now. Just a few moments more and . . .

Seth slipped. Not much, but just enough to make Lily yell out, her hands clasping at him in terror at the thought of falling off. It was the first time since finding himself sitting on the huge, muscled back of the horse that Seth had seen what was happening through his own eyes and not just those of the thing he had now become, a creature never meant to walk the Earth until that terrible, impossible-to-comprehend moment when humanity's time was up.

'Lily?'

No answer.

'Lily! Are you OK?'

This time an answer came, but it wasn't the one Seth was expecting as Lily slapped him hard across the back of his head before quickly wrapping her arms round him again.

'Don't you ever do that again, you hear? Don't fall! Don't even pretend to fall! Just DON'T!'

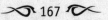

'It was an accident,' Seth replied. 'I . . . I had my eyes closed.'

'You what?' Lily yelled back in disbelief, then she realized something; Seth's voice was back to normal. She was talking to *him* again. 'Seth?'

'What?'

'No, I mean it's you again. Your voice isn't all weird and distant and echoey any more. You sound normal.'

'Thanks. I think.'

The conversation paused, seeming awkward considering where they were and the world they were racing through. Seth knew they had to stop, think about what they were doing. As if his thoughts were somehow connected to the horse, the beast started to slow until eventually it came to a complete halt. The world came back into focus then. Gone were the smudged horizon and seeping colours, the pained figure of shadows reaching for him, and instead they were standing in a world they recognized, albeit one of muddy fields, darkness and still the rain falling, falling, falling.

'I never meant this to happen,' whispered Lily, resting her forehead into the small of Seth's back. 'None of it, you understand? Please say that you do.'

Seth shrugged. 'You mean the big horse wasn't your idea? Are you absolutely sure?'

Lily nodded.

'The visions . . . all those lives and all those deaths,'

she muttered, her voice barely audible. 'I just wanted to save your life this time. It seemed the right thing to do. I never considered the implications.'

'Well, between you and me, I prefer it this way,' said Seth. 'Those visions of my deaths didn't make good viewing. This one though has definitely got a little more about it, don't you think?'

Lily sat up and, without warning, slid from the back of the horse.

'Who are you, Seth?' she asked. '*What* are you?'

Seth stared down at Lily, who was hugging herself and walking around to keep warm.

'We both know the answer to that,' he replied.

'But you can't be!' Lily snapped back. 'It's impossible! You're just a kid! How can you possibly be the one to herald the Apocalypse? What was that word Colin used? . . . *Harbinger*. It doesn't make any sense!'

'Ironic really, isn't it?' said Seth. 'Me, the Apocalypse Boy, used to telling people what their end would be and now, here I am, with the power to make it happen. Is that irony? I'm not sure I've never really understood it, but it seems pretty close.'

Lily was quiet. She had no idea what to say, what to do. She was terrified. But then who wouldn't be? It's not every day something you do starts the countdown to the end of the world.

'What made you decide to save me this time?' asked

Seth. 'What was it that made you change your mind?'

Lily walked over and tentatively reached a hand up to the nose of the horse. It leaned down and allowed her to stroke it. The beast was magnificent. A creature from another world where the perfect versions of everything were created first before the rest came into being on Earth.

'Colin and Saul,' she replied then. 'The Way wanted me for my visions, trained me to focus them to find you, and that's what I was doing when Saul found me.'

'Homeless and starving and nearly dead?'

'All part of it,' said Lily, blowing warm air into her hands. 'I was meant to escape. The doors were left open on purpose. The Way would track me, see? Because as soon as I was out of the house, the one thing I was looking for was you.'

'You're forgetting the nearly dead bit,' reminded Seth.

'The figure that found me first was one of The Chosen,' Lily explained. 'They'd been keeping tabs on me. Until I learned how to survive, to scavenge and steal to stay alive, they would take me in – drugged, if you remember – check me over, change my clothes, then send me back out with the pockets of my coat stuffed with food.'

Seth shook his head. 'It's twisted.'

'The Way believe they are saving the world from destruction,' said Lily. 'And seeing you like that, it strikes me that it's exactly what they've been doing. And we've really gone and messed that up more than a little, don't you think?'

'What about Saul?' asked Seth, and reached down to help Lily back up on to the horse. When she was comfortable, he tapped his heels gently into the horse's sides and it moved off slowly.

'He joined The Way to work as a double agent,' she explained. 'Colin and Saul took a gamble with me. If it had gone wrong, if they'd been found out, they'd have been killed, simple as that.'

'Colin was,' said Seth, remembering back to what had happened at the church.

To that Lily had nothing to say.

'I'm here to destroy the world,' said Seth, breaking the silence. 'And saying it doesn't make it seem any more real or possible. Though something deep inside me thinks it's a good idea, like I want to do it. But that's insane too!'

'Why?' asked Lily.

'Because I never truly believed in the Apocalypse!' Seth replied in frustration. 'My act was just that – an act! I fooled people, Lily! Just clever observation, cold reading and a good imagination. Anyone smart could do it. Anyone at all. Even you.'

Lily ignored the snub. 'What about your dad? Your family?'

'Oh, Dad was a true believer,' said Seth. 'He did his all to make me see it like he did, too. He hadn't time for much of the other stuff, the "other paths" as we're told to call them. But he tolerated them. It's how we made a living, remember? Mum used to read tea leaves and palms and stuff. But actually I'm not really sure I know what she ever truly believed.'

'What about Beth?'

At the mention of her name, Seth realized the silver shell round his neck was clenched in his fist, its sharp edges biting into his skin. 'Beth took after Dad,' said Seth, 'though I kind of think she was looking to go her own way sooner rather than later, find her own mind.'

'So what now?' asked Lily. 'You're the first Rider, Seth. The one spoken of in last part of *The Book*. You are the Revelation. And you're here to bring about the Apocalypse.'

Seth took a deep breath and exhaled slowly.

'Tempting,' he said, 'but if it's all the same with you, I think I'll give it a miss.'

'You say that like you think you have a choice in the matter.'

Seth swivelled round to face Lily. Though his voice was his own, those eyes still danced with an obsidian blackness.

'There's always a choice,' Seth said. 'And mine is to find the other Riders.'

Lily said no more and when Seth turned back round she was relieved. He terrified her now and froze her blood.

'Up ahead,' said Seth, raising a hand to point. 'That a town, do you think?'

Lily peered round Seth and nodded.

'Reckon we'd give people a fright if we turned up like this, don't you?'

'Isn't that the point?'

Seeing those lights, Seth found that he could sense the lives around them. People in lounges watching TV, out at a restaurant, sitting in a cinema, arguing over a spilled drink. And if he wanted to, he could snuff out each and every one of them, turn them all off like lamps, blow the flame of their lives to nothing but the sooty, dirty remains of an unremarkable fire.

'I have to find the other Riders,' said Seth then, in a moment of clarity. 'Saul was right, it's what I have to do.'

'I'm not sure that's such a good idea,' said Lily, trying to stay calm. 'Everyone knows what happens if the four of you get together. It's the end of everything, Seth. Everything!'

'Exactly,' Seth replied. 'Which is why I have to find them first and change their minds.'

'But—'

'There is no but,' Seth bit back. 'It's either that or sit back and let The Way seek them out and murder them before they turn. Is that what you want?'

'That's not what I'm saying and you know it! But what if it doesn't work out like you say? What then? What if you can't control them? Or yourself?'

Lily was trying to ignore that she was arguing with

someone who now had the power to wipe her from the face of the Earth in the blink of an eye.

'Free will, Lily,' said Seth. 'We always have a choice. To do good, do bad, do what we want, or not. You believe that, right?'

'But you're the end result of a prophecy!' cried Lily. 'You know you can't escape that easily! You just can't! That's the whole point of a prophecy!'

'No, but I can change it,' said Seth, excitement in his voice now. 'What I do with what I've become is down to me. Perhaps that's the point of all this. Perhaps—'

Lily thumped her fists hard against Seth's back, raining down such a flurry of blows that she only stopped when the pain in her own hands became too much to bear.

'You can't do it!' she yelled and before she could stop herself she was screaming at him. 'You just can't! It's too dangerous! You're supposed to be dead, Seth, not this thing you've become! And if you find the other Riders, together you'll have the power to destroy everything! I've seen it and so have you! SO HAVE YOU!'

Seth roared and kicked his heels hard into the horse's side. It responded instantly and despite its huge size and weight threw itself into a gallop with astonishing grace. The shock of the movement took Lily by surprise and she toppled from the back of the horse, landing painfully hard on the road. She screamed in pain and, amazed not to have broken anything, pulled herself to her feet and brushed herself down. Then a shadow fell upon her and she looked up into those dead-pool eyes of Seth's once more and knew, more than she'd known anything in her life, that for the first time ever, she – the hunter – was about to become the prey.

19

$S^{ETH...'}$
   He was leaning over the side of the horse, his arm resting on his thigh, staring at her.

Lily backed off immediately.

Seth followed, the *clip-clop* of the horse's hooves echoing all around and giving the countryside the odd feel of a gigantic, endless cavern deep inside the Earth.

Lily held up her hands, as if they would do anything at all should Seth charge her down with the horse.

'Seth – listen to me.'

'I've *been* listening to you,' said Seth, confused now. He sensed a fight inside him between who he really was and who this power he now had would turn him into. And there was something else, too. That figure of torn shadow he'd seen earlier. It was always there now, as if it had taken up residence inside his head. It was just on the edge of what he could see, what he could sense, but it was real. Calling him, begging . . . 'And you think I should be dead, right?'

'Yes . . . *No* . . . I mean . . . I don't know what I mean, Seth! I don't understand any of this! But you finding the other Riders? That's crazy! Can't you see that?'

The dark, faceless figure flickered once again in Seth's mind, like it was trying to catch his attention. Something about it drew him to it and the temptation to listen to it, to follow it was overpowering. But now he noticed that something was different to when he had first noticed it. It was becoming clearer . . . The edges were definitely not so torn now, and when he looked for it the figure didn't dodge so quickly from view.

'All I see,' said Seth, 'is fear in your eyes. It suits you.'

His voice was changing again, realized Lily. Whatever that power was inside him, it was gaining control once more. And she had a horrible feeling that if she lost him to it now, she'd lose him for ever. That would be it; game over, world. Been nice knowing you.

'You sound as though you like it.'

Seth shrugged. 'I suppose I do. A part of me does, at least.'

'Don't give in to it, Seth,' Lily said, working hard to stay calm. 'Don't let it control you.'

'What if I want it to?' Seth replied, a flicker of a smile dancing on his lips.

The figure swept into view, once again clearer than before. It was fully formed now, though its face was still hidden. Whatever it was, it was growing stronger.

'You don't want to!' said Lily as Seth spurred the horse towards her and she backed up. 'You're Seth, not *this*! What about free will? You just this moment said it yourself! Isn't that what this is about?'

'Maybe I'm not so sure now,' said Seth. 'Maybe free will isn't all it's cracked up to be. Ever thought of that?'

Inside, he reached out to the power and dared to touch it. The warmth of it crept through him then and he could think of nothing better than giving in to it completely, like he was given the choice between the icy waters of the Arctic and the sun-blessed seas of the Caribbean. When he caught another fleeting glance of the dark figure inside his head, Seth was sure it was smiling. Not that he could make out a face as such, but a cold sliver of silver had shone out ever so briefly.

'Yes you are, Seth!' cried Lily, tears welling unhindered. 'You have to be! For all our sakes!'

Seth kicked the horse. It started to walk towards Lily, who, with no idea of where she was going and no light to help her check, tripped and fell with a scream. The horse came closer until it was standing directly over her, its shadow the black, smothering cloak of death.

'Have you ever thought that all I'm really doing is giving the world what-it deserves, what it needs and wants? A chance to start again. A clean slate.'

The horse raised a great hoof and hovered it over Lily's head. It blocked out the world like a giant eclipse.

'Seth . . .'

'Think about it, Lily! The planet would be able to heal again. Doesn't it actually make sense? You must be able to see that, right?'

The hoof was poised just far enough away to allow Lily to catch a glimpse of Seth round its edge.

'You know there are trees that depend on fire to grow? The flames come and take the plants around them, leaving the trees with the space to grow and thrive. I'd only be doing the same; taking away the stuff that the Earth needs rid of so it can grow and breathe again.'

'It's not for you to decide,' she said. 'It's not for anyone or any*thing* to decide.'

'What about God? Does the creator have a say in this? And am I not God's messenger? The harbinger of doom?'

Lily laughed. The sound of it jarred with how scared she was, but she couldn't help herself. Seth was changing before her eyes, his voice sounded different, and the things he was saying were not the things a normal thirteen-year-old boy should even have on his mind.

'If you've been sent by God to do God's will, then how come we're here having this conversation at all?' she replied. 'Don't you see? That's how it's always supposed to be; we're given a choice. *You* have been given a choice. Don't waste it on becoming something you don't want to be! Don't be swallowed up by it like Beth!'

The mention of his sister's name was like a bell ringing clear inside his head and Seth sat bolt upright. The dark figure inside Seth's mind shrank away, as though afraid. The movement spooked the horse and it brought its foot crashing down towards Lily. She rolled out of the way just in time to see the hoof bury itself deep into the ground where her head had been. If she'd still been lying there when it had happened, it would have smashed her open like a coconut under a sledgehammer.

The horse removed its foot from the hole it had punched in the road and the tarmac glowed faintly red.

'Lily!' Seth yelled, pulling himself back, gaining control again.

'I'm fine,' she said, standing up. Seth's voice had again returned to normal. 'And by fine I mean still shaking and probably terrified of horses for the rest of my life.'

They looked at each other for a moment. Lily saw that the blackness had gone from Seth's eyes.

'I'm sorry,' said Seth and Lily could hear the tremble in his voice. 'This . . . whatever has happened to me, I don't know how to control it.'

'I know,' said Lily. 'Now, help me back up.' She held out a hand, trying not to be afraid of both the Rider and his horse. 'We're in this together. If we're not, then we may as well give up now.'

Seth pulled Lily up behind him.

'I still believe the only thing I can do is find the other three Riders,' he said. 'And I know it's risky, but it's either that or let three other kids get killed. And I can't live with that. I just can't, Lily. I'm sorry. But that's my choice.'

Lily rested a hand on Seth's shoulder. She understood.

'Let's go then,' she said. 'But if you will take just one piece of advice from me, then it's this: get Saul. He can help us. He knows The Protector's plans before anyone else – and The Way better than we ever could. Trust me on this.'

'You're the only one I do trust,' said Seth, 'because now, in this world, I've known you longer than I've known anyone else.'

Seth tugged on the horse's mane and with a whinny of excitement it spurred forward to a gallop that tore the road under its feet, the sparks lighting it up with flames that melted the tarmac and burned the wet grass of the verge to a tyre-black streak of mud and grime.

Lily wasn't about to ask how he knew which way to go because she figured that Seth probably wouldn't know the answer. There was something supernatural about him now, as if he didn't so much move in the world, as the world moved in him, like it was at his very command.

The world swept by like a movie stuck on fast forward. Lily tried to look at it, catch bits she recognized, but it was just ghosts and memories and pictures fading. So she focused on holding on. She was getting the hang of moving with the horse, much like she'd told Seth to when she'd taken him pillion on the scooter. He'd been the one frightened like a rabbit in headlights then. Now it was her.

The horse whipped itself out of the gallop and almost skidded to a halt, kicking its front legs high into the air as if smashing holes in reality.

They were back at Saul's car, only something else was there too. Lights were in the sky and there was a sound like an incoming swarm of seriously angry bees.

'Helicopter!' yelled Lily, pointing at the lights, but her voice was snatched away by the sound of the rotors in the air above them.

The helicopter was still high in the sky, but the searchlight pinned to its nose was sweeping the ground around Saul's car as though it was trying to sniff something out.

Saul and the wolf-sized dog, Snuggles, were nowhere to be seen.

'It's looking for us!' shouted Lily. 'It's looking for Saul! Where is he?'

Seth saw a shadow move in the trees.

'Saul . . .'

He was waving at them with his pistol and shouting. Snuggles was with him.

'They know what went down at the church! You

have to get away now or all this will have been for nothing! Go!'

'We can't leave!' screamed Lily. 'Not without you!'

Saul raised his pistol again, but as he went to pull the trigger, he dropped the weapon. His hands went to his head and Lily saw pain scratch across his face.

'He's done bad things, Lily,' said Seth. He could see them, sense them, taste them. Seth's power became a key to every door in anyone's mind. He could pick the lock, walk right in. And at that moment, he was in Saul's mind, walking corridors hung with dark memories, the horrors of his life. Yes, there was good too, but it was the darkness that drew Seth in. A gun in Saul's hand aiming at a shaking silhouette, hands held up in fear. Money changing hands to pay for information. Bloodied fists being dragged off before too much damage was done. Smashed photographs of friends, family. And a half-empty whisky bottle next to a lonely bed. And peeking round from behind Seth was that figure again, like it was leaning in to get a better look at Saul, a ringside seat at his destruction.

Lily heard that change in Seth's voice again. She saw the helicopter closing in. This was not going well. Without thinking what she was doing, Lily grabbed Seth, heaved him round to face her, then backhanded him hard across the face, so hard she thought her knuckles had burst.

Hell blazed in Seth's eyes.

'You want to get angry, that's fine by me!' screamed

Lily, wind whistling round them, rain approaching again, making the air damp and cold. 'But save it for someone worth getting angry at – not Saul, OK? Not Saul!'

Seth let out a long, slow breath.

'Get him,' he ordered. 'Quickly!'

Lily made to slide from the horse but Saul fired another shot. The helicopter had them under the searchlight now, like actors on a stage.

'Snuggles won't get on, even if you beg him to,' Saul shouted. 'And I'll only slow you down! And don't go telling me you don't know it, because you do, Lily, don't you?'

Of course I know it, thought Lily, tears in her eyes.

'If they know what happened,' she started, but Saul stopped her with an upheld hand.

'I'll deal with it, Lily. You have to go.'

Lily hesitated. Saul raised his pistol again then sent off a volley of shots at the helicopter. It backed off, like it had been stung.

'Just take this and go!' Saul roared, throwing something in the air. 'Get out of here! GO!'

When Lily caught it and saw that it was a roll of banknotes, she knew that Saul meant it. He was not coming with them.

With no time to think, Lily reached up to Seth, who pulled her up behind him. She gripped her arms tightly round Seth's waist as he kicked the horse away from Saul and Snuggles, the ruined truck, and the helicopter coming back in to find them.

'He'll be fine,' Seth called back. 'Saul can look after himself.'

The horse was gathering speed and the world around them was starting to fade and bleed into one. Then a white flash smashed the night and Seth and Lily snapped round to see Saul's car and the whole clearing where it had crashed explode in a fireball.

The explosion sucked all other sound from the moment and Lily and Seth stared at the bubbling, boiling mushroom of fire as it grew and grew, breaking eventually into a terrible image of flaming hands reaching desperately for the sky.

'Saul . . .' breathed Lily. 'Snu—' but her voice caught in her throat like wool on barbed wire.

Seth raised his bow, notched an arrow, and drew the string, locking the hand holding it against his cheekbone.

Lily said nothing, her vision stained with tears.

Like the tail of a comet the arrow sped through the black. When it impacted with the helicopter, the craft didn't so much explode as vaporize. Lily expected to see huge chunks of it falling to the air to clang as they landed on the ground, but instead, all they heard was the sound of faint rain.

A beat.

As darkness poured itself back into the space caused by

the explosion, and as the flames started to die down, Seth tapped his horse to turn it away. As it started to pick up speed he called back to Lily.

'That time Saul bought us at the church?'

'What about it?'

'It just ran out.'

20

THE HORSE WAS MOTIONLESS. A block of white against the darks and greys of the night world. If you looked close enough and stared at its edges, where the horsehair ended and the rest of the world began, it was as if that world was bending slightly, like light through a prism, refracting and splitting and breaking. Yet instead of a rainbow, it became shadow and emptiness.

On the huge, wide back of the horse its passengers sat, each lost to their own thoughts. Behind the Rider was a girl, hunched up tight and thankful for the additional warmth. She was on the back of a horse whose hooves would crack the earth and send up spitting fountains of fire and lava to scorch history clean. And she could do nothing about it. What made it worse was that if she looked back at all her decisions, the good and the bad, they'd all led right here. Destiny, it seemed, was a nasty piece of work.

And in front of the girl, with one hand grasping a thick clump of the horse's mane, the other holding a pale wooden bow, was a boy, staring out into a world that now seemed in his mind to be utterly different to the one he'd looked out on a few hours ago. What he saw now was a world that was dying and falling apart. A tree to him was already rotting into the ground to decay. The sky had no colour, unless that colour was the absence of all other hues and shades and tints. And humanity was on the cusp of collapse. This was a place condemned, and all he really wanted to do was the decent thing, the thing anyone who saw an injured animal suffering from unfixable injuries would do: end it. Yet something inside was stopping him. And it was that something that looked through all the helplessness before him towards the lights of a town blinking in the night like stars on the surface of a lake.

Seth got Lily's attention and pointed down the road ahead to a transport café. Its car park was filled with sleeping trucks. On the way they'd seen another car wreck, though with so much going on, neither of them took much notice, not even of the unmoving bodies still inside the vehicles.

A flashing neon sign told them that the café was a

twenty-four/seven. Neither of them cared at that moment how grubby the place might be. That it was also a motel meant it could provide them with shelter and somewhere to stop and work out what to do next, and that, for now at least, was more than enough.

'We eat, we rest, then we decide,' said Seth, sliding from the horse and down on to the road.

The horse swung its huge head round and, in a thick cloud of its own breath condensing in the cool night air, nudged Seth with something close to affection. Or perhaps it was impatience.

'Decide what?' asked Lily, her voice snapping at Seth like a crocodile as she slid down to stand beside him. She was still in shock from what she had seen happen to Saul and Snuggles. No matter how many times she played it over and over in her mind, it still seemed unreal. She just couldn't accept that they were dead. Not yet.

'I don't know,' said Seth, and started to walk down the road towards the café.

Lily caught up. 'What about the horse?'

'It will come when I call,' said Seth, as though it was the most obvious and natural thing in the world and something he'd always known.

Lily glanced back to see the horse begin to fade, as if it was made up of a million tiny light bulbs and they were all snapping out. One. By. One. Then it was gone, the remaining image of it nothing more than the memory in

Lily's mind of the space it had once occupied. Seth's bow and quiver of arrows was gone, too.

No further words were said.

Stepping into the café was like stepping back in time. The place had been decked out to look like a nineteen-fifties American diner, but by someone who'd clearly never been to the USA. The furniture was tired, the windows grubby, and the air thick with the smell of grease and steam. Perched on a shelf screwed to the wall was a television, old and tired and desperate for retirement. It was streaming twenty-four-hour news into the room, not that any of the current customers were watching. They were all much more interested in the mountains of fried food and the giant mugs of tea sitting in front of them. The clock on the wall was a faded picture of Elvis Presley and had the king of rock 'n' roll's arms swirling round to tell the time. As Seth and Lily walked through the café to find a table, the clock hit the hour and Elvis said, 'Uh huh! Thank you very much.' It would soon be morning. But even here The Protector was visible, his face smiling down from a grease-covered photograph hung on the wall above the counter, as if he was looking down to check that no one was given the wrong change.

'What do you want?' Lily asked, passing Seth a menu and trying to ignore how it stuck to her fingers. She wiped away a circle in the condensation on the window next to her and glanced outside. It was hard to believe that beyond it was an oblivious world on the brink of annihilation. Even more hard to believe that Colin, and now Saul and Snuggles, were gone.

'Food,' said Seth. 'You decide.'

Lily took the menu and went over to the till to order. The food arrived within minutes and they demolished it just as quickly. Their appetites sated, Lily and Seth sat in silence until a sound from the grubby television caught their attention. Lily noticed that the rest of the late-night customers were staring at what was happening on the screen, some with food pinned to their forks halfway to their mouths.

It was a nationwide news alert and one of the highest possible priority. People were asked not to panic, but to understand, and to take the necessary precautions (whatever they were), because the threat level to the country had just jumped from moderate to critical.

A reporter was at a news conference. Standing at the podium was a man that everyone knew, and pinned to his face that smile everyone recognized from the television adverts and the billboards and the junk mail.

'What's happened?' asked Lily. 'What's he saying?'

Seth did not answer.

'. . . unable to comment further,' said The Protector, his face calm, collected, his voice measured as though he was speaking in perfect time with an internal metronome. 'Our current status is simply a precautionary measure, the safety of our people our highest priority.'

A reporter asked, 'So The Way has lost control, Protector, correct? That's what you're really saying, isn't it? That in the face of such anarchy it is powerless!'

The Protector's face displayed not a flicker of a reaction. 'As you all now know, in the past few hours, the country has experienced an inexplicable wave of civil disorder and violence. Yes, we have seen our fair share of this kind of behaviour before, but never on this scale.'

In the bottom-left corner of the screen, images were bumping into each other in their urgency to be seen by the world; burning cars and shops looted and crowds on the street and petrol bombs and riots and people running for their lives and the territorial army mobilized . . .

'It's . . . started,' said Lily to Seth, stunned to be witnessing society in full-scale meltdown. And she remembered the car wrecks they'd seen. Were they a part of this, too? 'The end of the world. And believe me, I do know just how crazy that sounds but that's what this is, isn't it? What *you* are, Seth, right?'

But Seth wasn't listening. Something else was now bugging his mind, like a moth thumping relentlessly against a lightbulb. He'd started to sense the thoughts of those around him in the café. It had happened earlier with Saul but here it was much more intense and before he could do anything about it, it was as if he'd opened a flood gate.

Everything about everyone in that room spilled into him like a drink sploshed into a glass way too small. Seth squeezed his eyes shut but it did no good, not even when he shook his head in a desperate attempt to knock the stuff out.

Lily knew something was up and rested a hand on Seth's shoulder. 'Seth? What's wrong?'

Seth didn't answer because he didn't hear. His mind was elsewhere now. He could sense everything about everyone in the café. Their inner conflicts, their good and their bad, their violent selves which they kept buried so deep, their secrets not so secret any more.

Seth slipped into their minds easily, a thief in the night they'd never catch. He saw their waitress racing down a street, raindrops mixing with tears, behind her a blanket-wrapped bundle screaming and screaming on the steps of a hospital, a nurse reaching down, staring out into the storm for the mother, now gone for good. He followed the man in the far corner of the café as he walked away from a house ruptured by tongues of fire, petrol fumes in the air, the thrill of the flames not healing his broken heart like he'd wanted them to.

Then a fight broke out at the far end of the café.

Two truckers in oil-stained trousers, faded T-shirts and scuffed work boots had been strangers until the first fists had been thrown for no apparent reason whatsoever. It was like watching two giant schoolboys dancing round each other in childish rivalry. Hands slapped, punches missed, arms grabbed and dragged.

Seth stared not at the men, but into them, took a hold of what was inside, and twisted it as if conducting their thoughts. The fight started again with renewed vigor as the men fell and rolled across the floor. Seth turned his attention elsewhere, to the weary waitress whose face turned to a snarl as she refilled a customer's mug of tea then poured it all over his food. Soon, the once-quiet café was a battlefield, with plastic forks and newspapers and wallets and ketchup bottles used as both weapon and shield. And it was all down to Seth. He was controlling it all.

'Seth!' Lily yelled, shaking him hard. 'What's going on? What's happening?'

Seth wasn't listening. He was lost to the play now being performed in front of him, he the puppet master. All he had to do was reach in, unlock a door, release a darkness. And it was fun! So much fun! The shadow man inside his head was enjoying it too. No longer hiding just out of sight, he was in full view now, encouraging Seth, whispering to him. He couldn't make out the words, but he could sense what was their meaning, to destroy, to bring conflict!

Lily ducked as a magazine, rolled up and twisted really tight, flew over her head to bounce off the window.

She grabbed from the floor a can of Coke that had fallen from the waitress's tray. It was icy cold and she shook it hard before snapping it open to spray it into Seth's face.

Seth shook like he'd just bitten an electric fence.

'You have to stop this!' Lily screamed. 'Now! You understand? These people . . . you can't do it to them! Make it stop!'

But the fight had already begun to fade and the customers were starting to look at each other confused, as though waking from an awful nightmare to find it was shockingly real. Gradually, with apologies and excuse-mes fluttering around like escaped butterflies, everyone made their way back to their tables and quietly settled where a storm had been. The only sound that followed it was that of the mess being cleaned up by the confused, crying waitress.

Lily waited for an explanation, but nothing came. Seth just fell back in his seat, all colour drained from him and his eyes sunk deep into shadow. She spotted something caught on one of Seth's shoes. It was Beth's necklace and she picked it up. She glanced back at Seth to see if he was fully back to himself, but his eyes were flickering and she knew he'd soon be asleep. They both would.

Pocketing the necklace, Lily heaved herself out of her chair, pulled Seth to his feet and walked them both out of the café and across the car park to the motel. Seth leaned on her all the way like a wounded soldier. The air was still and dawn was now breaking, the sun rising slowly over the horizon like it was scared to see the aftermath of the night before. Dotted here and there Lily spotted faint black streaks of smoke lifting and swirling upwards, like a dozen oil wells burning. But judging by those nearest to them, they weren't oil wells at all, but buildings, homes, warehouses. Lily remembered what she'd seen on the news. The disorder was spreading quickly.

At the motel, she checked them into a basic room, using Saul's money to pay for it. She'd expected the receptionist to ask questions about why two young kids were alone and booking into a motel, but the man didn't even raise an eye from his book to look at them.

Locking the door behind them, Seth collapsed on to the bed. He was asleep before his head hit the pillow. Lily lay next to him and stared at the ceiling fan, which spun pathetically above her. Then, as the past two days came crashing down on her, she cried out in pain and eventually fell to sleep, tears still wet on her cheeks.

21

LILY WOKE TO FIND Seth standing in front of the television that was chained to the wall at the bottom of the bed. He was watching the news. And it had only got worse. More riots, more looting, more violence. Lily squeezed her eyes tight then opened them to check the time. The digital clock on the cabinet at her side, and the odd light coming in through the window, told her that they'd slept through the whole day. Dawn till dusk, and it was already evening again. But she didn't feel rested at all, if anything she was even more exhausted.

'Seth?'

Seth just continued to stare at the screen.

Lily sat up and swung her legs off the bed, leaning her head forwards to rest in her hands. Movement caught

her eye and she watched as Seth reached his hand out to the screen like a child touching the surface of a lake for the first time, afraid that something might come up and bite a finger. Just as Lily was about to ask what he was doing, Seth made contact with the screen and as he touched it a crackle of static exploded into the room and Lily jumped back and hit her skull on the headboard, her eyes wide and staring.

Lily couldn't be entirely sure if she was seeing things or not. But it was as though the pictures from the television were flowing like water, spilling and splashing out of it to run up Seth's arm, then reaching like the tentacles of an oily squid into his mouth, his nose, his eyes.

A pain inside Seth's head, like a chainsaw chewing though his brain, forced his head to snap back, yet it wasn't the ceiling he was staring at but something much more distant. As the images from the news drove into him, contaminating his every thought, he started to sort through them, searching for something hidden inside them, the pain dragging him on to find its source. He pushed on through burning streets crowded with gangs, past police cars and helicopters and ambulances and violence, shifting from city to city until something hooked him in and he followed it. The world rushed past like a movie on fast forward and he was in the suburbs somewhere, standing outside a modest detached house with an SUV parked outside. The wide street was littered with bodies, dead or unconscious he didn't know, but the source of the pain was close, inside the house, up the stairs, in a very neat and tidy bedroom where—

Seth's eyes snapped open.

'Strife . . .' he muttered weakly and didn't just sense but *knew* that a red horse far off was galloping.

Lily was staring out through the window of the motel room. Below her, Seth was standing in the car park.

Now alone, Seth was briefly the boy he'd been before turning thirteen. He wanted to call his parents and ask them to come and get him. He wanted to apologize for being such an idiot and running away. He wanted to see Beth again and to hear her have a go at him for doing a runner in the first place.

None of this would happen. None of it ever could.

Seth remembered the white horse that had come to him. It was like an image from a dream, but he knew it was real. Even more so when, from the darkness in front of him, folding out of nothing into reality, under the lights still spilling across the car park with a sad, yellow glow, the horse walked forth. It came up to Seth as though it was the most normal thing in the world for a creature such as this, a giant horse the colour of fresh coconut flesh, to be in a deserted car park to meet its master.

Seth reached out a hand to feel the warmth of the animal's nose against his palm. The hot breath that chased up his arm was deeply comforting. The horse then lowered its neck and raised its front right hoof. Seth stepped up on to it and the horse raised him up to swing his leg over its neck and slide down on to its back. As he sat down he found the bow in his hand and the quiver of arrows on his back. The crown was there too, knotted in the horse's mane.

The horse scratched its hooves against the ground, sending sparks to spill and spit and dance across the cold, grey surface like lost sprites. Seth reached forward, took a hold of a great clump of the horse's mane, then tapped its sides with his heels. He glanced back to see Lily staring at him from behind the window. Then – as the horse shook with anticipation, rose its front legs into the air, and charged forward – he saw her turn away as though to go and answer the door. But his mind was on other things now. It was time to find the source of the pain in his head. It was time to find the second Rider.

The street was just as he'd seen in his mind.

The horse walked Seth forward, past a car that had crashed into one of the trees lining both sides of the road, round the bodies of those who had fallen to the ground and stayed there, through rubbish spilled from bins tumbling into each other like empty Coke cans. Everywhere Seth looked, something was broken or twisted or smashed. Mostly though, what really had him staring, were the bodies. Men, women, children even, were on the ground, scattered across gardens and pavement and road as though something had dropped them where they stood.

Seth moved on. The source of the pain was close now and, after about another hundred metres or so, he saw the house, with the SUV parked outside. Displayed in the back window was a sticker displaying in a decorative celtic scrawl the words *The Lord of All Things*. It was then that Seth noticed that this was the only house in the whole street with a single light on. It was coming from upstairs. Seth slid off the horse and made his way towards the front door. He expected it to be locked. Instead, it was open and when he pushed it, the door hit upon something on the other side. Inside Seth found that the thing resisting the door was the body of a man. Opposite the door was the staircase sweeping its way to the upper floor. On this were two more bodies, a woman and a boy no older than nine or ten. And when Seth passed them he noticed they were breathing. It hadn't occurred to him until that moment that anyone he'd seen might have been alive. He'd assumed all the bodies were just a litter of the dead, the souls swept away by some unknown force. He doubled back and checked the man at the door. He was also breathing. Seth wasn't sure if he was relieved or just intrigued by this turn of events, but it made no difference to why he was there in the first place. He moved back up the stairs, passed the boy and the woman, and on towards the only room with a light showing.

The girl was sitting at a keyboard. Clamped over her head was a pair of earphones that covered her ears completely. Her fingers were moving up and down the keys, hammering out a tune Seth couldn't hear. The girl's eyes were red from tears, though the tears themselves had long since dried up. And across her lap rested a huge sword.

Seth fell back on his old skills of observation to try and get a sense of what the girl was about. She was dressed in her school uniform. A dark-blue blazer striped with light-blue lines, a tie, a shirt and a dark-blue skirt. The skirt was crumpled, probably from sitting so long at the keyboard, but the rest looked pristine, and from that Seth knew she was someone to whom school wasn't just somewhere you had to go – it really meant something. The room gave even more away. The posters on the wall were of the usual almost-naked-but-not-quite hunks who sing well but look prettier, but it was neat and ordered and nothing was out of place. Her desk displayed such an attention to detail that he was pleased the girl would never have to see his old caravan, where there had never been anything other than a disorder occasionally disguised as homeliness.

Seth didn't want to spook the girl so he walked calmly towards her. But he didn't wait around either. If he'd found her then The Way were probably not far behind and he had to fight to stop himself racing over to her. Because this girl, he knew, was the second Rider, and her life was forfeit.

The girl, clearly sensing Seth's presence, turned her weary face towards him.

'I . . . I can't stop . . .'

Seth nodded and gently removed the sword from where it was resting across her legs. If he had ever imagined the type of sword a Rider sent to destroy the world would carry, it would have been a thing of terrible beauty, all gold and silver and jewels. But this was a world away from anything like that. It was a killing tool and nothing more. In his hand it was light and balanced and it seemed to come alive at his touch, dance almost, as though desperate to get on with its hideous work. The handle, large enough to take two hands, was wrapped in soft, worn brown leather, the hilt a knot of dull brass, the cross guard broad and flat and strong. As for the blade, it was utterly unremarkable, with a thin groove running down its very centre and edges keen enough to split light in two. No ornamental sword for show, this was made with the sole purpose to destroy. And now it was in the hands of a girl taking her first tentative steps into the life of a teenager.

Seth rested the blade against the wall and turned back to the girl.

'Help me . . .' she whimpered, her voice brittle as the thinest of ice. 'Please . . .'

With a firm gentleness he'd never realized he'd possessed, Seth wrapped his arms around her. He knew

there would be no persuading her to leave what she was doing. Force was the only way.

'Ready?' he mouthed clearly so that she could understand and she nodded.

Seth gave no warning. With all his strength and with his arms wrapped tightly round her, he pulled, sending them both back and away from the keyboard. The stool fell and the keyboard smashed to the floor.

Free now of the source of the music she'd been playing the girl lashed out, screaming, scratching at Seth, begging him to let her go, but he held on. And soon her thrashing eased, her yelling dimmed to a pitiful sob.

Touching her had given Seth all the certain knowledge he needed about who she was and what she would become.

'I know who you are, Kelly,' he said, her name falling from his lips like that of a distant friend's, though he had not known it a second earlier. 'I know you have seen terrible things, that your mind has shown you things you never thought possible, and I know that the power inside you that created that music is telling you to give in to it.'

Kelly just stared at Seth as though from inside a deep, dark cave.

'People are coming for you, Kelly,' explained Seth. 'And they will kill you if they find you.'

The sword caught Seth's eye and he remembered the power that had blasted through him when the white horse had arrived, and then even more strongly when the bow had come into his hand, and the arrow.

'Though I reckon the moment you pick up that sword and think about using it, no one will be able to get close enough to you to do harm ever again.'

Kelly wiped her eyes clear.

'What I saw . . .' she said, 'while I was playing . . . All that destruction, the death. You were there, too. I saw your face. We weren't alone.'

'We've two more to find,' said Seth. 'Then—' But he wasn't given time to finish as the sound of a helicopter over the house broke the moment like a rock through a frozen pond.

'We have to move!' Seth ordered, pulling the girl off the bed and handing her the sword as the sound of something, some*one*, crashing through the front door downstairs echoed through the house.

The girl said nothing and Seth shook her for a response.

'How do we get out?'

Kelly said nothing.

Seth shook her and this time shouted to get her to take notice. 'Kelly! How do we get out?'

A light broke the shadows in Kelly's eyes.

'The loft,' she said, her voice hesitant, as though she wasn't yet clearly aware of what was going on around her. 'There's a skylight, heads out on to the roof.'

'That's the only way?'

With a nod Kelly said, 'There's a huge tree that hangs

over the back of the house. We might be able to get to it before they know where we are.'

'Not like we have much choice, is it?'

'No,' said Kelly, more alert now, her voice at last returning to normal. 'It isn't.'

Kelly locked the door and, as Seth rammed a cupboard up against it to stop anyone getting through, opened a latch in the ceiling to the loft and pulled down a set of ladders that clicked into place and rested on the floor. Seth climbed up first, and once Kelly was up with him she pulled on a rope that clicked the ladder back into place and shut the door in the loft floor behind them.

Moonlight draped through a skylight in the roof like delicate curtains of gossamer.

'Now what?' whispered Kelly. 'You have a plan, right?'

He wasn't about to say it out loud, but Seth had no plan at all. If he was honest, none of this was planned. He was just following his gut. And doing that wasn't easy, not with the power he had at his command, and the growing urgency inside him, deep in his soul, to use it.

Seth glanced around the quiet, claustrophobic loft. Grey shapes and odd shadows moved in and out of focus. It was as though he was standing inside his own mind and trying to make sense of what was hidden in the darkness. Momentarily lost to his thoughts, Seth's mind caught itself on something that, in the past few hours, had become almost comforting: a horse as white as mountain ice.

A thump from below punched Seth out of his silence.

'We have to go,' he said.

'No kidding,' said Kelly and pointed at the skylight. 'But the only way out is that and—'

She was about to say something about not wanting to fall off the roof, and then something else about trying to make it to an old tree that bent over the far end of the house, one that had clutched in its branches the decaying remains of a treehouse her dad had built her years ago, and that her idiotic brother now practically lived in like some tree-dwelling troll, when a great thunderous crash ripped its way across the roof and she yelled out and dropped to the floor like the house had been hit by an earthquake. Dust and wood and slate tumbled into the loft.

Seth reached down and heaved Kelly back up on to her feet.

'Come on. It's time to go.'

'What on earth was that?' hissed Kelly as Seth pulled her along, her eyes blinking away the dust. 'It sounded like a plane just dropped out of the sky!'

Seth said nothing as the answer to Kelly's question walked towards them through the rubble.

'Horses . . .' Kelly breathed, eyes wide in wonder, her voice saturated with disbelief. 'Horses in the loft.'

Seth's own beast, resplendent and terrifying all at once, led the way, walking straight up to him and lowering itself to allow him to climb up on to its back. At its side, the other horse, the one that had come for Kelly, was the deepest of reds, the colour of the heart of the sun burning, burning, burning.

And fire was in its eyes.

22

LILY'S ROOM AT THE motel was empty. But she'd clearly put up a fight – Seth could tell that just by looking at the destruction all around them. Kelly was at his side, brighter now, but still confused.

The television was hanging by the security chain but still working, and spilling out yet more coverage of chaos and blood running on the streets. Things were getting worse, not just with disorder breaking out, but organized and violent gangs taking to the streets. Seth stared at the flickering screen as a car was overturned and set alight, a shop window was smashed in by looters desperately grabbing flat-screen televisions, a group of men armed with cricket bats and hockey sticks walked the streets.

'The world's gone mad,' said Kelly, standing next to

him, her hand slipping into his and squeezing it.

'Not the world,' said Seth. 'Us.'

Seth reached out and switched the television off. Right then, none of what they had seen mattered to Seth. Lily did, and that was that. He'd known her hardly any time at all, yet felt as close to her as he'd felt to his own sister.

Beth.

That memory, painful and hard like a thorn buried deep, made him reach for his neck and the little silver shell that hung round it. But it was gone.

'What's wrong?' asked Kelly, noticing a change rake across Seth's face.

Seth couldn't answer. He'd lost his last remaining physical connection to his family. It was gone, where to he had no idea. But it was enough to force hot tears to his eyes. He wiped them quickly away with the back of his hand. He had to find Lily. He couldn't lose her as well. He *wouldn't* . . .

The mirror from the wall was now a broken picture of the reflected ceiling, lying on the floor. The bedclothes were all screwed up and across the walls and on the floor too, splatters of blood were visible. The fan was still spinning.

Seth roared, and the sound of it blasted through the room like the shockwave from a bomb. Plaster fell from the ceiling. Cracks split the walls. Furniture danced and spun and fell.

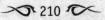

Kelly, hit by the sound, staggered back, pushed herself into the wall.

Seth, his voice dying, could see only the blood. Smell it. Know it was Lily's. He wanted to tear the world down to find those responsible. It was exactly what he was now going to do.

Kelly found her voice again now that Seth had fallen still. 'What happened?'

Seth didn't answer right away. He was sucking in deep breaths, trying to take it all in, to seek out some faint hint of where she had been taken, because it was clear as the morning sun on a crisp, winter's day, that she hadn't gone willingly.

'They took her,' he said at last, circling the room, praying for a sign, anything, that would help. 'The same ones who came for me, and who came for you.'

'Who?'

'The Chosen,' replied Seth.

Lily had no choice but to breathe in the stink of the sweat-and-grime-soaked balaclava that had been pulled over her head, its eyes sewn shut with thick scraps of rough canvas. She was blind, disorientated and terrified. And she was completely and utterly alone.

When they'd come for her, only moments after Seth had disappeared on the back of his horse, she'd done her best to fight back: terror was always a good fuel for a fist. But

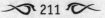

despite knocking the teeth out of one man, bloodying the nose of another and sending yet another to the floor grabbing his crotch, Lily had been overcome. They had, after all, had the advantage not just of surprise but of numbers too.

After the fight, Lily had been thrown across the passenger seats in the back of a car. She'd crunched her head hard against the far door, before being sat upright, clipped in, then blindfolded by the stinking balaclava. Her hands were tied behind her with a plastic tag tight enough that with every bump and thump on the journey it cut into her skin and was soon drawing blood. Then the car had started moving and the man sat next to her had leaned in and, with a voice of misplaced calm, whispered, 'Move, make a sound, and I'll rip your arms off. Understand?'

Lily had believed the voice and the huge hand that had squeezed her arm a little too tightly before giving it a sharp jerk as a final warning. Then a rag had been pushed over her mouth and nose, an acrid vapour had exploded in her lungs and she'd passed out.

Now, though, she was awake and no longer in the car.

'Where am I?' she yelled out. Someone had to be listening and she wanted answers. 'What do you want with me?'

Lily had no idea how long she'd been unconscious, but now awake she was looking for a way out. The room she was in was cold and damp. The only light came from a sliver of light, like a shard of glass, from under a door a few metres away. The chair she was sitting on wobbled badly. And she was feeling woozy, which was probably partly due to whatever they'd drugged her with, but had also always been a warning sign, and one she'd grown accustomed to.

Lily shouted out again, but no response came.

She'd been asked no questions, given no information about what was to happen to her. The last voice she'd heard was the one that had threatened to relieve her of her arms. But she knew the silence wouldn't last for ever, just as well as she knew that the ones who'd come for her and blindfolded her and got on the wrong end of her fists and feet and knees were The Chosen. The ones who'd watched her grow in that awful house, filled her mind with visions, put voices in her head.

A scuffling sound from outside the door. It clanged open, blasting her blind with white light.

'What do you want from me?' Lily yelled, unable to stare into the light.

A rough hand grabbed her chin.

'We want nothing from you at all, Lily,' said a voice close enough for Lily to smell the sweet reek of tomato sauce on his breath. 'You have done your job well.'

Realization lit up like a sparkler in Lily's brain.

'You came for Seth but only found me.'

'Clever girl.'

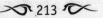

'And now I'm the bait, right? He won't fall for it. He won't.'

'That's a gamble I'm willing to take,' said the voice, pulling away. 'And he will have found your insulin pen by now, I'm sure.'

Lily bit her lip in fear. Not just at the loss of her pen, but at the trap set for Seth.

'You have no idea what you're taking on,' she said. 'No idea at all.'

'He is a boy, Lily,' said the voice. 'That is all.'

Despite everything, Lily couldn't stop the laugh that shot out of her. It was hard and brittle and barbed.

The voice spoke again as though Lily's laugh hadn't even happened. 'A boy who will now be on his way to help his friend: you.'

Lily laughed again, only this time it was cut short by a slap that stung her face. Then that acrid smell again as another rag was pushed into her face. Briefly, Lily wondered what her parents would say if they saw her now.

She blacked out.

Seth spotted something on the floor and under the bed. He walked over to it, knelt down. He knew what it was straight away.

'What is it?' Kelly asked.

'Something that belongs to Lily,' Seth replied. 'Something important.'

As soon as he touched it a blast of energy from it made him catch himself before he fell backwards. It was as though Lily was right beside him in the room. His breath caught in his throat.

Kelly saw Seth wobble on his feet a little and grabbed him.

'What's up? What did you find?'

Seth held it up.

'A bumbag?'

Seth looked anxious. 'It's got all Lily's diabetes kit in it – her insulin and glucose and blood-sugar testing stuff. She needs this to survive.'

Now, with the kit in his hand, his senses drove into him as a vision of what had happened played out before him like a 3D movie in real-time.

He saw Lily staring out through the window across the car park, the door bursting open, the now familiar figures in grey coats rushing in to grab her. He saw Lily jump up on the bed, bring an elbow in hard to the jaw of the first to grab her, smashing his teeth, before rounding on one coming at her from the other side, and driving her knee into his nose. The third fared worse and dropped to the ground like a sack of ball bearings. But others came in then and Lily was dragged screaming from the room and out into the evening.

Seth pushed past Kelly and stood outside, Lily's bumbag gripped tightly in his hand. He didn't need anyone to tell him where Lily was, he realized, annoyed that he'd already wasted time, though thankful he'd found her kit.

'Where are you going?' asked Kelly, hurrying after Seth. 'We go together now, right?'

'We're going to find Lily,' said Seth.

He could find her. He could find anyone now, if he wanted to, anyone at all.

'But what about—' Kelly began, but Seth cut her off.

'It can wait!' said Seth, his voice laced with the deep thunder of a storm at sea. 'And yes, I know it's a trap. But what choice do I have? She's my friend, Kelly! The only one I've got!'

Out in the car park Seth and Kelly found their horses patiently waiting for them, excitement rippling through their huge bodies, their skin shivering.

Seth let his eyes glide over the parking lot. Most of the trucks had now gone. The only one left was on fire, its tyres melted into the gravel, its load smouldering and sending a thick, black pillar of smoke up into the sky. The driver was nowhere to be seen. Seth then noticed that some of the windows of the café had been smashed in. Inside, the place looked like the aftermath of a bar brawl, with tables turned, chairs broken, food and drink everywhere, running down the windows and walls. He hadn't spotted it when they'd arrived because he'd been too deep in thought about what he and Kelly and Lily were going to do next. But that was all now decided and whatever had gone down here Seth knew with absolute certainty that it would only get worse. That was unless he did something to stop it. But first, Lily.

With the ground falling away beneath them and the world blurring, the horses heaving them forwards with a momentum that could warp and twist space and time, Seth focused his mind on Lily. Nothing else mattered. And wherever she was, those who had taken her would very soon regret it.

23

'Y OUR FRIEND IS IN there?' asked Kelly.

Seth nodded.

'Doesn't look very inviting, does it?'

Standing in bleak moorland, bathed in moonlight so bright that they could see for miles, Seth drank in their new surroundings. A few hundred metres away was a military compound – or at least it looked like one. Except that it was built around what looked to Seth like an old church, its weather-worn tower jutting up from behind the high, razor-wired walls like a dog trying to jump out of its run. Gun towers were clearly visible at various points in the walls and, between where he and Kelly were standing and the gate, a large sign made it absolutely clear that from there on in, the place was littered with mines. Around the outside of the wall were the skeletal remains of other buildings. Seth guessed they were the crumbling memory of what had once been a small, isolated community, built around the church. It was a sad place. And a chill wind blew despite the sun.

'I guess they're just not used to having visitors,' said Seth, then pointed to the gun towers, 'but I think they know we're here.'

A drum tattoo of weapons opening up on them crashed through the air.

Neither Seth nor Kelly moved. Bullets exploded all around and tracer fire lit the air like fireflies, but none were close. Not yet.

Kelly's horse took a few steps back, as though readying itself to charge, then stamped its front hooves down hard. The ground split and cracked like ice on a lake. Dust shot out of the cracks. Then Kelly whistled.

At first, Seth couldn't make out much of a tune, just a faint blowing sound with a hint of a note wrapped up in it. But quickly the note grew in strength and the hairs on the back of Seth's neck stood on end.

The tune itself spun out into the air and twisted the dust into a thick rope of wind and grit. Kelly continued to whistle, controlling it, flicking it around them like a huge bull whip.

In front of them the gate swung open and a heavily armoured convoy emerged, like an angry snake stirred from its dark, cool nest. And at that precise moment Seth heard Kelly's faint, pure whistle twist itself into a whirling trill that grew and grew until Kelly snapped her mouth open, broke the whistle, and was singing. In her hand was the sword.

The trucks were gaining. No sooner had Seth thought about his bow than it was in his hand and he drew an arrow, clipped it to the string. But before he had a chance to loose it and send the trucks spinning like toy cars thrown by a tired child, Kelly's voice was raised to an almighty crescendo, almost as though it was sucking all sound from around her. Then she raised the sword and pointed it at the trucks.

Seth's ears popped as the sound, so huge now it was like it was being pulled from the world itself like stitching from an old wound, channelled itself into the sword. The blade vibrated and a spiralling sonic wave, blue and bright and terrible, flashed out from its deadly point and smashed into the oncoming traffic.

The first truck bore the brunt of the force. It didn't explode or tumble from the road and down a ravine, or even flip into the minefield. Instead, it just crumbled, bits of it falling and turning to dust and spilling out in twirls and swirls till nothing at all of it was left. The rest of the convoy followed in another single devastating blow.

Kelly turned her attention then to the compound, this time instead of pointing the sword she swung it in a great arc, left to right, as though trying to cut the air in two. A tidal wave of destruction threw itself against the walls. The razor wire and the walls vaporized. Inside the compound, windows shattered, doors splintered, roofs were torn off.

Then a voice, a rumbling, tumbling thing as though the mountains were speaking.

'And there came forth another horse, blood-red in colour,
and to him that sat upon it there
was given to take peace from the Earth,
and to bring it about that men should slay each other,
and a great sword was given to him.'

Kelly stared at Seth, eyes wide in shock, not just at the voice they had both clearly heard, but at what she had done and what she now knew she had become.

'I . . . I am Strife,' she said.

And that was enough.

More than.

'It's the music,' said Seth.

Kelly nodded, a fear in her eyes about what she had just done, almost without thinking, but also a desperate thirst to do it again. 'I know. It's like it's a part of me now.'

'But what were you whistling and singing?' asked Seth. 'The sounds, the notes, it was impossible to hear them, or at least when I tried it was like they were always just out of reach.'

'It's like everything has a tune that only I can hear,' said Kelly. 'Rocks, trees, the sky, you. Does that make sense?'

Seth said, 'Yes, even though it shouldn't, right?'

Tears welled up in Kelly's eyes. 'I want to go home, Seth.'

'I have no home to want to go to,' Seth replied. 'You're lucky.'

'Oh, I'm sorry,' Kelly apologized. 'I didn't mean . . .'

Seth shook his head. 'Your parents, your brother, they were alive?'

'I thought . . .'

'No,' said Seth, happy to make someone smile for a change. 'Just unconscious. That tune you were playing when I found you. I think it's what's set all this off. And me.'

Kelly didn't understand.

'When did you first hear it? That tune in your head? The one you were playing?'

'How did you know that's what it was?'

'Educated guess,' said Seth. 'So here's another one. It woke you up, didn't it? Early this morning when it was still dark?'

Kelly was dumbstruck.

'But . . .'

'It's a long story,' said Seth. 'I'm supposed to be dead. Murdered. But I'm not. And because of that little error, I turned thirteen and now here we are. OK, so there's more to it than that, but it'll have to do.'

'It was my birthday too,' said Kelly.

'Figures,' replied Seth, then added, 'Sorry. You should've had a better present than the power to destroy the world.'

'Chocolates would've been nice,' said Kelly.

At that, Seth knew he liked Kelly. She wasn't edgy or desperately-seeking-danger like Lily, and there was something about her which made him warm to her. Seth thought about the mates he'd had in his life and realized then that he'd never really had any. A dad for a showman preacher was up there with a leper's bell. Weird then, he thought, that now, of all times, he knew two people he hoped he could call friends.

In front of them, the dust was settling on the pulverized compound, and the air was starting to echo to the sound of panicking voices.

Kelly spurred her horse forward. 'Come on,' she said. 'Let's go find your friend.'

Yep, thought Seth, *I like Kelly*, and followed on behind.

24

WHEN SETH AND KELLY rode into the compound, those unfortunate enough to still be either alive or conscious after what had just happened quickly wished they weren't. The sight of the huge horses tramping through the burning rubble, sparks and flames torching the ground beneath them, great cracks opening up to cough dust, seared into their minds. Some ran and kept on running, refusing to look back, preferring the deadly lottery of the minefield to what was now before them. Others could do nothing but stay frozen as they were, caught in the horror and unable to wake from the nightmare before them.

'She's this way,' said Seth, moving forward purposefully, looking neither left nor right. He was holding himself together, but only just. What had just happened was too much to comprehend. A ferocious destruction of unmatchable violence. And now, somewhere in its smouldering, crushed remains, was Lily. If she was hurt . . .

Seth held back the tears, focused on Lily and led Kelly to a patch of ground in the middle of the compound. It was covered with four-wheel drives and armoured personnel carriers, all of them tossed into a pile like a bonfire.

'But there's no building,' said Kelly. 'You're standing in what used to be a car park.'

'I know,' said Seth. 'Just let me focus!'

He immediately regretted snapping at Kelly, but he was worried about Lily. She had to be here, and she had to be alive, because if she wasn't, then none of this was worthwhile. And the consequences, he knew, were terrible.

Then, as Lily's face floated in Seth's mind, almost if an unspoken command had passed between himself and his horse, the beast brought its left foot down with a force that could crack granite. The ground opened up beneath it. Not that it had much choice.

Seth leaped off the horse and dropped to the ground to stare into the hole. It was dark and stank of damp and the cold and other not so recognizable things that he didn't want to imagine.

'Lily?'

Nothing.

She's down there! I know it!

'Lily! It's Seth! Answer me! You have to be alive! You have to be! So speak to me! Please!'

A murmur then, followed by mumbling, but it was enough.

'Rope!' Seth shouted out. 'We need rope! I have to get her out of there!'

He didn't expect a coil to be tossed over to him by Kelly.

'I've found a first-aid kit too,' she said. 'Just in case we need it.'

Seth, wiping tears that were now freely flowing from his eyes, was at last able to see into the dark below. Lily was there, arms tied behind her to the chair she was sitting on, blinking up at the light from the hole his horse had made.

'Lily! It's OK! I can see you! I'm coming to get you!'

The floor didn't look too far away and with little thought Seth slipped his feet into the hole and dropped down. He was with Lily in three quick steps. His arms were around her not a second later.

'Lily! Are you OK? Did they hurt you?'

The plastic tag holding Lily's hands tight was no match for the power in Seth and it gave way immediately.

Lily mumbled something, her arms hanging weakly down by her sides, but Seth couldn't make it out. He held up the kit.

Look, I've got your stuff – but what do you need? What do I have to give you?

Lily's eyes rolled in her head and she murmured, 'Blood

sugar too low . . . Need glucagon shot . . .'

Seth tore open the bag and found the syringe he thought she was talking about.

Lily, her limbs floppy like a puppet's, pointed to an area on the inside of her leg.

'There,' she mumbled. 'Jab . . .'

Seth pressed in the needle and pushed down the plunger.

'Thank . . . you . . .' breathed Lily, then with an attempt at smiling asked, 'Is this a rescue?'

'It will be,' said Seth, 'once we work out the best way to get you out. Anyway, we need to give you a bit of time to at least be steady on your feet.'

Lily said nothing, allowing the glucagon to slip its way through her body. She tried to get up but fell forward on to Seth, who caught her easily.

With Lily in his arms, the glucagon gradually doing its work, Seth stared round at the room in which Lily had been kept. The revulsion inside him at the thought of her being in such a place was overpowering. It was all he could do to not drop to his knees and scream.

Lily raised herself from Seth's shoulders. With relief he saw a little life in her eyes, colour to her cheeks.

'Feel human yet?' Seth asked Lily, trying to make light of what she'd been through.

'Not sure I want to,' Lily said. She pushed away from Seth and tried to stand, but her legs were still too weak.

'Lean on me,' said Seth, and slowly, carefully, helped Lily to her feet, his arms holding her tight. 'We need to get you out of here.'

Seth walked them both slowly over to the hole he'd dropped through.

'Kelly? Can you . . .'

The rope fell through the hole. On the end of it was a makeshift harness. Seth examined it, impressed with Kelly's improvisation. She'd threaded rope through the arms of a thick, padded jacket and tied it in a loop.

'It's not much,' Kelly shouted down, 'but at least it won't cut into her too much.' She waved then at Lily. 'I'm Kelly,' she said.

Lily lifted a hand and almost managed to wave back. 'Lily,' she said.

Seth looped the jacket under Lily's arms then gave a shout for Kelly to haul her up. Within minutes he was following.

'Thanks,' he said to Kelly.

Kelly hushed him and pulled open the medical kit she'd found.

'Know how to use any of this stuff?'

'Totally,' said Kelly. 'I'm a school first-aider.'

Seth rested Lily against him as Kelly cleaned her grazes and cuts.

'You've looked better,' said Seth, and that brought a smile to Lily's face. He was pleased to see her, more pleased than he'd ever been to see anyone in his life before. The warmth of the sensation made him blush.

'Nice of you to notice,' she said, a weak smile plucking up the courage to slip across her weary, grubby face.

'You need food, don't you?' said Kelly, finishing off wiping Lily's face. She handed over a box. 'MREs. Whatever this place was, it was certainly well stocked.'

'MR whats?' asked Seth.

'Meals Ready to Eat,' said Kelly. 'American army rations. Dad's ex-forces so I've seen a few of these. He'd always come home with spares and loved trying out what soldiers from other countries had to eat.'

Seth wasn't so sure.

'They're pretty cool actually,' said Kelly. 'They come with a flameless heater too that you activate by adding water. Check this out!'

Kelly poured a little of the water from a bottle of water she'd also found into an olive-green pouch, then added the MRE.

'It's just iron, magnesium and salt,' she explained as the bag containing the food started to heat up. 'Works like a battery. There!'

Kelly passed it to Seth to share with Lily.

'Meatballs, I think,' she said. 'You both eat. I'm going to look around. This is the type of place my dad used to work in. Kind of interesting to see it up close.'

Seth finished the food so quickly he immediately had

indigestion. He tried to stop himself burping all the food back up again. Lily, who was eating and already looking healthier than when he'd found her in the hole, sipped slowly at some water.

Moments later Kelly returned with a folder.

'Look, I found this,' she said.

Lily took the folder and the torch from Kelly and saw the mark on the front of it that she recognized all too well.

'It belongs to The Way,' she said. Before the others could ask how she knew that without even opening the file, Lily stopped eating and pulled her top down over her left shoulder. The black tattoo stared back.

'It's kind of a secret mark,' she said. 'I believed taking it was the right thing to do at the time. Not so much now though, right? I like to keep it covered. Time changes you. Not always for the best, but this time, I reckon so.'

Lily flipped the folder open and started to read. She soon wished she hadn't.

Seth noticed a change in her immediately. 'Something wrong?'

'What is it?' asked Kelly.

'This . . .' said Lily, tapping a finger on the folder as she flicked through it. 'I've never seen it before in my life, but I know it.'

'How do you mean?' Seth asked, taking more interest now.

Lily pulled some of the papers out from the file for Kelly and Seth to see.

'It's just a list of names,' Kelly observed. 'Like from a phone book or something.'

'But it's not just a list at all,' said Lily. 'The names: they're *all* potential Riders!'

Saying it out loud made the reality of it crash home like a well-aimed penalty kick. Lily involuntarily covered her mouth with her hands as though appalled at what she'd just said. But it wasn't that which had shocked her, but something else. A deeper meaning behind the existence of such a list, a darker mystery about everything her life had been about.

'Lily?' said Seth, reaching out to gently squeeze her hand. 'What's wrong?'

The words couldn't come immediately because the realization as it sunk in was too much to bear. At last she spoke.

'These names, they're all targets,' she said, trying to not let her voice shake too much.

Seth cut in, his voice almost breaking. 'But there must be hundreds here!' he said, staring at the list, shock raw in his eyes. 'And they're from all over the world! How is that possible? Even if what you're saying is true . . .'

'I know,' said Lily, guessing where Seth was going. 'There's no way I could get to them all. Not on my own. And that means—'

'That you're not the only Finder employed by The Way,' Seth finished.

Lily stared back at the folder, flicking through the hundreds of pages it contained. Of the names that were circled, some were also crossed out and others made no sense at all. Two names caught her eye, made her wonder just why they were there in the first place, but she thought nothing more of it.

'I think I understand how it works,' Lily said at last. 'Everyone of these is a potential Rider, or target,' she said. 'Like both of you. So your names must be in here, too.'

Kelly and Seth nodded, said nothing, listened.

'The names are all taken from here,' continued Lily, tapping a logo at the top of one of the pages.

'Prophet,' said Seth, and then for Kelly's benefit explained exactly what it was.

'That can't actually exist!'

'Neither can those horses,' said Seth, nodding back at the huge animals. 'Neither can *we*. But they – and we – do. Right?'

Kelly's nod was answer enough for everyone.

'Prophet must monitor the names,' said Lily. 'It would make sense to use it in such a way, assuming it was accurate, which The Way clearly believes that it is.'

'Then what?' asked Kelly. 'Why are some circled?'

'They're the ones that Prophet deems to be a threat,'

said Lily. 'And I'm guessing this is where I come in, and those like me.'

'To make sure?'

Lily nodded.

'But what's the point in that?' asked Seth. 'Can't Prophet find these people? Surely that's the easy part. Why bother with you at all?'

'You're forgetting something,' Lily said. 'I've been doing this not just for a few years, but a few lifetimes. The Way will trust only Prophet so far. Then it's down to me. I go in, I find the target, and I check if the threat is real.'

Seth stared at Lily with renewed horror.

'How many people have you tracked down?'

Lily shrugged, shook her head.

'How many in this lifetime, Lily? And how many before you found me?'

'I've lost count,' she said, her voice quiet, sorrowful. 'But none of them matter. *You* do, Seth. It's you I had to find. The others were only possibles. I went through them to find you. You're the real deal.'

Seth wasn't listening. Having flicked through the file himself, he'd found at the back a number of other pages all clipped together. On them was yet another list of names. None were circled, but many had been crossed out. Without lifting his eyes he asked Lily, 'So what happened to them?'

'Nothing!' Lily snapped back, irritated now at what Seth

was implying. 'The Way doesn't kill people unless they know they're a threat!'

Seth started to read out the names in front of him.

'What are you doing?' asked Lily.

'. . . Debbie Wright, George McGrath, Dennis Robb . . .'

Lily snatched the list from Seth's hand. But the act of doing it made her fall a little and she only just caught herself from falling further.

'Just stop it, all right? Enough!' She clenched the list in her hands and shook it at Seth. 'I don't know any of these names, you hear me? Not one of them!'

'It's a different list!' Seth snapped back, brandishing the list in front of Lily's eyes. Many of the names were crossed out. He jabbed his finger at one name in particular. 'You're on the list, Lily, only your name isn't crossed out because you're still alive. But the same can't be said for the others, can it?'

'No . . .'

Seth nodded coldly. 'It's the only answer, isn't it? The Way, it seems, are more thorough than you gave them credit for. They send you in, yes, but only because they know that when you do eventually find a potential Rider they can dispose of you too, right? And they erase the others just to make sure!'

'That's not true!'

'Yes it is!' Seth shouted, tasting anger. 'All those lives you've lived before?' he asked. 'Why haven't you got any memories of adulthood? Why are they all about hunting for me? It's because you *had* no adulthood, Lily! All along you've been hunting me down, yet completely unaware of the hunter waiting in the dark to kill you too!'

Lily scrabbled backwards in the dirt, away from the list, away from Kelly and Seth, shaking her head.

'No . . .'

'Who does the killing, Lily?'

Lily couldn't speak, but Seth pressed until she answered.

'There are . . . four of them,' said Lily, like she was afraid of the words as they came to her. 'They are known simply as The Calling. The final kill is their responsibility.'

Seth froze as a flashback pushed its way to the front of his mind. He was on the back of Lily's scooter at a road junction, and he was staring into the fields of Glastonbury Festival, gazing back towards his parents' caravan, as four figures slipped out into the night.

'They were at Glastonbury. The Calling. I saw them when we were escaping on that scooter. They'd come to make sure I was dead, or find me and finish the job themselves.'

'And they were here, too,' said Lily looking again at the file. 'This belongs to them. It has to. They never thought it would fall into the wrong hands.'

Kelly had hold of a sheet that had fallen loose.

'The dates stretch back decades,' she said. 'But some of these are like right now. I mean, this one here, right?

Jason MacKenzie?' She showed the others the name on her list. 'His name's circled and he turns thirteen today! And these two, and—'

Lily interrupted, her eyes wide. 'Which means . . .'

'That time is running out,' said Seth. 'And that these names are being crossed off, one by one.'

25

WITHOUT ANY WARNING, SETH jumped up and called his horse over.

'We can save him!' he shouted. 'We can save all of them!'

With a shake of its mane, clearly excited to be moving again, Seth's horse trotted over. The red horse followed, alert and keen. The ground shook as they approached, as if they brought with them their own personal earthquakes. Seth was already on his horse by the time Kelly and Lily had joined him, Lily with the folder stuffed securely inside her jacket.

'Have you completely lost the plot, Seth?' asked Lily, still wary of the horses, even more so now that there were two of them. Yet her fear seemed to mean little to the creatures, who nudged her softly with their noses as

though they were expecting a sugar cube.

'We have the power to do it,' said Seth, looking down at Lily from his seat upon the horse. 'To change things. And I saved you, didn't I? So I can save the others! Jason's just the start!'

'No,' answered Lily. 'What you do is destroy!' She swept her arms around at what remained of the compound to get her point across.

'That was Kelly, not me,' said Seth, attempting a very poor excuse.

'Doesn't matter,' said Lily. 'This is what you do. How the hell do you think you can save these others?'

'I don't know!' Seth barked back. 'But doing so will change everything, won't it? It's back to choice again, Lily, don't you see that? If I choose to save them, then there's still a chance for us! For everyone!'

'Aren't you forgetting something?'

'Like what?'

Lily glanced over to Kelly, who was now on the back of her horse, then to Seth again.

'There's only two of you,' she said. 'And there should be four.'

'She's right,' agreed Kelly. 'Thinking back to all those church groups and Sunday services I've gone to, we're Conquest and Strife, right?'

Seth nodded.

'Then we're missing Famine and Death.'

'You need to find them,' said Lily. 'If you really want to make a difference, become the four Riders and . . .' Lily's voice faltered. What on earth was she doing?

'And what?' asked Seth.

'Just shut up and let me think!' Lily snapped back. 'Please!'

Lily turned her back on Seth. Her brain was melting. That's what it felt like, as she fought with herself about what she was doing. What any of them were doing. She was persuading Seth, the first Rider, to bring all four of the Riders together! How was that in any way a good thing? But she had to trust Seth and, deep down, she did. He had a good heart, albeit it was an argumentative, headstrong one, and he wanted to do what he thought was right. And perhaps this was something that The Way had never counted on. To them, the Riders had always been a force bent on nothing but crushing the world completely. But what if – *what if!* – the whole point of all this was to have the Riders decide? Then perhaps the Riders hadn't come here to destroy the world at all, but to change it. It was possible . . . It *had* to be!

'Lily?' It was Seth. 'Penny for your thoughts?'

'You really have to find the other Riders,' she said. 'If you don't, two things could happen.'

'Two?' said Kelly. 'I thought it was just The Way we had to worry about.'

'That's one,' said Lily. 'The Way will try to find them

before *you* find them, before they become like you, and kill them.'

'So what's the other?' asked Seth.

Lily squeezed her eyes tight then snapped them back open to stare into Seth. 'What if they become Riders before anyone finds them at all?' she asked. 'Have you thought about *that*? I don't know about you, but I don't really like the idea of Famine and Death riding out without you to lead them or at least hold them back and help make them change direction!'

'I haven't sensed them yet!' Seth said, taking what Lily had said, trying his best to ignore the implications. 'And until I do, if I can save a life, I will! Starting with Jason!'

'Seth . . .'

'Are you coming with us?' Seth asked. 'Because we're going now.'

Kelly turned from Seth to Lily. 'Ride with me. What you're saying makes sense, but so does Seth. And we can't just stand around doing nothing if we can save someone.'

Lily knew she had no choice, not unless she wanted to be left out here. So she walked round to the side of Kelly's horse, which lowered itself enough for Kelly to reach down and help Lily up.

Seth gave no instruction, just tapped his horse forward and they were gone.

* * *

The house, when they found it, was out on its own in the middle of nowhere. They had ridden for what seemed like only a few moments and although it had been night when they had left the compound, Seth noticed that a new day had broken. He wondered at the power flowing through the horses, something that seemed to defy time itself.

Fields lay about the house like a vast quilt draped across the land, and the crops danced and swayed in the wind. Around the house were various farm buildings. The place was neat and tidy; a farm that wasn't just a living but a place the owners were proud of.

Seth was filled with hope.

'We're in time!' he called out. 'Come on!'

But as they drew closer, his hope didn't fade so much as catch light and start to burn. Much like the window on the first floor of the house.

Seth spurred on his horse, slipping from it as they came up to the house and the four-wheel drive parked outside, engine still running, radio on.

'You can't go in there!' Lily yelled out, jumping from the horse to get between him and his clear purpose. 'Don't be an idiot!' She saw something then, distant, but definitely the dust kicked up by a truck racing away. It could've been anyone, but something told her that she knew exactly who was in that truck and why they were in such a hurry.

Seth caught Lily's gaze and saw the dust for himself.

'You think . . .' said Lily.

'No,' said Seth, 'I *know*,' then did little more than look at Kelly, who raised her sword. Then sang.

Kelly's voice was beautiful and haunting, as though calling the notes from all around her, dragging them out of the ground, out of the plants and fields and the far-off, hidden mountains. Then she raised her sword to point at the shrinking cloud, and the vehicle it hid from view, and hit a note so high and pure and perfect Lily wanted to hear it in her head for ever, even if the power of it dissolved her to nothing but dust.

The sonic wave shook Kelly's arm as she held the sword. It blasted out from the point and almost instantaneously reached the retreating vehicle. There was a pause, Lily's ears popped and then, like the foot of an invisible giant, a solid block of air slammed down on to the vehicle, crushing it to nothing.

When Lily turned back to Seth, he had already gone, and she only just managed to catch sight of him as he crashed through the front door, eyes searching.

An explosion knocked Seth off his feet as a fireball raced down the hall and over his head, smashing through the front of the house. Lily dropped to the ground and she and Kelly shielded their eyes. The horses didn't even flinch.

Seth wasn't giving up. If there was a chance of someone being alive still, he had to do something. As he stood up a shadow swept across the floor from behind him, blocking out the day's light. His horse had come for him.

The beast lowered itself and Seth clambered on. It moved down the hall and up the stairs to the next floor. The weight of the creature made the staircase groan, yet the old wood of which it was made did not yield and they were soon on the landing. Fire was everywhere now, but Seth and the horse were unharmed, the flames swirling around them like ribbons, the smoke parting like the sea for Moses.

At the room where Seth had first seen the fire, the door was still shut. The horse raised a hoof and splintered the thing into a million matchsticks, then stepped inside.

It was as though they had stumbled into a furnace. Everything was aflame, the yellows and reds of the fire tumbling and fighting with each other, desperately seeking a way to escape, to find more things to burn. Then, in the corner of the room, Seth caught sight of what he'd come here to save.

His rage boiled over.

Lily and Kelly heard the roar from outside. The house was an inferno now and they'd stepped back from it as the flames reached higher and the sparks danced far enough away from their mother to light small hearts of fire in the land around and about them. Then they saw an explosion of wood and glass and flame from the upper floor and from it shot Seth and his horse, like a rocket from a cannon. The fire whipped after them, curling round them like a giant cape caught in the wind and, when they landed with a grace utterly impossible for such a leap, the ground shuddered and split. Seconds later the house collapsed in on itself like it was made of playing cards.

Seth approached. With every step of his horse's hooves, more cracks appeared, the ground opening up like crazy paving.

Lily backed away, saw the white of the salt from Seth's tears dried on his face by the furnace he'd just escaped from. She did not need to know what he had found inside the house; his face was answer enough.

'So this is how The Way serves to save the world,' said Seth, the house crackling with the heat consuming it. 'This is how The Protector protects.'

'They do it out of love,' said Lily. 'Twisted, I know, but it's how they would answer you.'

Seth opened out his arms as if he was pinned to an invisible cross.

'How many thousands have died to prevent me becoming this?' he asked. 'How many, Lily?'

Lily said, 'But look at you, Seth! Surely you can see their reasoning!'

Seth snapped his arms back in.

'Look at what you are!' Lily continued. 'You're our doom, Seth! In their position, who wouldn't do the same? Who wouldn't put the needs of the many before the needs of the few?'

'So they're afraid of me?' said Seth.

'The whole damned *world* is afraid of you!' Lily cried back. 'Can't you see that?'

Seth was still. For a moment, the world around them slowed, the fire in the house now a smooth blending of beautiful autumn colours, the clouds stalling slightly, trees half bent in the wind refusing to return upright.

'Well,' said Seth, 'it ain't seen nothing yet . . .'

26

THE BLACK FIGURE WAS back. Seth could see it clearly, standing before him, built of shadows and destruction. Though his own eyes were closed, Seth could clearly make out the figure's face. Above that silver glimmer of a smile he'd seen before, two shimmering eyes glared back. Their edges were ragged, as though flickering with intense heat. The figure's hands beckoned to him once more, calling him forwards. Seth followed and as he drew closer, the figure's fingers drew lines of fire in the air which twisted and converged in the darkness, knitting together into a rope for Seth to follow. Around him and in him and beneath him, Seth could sense the world's pain, hear its cries. The suffering broke his heart.

Lily was staring at Seth, could not ignore the terror

scoring its claws across her skin at the fierce look of purpose now set on Seth's face, like ancient runes chiselled into stone. His eyes were closed, and he was mumbling. His horse was still. She reached out to him, but drew away at the last moment, as though she was afraid of getting burned.

'What's he doing?' she asked, hoping for an answer from Kelly.

Kelly too was as stone and mumbling.

Lily stumbled back. She'd made a terrible mistake. Seth should be dead. The Way was right all along. And now, because of what she'd done, Seth was going to do what his destiny had meant for him all along: destroy the world.

Seth was unaware of Lily. Kelly, though, he now called on. And she came, riding into his vision as though it was the most natural thing in the world to do. Seth did not speak to her for words were not needed. Just a connection to help him find what lay at the end of the rope. He turned his attention to the flaming rope stretching out before him and Kelly now, a rope laid there by the figure of shadows. Reaching for it, grasping tightly, expecting pain, Seth felt nothing. The rope yanked him forward. Below, the Earth seemed to flicker from apparent calm to Armageddon, as if it couldn't quite make up its mind. Then the rope came to an end and ahead shadows swirled and bubbled. Something in them drew Seth in, called for him. Seth pushed into the shadows. Was swallowed by the darkness.

He saw thick jungle, could smell it in the air, a warm dampness of relentless life, and hidden deep inside it something waiting for him. Then he saw a land bleak and cold and ravaged by rain, but what was waiting for him didn't just feel bad, it smelled bad too. The fog parted. Seth came face-to-face with . . .

Lily had to do something. Panic and terror pulled at her, Lily searched for anything that would help. And spotted, leaning up against a fence, an axe. It was new, and on a stool beside it was an older axe with a snapped shaft. Clearly it had been purchased for a fix-it job. A job that now, with the fire still burning in the heart of the remains of the house, would never happen.

Lily raced over, picked up the wood, then ran back over to the horses, who eyed her with little interest now. She raised the axe over her shoulder, prepared herself, but then, in the presence of Seth and Kelly, felt immediately shrunken and powerless, like a flower blasted by the sun. What was she thinking? That she could knock them from their horses and bash some sense into them? As if that would work! It didn't stand a chance. What was she thi—

Seth opened his eyes.

'Lily . . .'

Kelly was back online too.

'What have you done, Seth?'

His face was grey and he was slumped forward. He

looked like a huge syringe had been rammed into his back to suck out his life force.

'I . . .'

Seth toppled from the horse and Lily, with no time to react, could do nothing but watch him fall. His landing wasn't soft, as if he'd jumped from a plane without a parachute. His body crashed down with enough force to bury it in a hole two feet deep. The shock of it knocked Lily back. She ran to Kelly before the same thing happened to her, catching her just in time.

Lily lay Kelly on the ground, then went over to check Seth, pulling him from the hole and over to the grass Kelly was resting on. She was awake now, and looked close to vomiting.

'I found them,' said Seth, the rope of fire still scorching his mind with the memory of what he'd found at the end of it. His voice was weak, as if he had but a few moments left in this life. 'I searched for them and I found them, Lily! Like I was supposed to!'

Lily didn't understand. 'The other two Riders? How? What did you do, Seth?'

'Water . . .'

Lily had seen the old pump at the corner of one of the barns outside the house when they arrived. It wasn't too far away and, hoping it worked, she raced over and gave the handle a heave. It complained a little but, miraculously, drew out such a clear stream of crystal-like water she

almost wept with happiness. It didn't take long to find a bucket and she swilled it out, filled it and took it to Seth and Kelly.

Seth drank deeply.

'I needed Kelly,' Seth explained as she leaned over to take some water in her hands and sip it slowly like someone parched by the desert sun. 'Alone, I wasn't strong enough, but with her I could focus more clearly, search wider and further. And I found them.'

'But there were *three*, Lily!' said Seth, pouring water over his face. 'I know that doesn't make sense, but it's what I saw; three other Riders, not two! How is that possible?'

Lily wondered then if what had happened to Seth was now really beginning to take its toll. She couldn't tell how much longer he'd be able to last. She choked back tears as her mind kept yelling at her, *It's all your fault . . . your fault . . . your fault . . .*

'What happened?'

Seth had cupped water in his hands but rather than drink it, just watched it seep through his fingers back into the bucket. It glistened silver in the light of the day like liquid mercury.

'I called them,' Seth said, his voice a whisper flickering its way through a deep, rocky valley. 'I don't understand how, but that's what I did, but two didn't hear me, at least they couldn't. I don't know, something was wrong.'

Lily slumped back on the grass, hopelessness seeping into her like a creeping dampness. On the horizon a grey cloud was gathering. It was thick and wide and seemed to be moving at a ferocious pace, rolling and tumbling towards them. Whatever kind of storm it was she didn't want to wait around to find out.

Moving then to stand up and get Seth and Kelly back on their horses, Lily was acutely aware of the muffled radio still switched on in the vehicle outside the house. Music had been playing, but now it was the news. More of the same she thought; disorder, destruction and death. But then a newsflash interrupted the broadcast. Lily couldn't catch much of it, but she heard one word clearly: locusts.

A wind hushed across the yard between the smouldering remains of the house and the barns, kicking up a squall of dust and burned grass and ash. It got into Lily's eyes, made them water. Rubbing them clear, she was drawn again to the approaching cloud. Something about it wasn't quite right. The way it was moving was nothing like a normal storm. If anything, it appeared to be going in the opposite direction to rest of the clouds in the sky and it was kicking up dust in front of it like a tornado.

Then she knew. Not because of how the cloud moved or behaved, but because of what landed on her arm.

'Locusts . . .' she said, repeating what she'd heard on the radio. 'Locusts!'

Lily's skin crawled as she looked back up and saw now

that the cloud wasn't a cloud at all, but a towering, ever falling wall of locusts racing towards them, expanding outwards to block off any escape.

'Locusts!' she screamed at last, her voice finally able to escape her strangled throat. 'Seth! Kelly! We have to move!'

But Seth and Kelly made no effort to. Not even when Lily dropped down to try and heave them on to their feet. Instead, they just stared and stared as the plague of locusts swept closer and closer, until they were at the edge of the last field beyond the farm, then halfway across it, then at the beautifully painted white picket fence that stood guard around the farm's border, then . . .

Lily fell to the ground and covered her ears. The sound swarming towards them was a cacophony of bones being crushed, as the locusts' wings beat and beat and beat. Some of the insects caught in her hair and Lily had to fight against every instinct inside her not to panic and scream and yell. She could feel them crawling over her, their light bodies given weight by the sheer number of them in the air. And she dared not open her eyes because then she would see it and it would be real and they'd fly into her then, wouldn't they, into her eyes and her mouth and down her throat and she'd choke on them as they filled her belly and crawled into her lungs . . .

Then calm.

Lily didn't notice it at first, too focused as she was on keeping her head down and her hands over her ears so that the hideous things didn't just go crawling in there and start burrowing. But when she did, when she realized that although the air was still alive with the sound of the flight of a billion insects, she could no longer feel them crawling over her.

She dared to look.

They were in the eye of a storm. Around the farm, swirling in a vast maelstrom and miles high, was a hurricane of devouring destruction. It was impossible to comprehend what she was witnessing, it was so huge and implausible that all she could do was stare. Then she realized something else: they were no longer alone.

Seth, still exhausted from going into the house to look for survivors, viewed the locusts with indifference. But he immediately recognized the figure standing in the yard before them, and knew why he was here; because Seth had called.

Seth stood up and with him Lily and Kelly got to their feet. He led them forward and the white and red horses trotted on behind them. The boy in front of them did not move, and neither did the huge black horse standing next to him. The boy was holding something in his hands. Locusts were on him, not crawling, but sitting, calm and content, as though completely at home.

The boy moved towards them, the black horse at his side, its eyes dark, hollow almost, but with a glint of hardest diamond within each of them.

They all stood for a moment, staring at each other. Kelly, sword in her hand, and the red horse by her side. Seth, his bow in his hand, the white horse tapping its nose against the back of his head. The boy held a small set of brass balance scales, and his own horse was so black it was as though it had been formed of the darkest reaches of the cosmos. And Lily, with nothing but despair in her eyes for what she had started and now couldn't stop even if she'd tried.

Then that voice again, the one that seeped from everything, yet came from nothing.

'I looked and there before me was a black horse! Its rider was holding a pair of scales in its hand!'

'Famine,' said Seth.

The boy, eyes wide in terror, said nothing in reply.

27

'AM I DREAMING?'

Lily shook her head as the boy glanced at each of them in turn.

'No,' she said. 'Though I spend most of my time now hoping I am and that soon I'll wake up. But it doesn't happen. It's just a nightmare we're all living through. Sorry.'

'I was at home,' continued the boy, dazed almost, as though he'd just woken up from being unconscious. 'I had to clean out my pets, so that's what I was doing, you know? Mum always prefers it if I do it, says it teaches me responsibility or something. Not that I mind, because it's fun really, and I like to make sure they're all fed and watered and clean. You can't keep pets – well, I don't think you should be allowed to anyway, not if you can't look after them properly.'

Lily stepped a little closer and introduced herself and Seth and Kelly.

'I'm Demetrius,' said the boy, sounding almost embarrassed by it. 'Mum's into Shakespeare. Most people call me Dem. Who are you? Why am I here?'

'You were cleaning your pets; then what?' Seth prompted, as much to clarify his own visions as anything else. Dem had been at the end of the flaming rope. That much Seth was sure of. But so had something else, something worse than all of them put together.

'I want to be an insectologist,' said Demetrius. 'Just like my parents. They travel all over the world finding new species. That's why I've got my pets, you see? Practical experience. I've got stick insects and a few praying mantis, but my favourites are the cockroaches, just because they're so hardcore!'

Seth heard the enthusiasm and excitement in Dem's voice. It was a little weird.

'Cockroaches can basically survive anything,' said Demetrius. 'Even the end of the world.'

'We could probably test that hypothesis if you wanted,' said Lily. 'But I'd prefer it if we didn't, if it's all the same with you.'

'Then what happened?' asked Kelly, pushing for more detail.

'The windows in my bedroom burst in,' said Demetrius, clearly remembering something bad as the words caused him to shudder. 'My pets went crazy and then the room was just filled with insects. I could hardly breathe. They were everywhere, all over me. I screamed for help, but no one came. Then I think I heard something, I'm not sure; a voice, I think, or an echo, and it was coming from outside. Sounded like just one word, *follow*.'

'Go on,' said Seth, knowing it was his voice Demetrius had heard.

'I wanted to follow it, but I couldn't move because of the insects, but then it was as if they just lifted me up! How insane does that sound? They're just insects, but they actually picked me up! Outside, it was as though I was floating on this huge cloud of insects. It was disgusting really, but fascinating too! Then the horse appeared and now . . .'

'You're here,' said Seth. 'With us.'

Demetrius shrugged. 'I guess.'

'It makes sense,' said Kelly. 'You're into insects and here you are as Famine, controlling a cloud of locusts.'

'I'm what?'

'You really have no idea, do you?' asked Seth. 'Conquest, Strife, Famine and Death?'

Demetrius was blank.

'You go to church, right?' asked Kelly.

Demetrius shook his head.

'But what about The Way?' asked Lily disbelievingly.

Demetrius shrugged. 'I hear stuff on the news but Mum and Dad aren't big on any religion or belief that thinks it has all the answers.'

'You're more of a questions kid, aren't you?' said Seth, and knew he had Demetrius in a nutshell.

'Can't learn unless you ask questions,' replied Demetrius.

A voice on the radio interrupted with the latest news of a locust swarm and the wiping out of thousands of acres of crops. The voice sounded almost out of breath with panic.

'It's not my fault!' said Demetrius, glancing from where the radio had spoken back to the others. 'I didn't ask for this! It just happened!'

'None of us asked for it,' said Seth. 'It just did.'

The radio continued with its broadcast. And it wasn't just the locusts it was bothered about either. Reports were coming in from all over the world:

'. . . unable to hold out much longer, with the streets in flames, people looting, the police will be hard pushed to control . . .'

'. . . talks broke down and now both countries are massing their forces at the borders. Indeed, reports are coming in that shots have already been fired . . .'

'. . . disputed lands at the heart of this, but it runs deeper and it seems that now for both sides the only way to solve this is with violence . . .'

Demetrius was crying.

'I don't understand this,' he said, his voice breaking. 'I'm meant to be at home! It's my birthday and Mum and Dad won't know where I am! They'll be worried! I have to go back! I can't do this! I won't!'

Seth rested his hand on Demetrius's shoulder and squeezed it.

'I'm sorry, Dem, but this isn't over,' he said. 'Not yet. Not by a long way.'

'No,' said Kelly, 'not until we find the fourth Rider.'

'And if it's any consolation,' added Lily, 'coming here probably saved your life. For the moment anyway.'

Seth was back to thinking about the fourth Rider, but the image flickering in his mind was confusing.

'I tried,' he said, 'but I could only find Dem. The other two . . .'

'Two?' said Demetrius. 'But I thought you said there were four Riders?'

It was this that jemmied open a window in Lily's mind. She pulled the folder from out of her jacket and flicked through it.

'There!' she said, jabbing her finger on a page. 'Two names! I spotted it earlier, but didn't think anything of it.'

'Twins,' said Kelly.

Seth read the names, saw the note jotted in next to them.

'Can't be them,' he said. 'Look, it says they've got a rare medical condition or something and that they probably

won't survive till they're thirteen.'

'Then why are their names circled?' said Lily. 'It's them, Seth. It has to be. And you said yourself that you sensed two others, not just one. Which means they're alive!'

Seth was astride his horse in seconds. He pulled Lily up behind him with ease.

'We have to find them!' he said. 'And we need to shift. I failed here, and people died, but I'm not going to fail this time.'

'You don't know where they are though,' said Kelly, now on her own horse, the one whose coat shimmered like the surface of the sun.

'Scotland,' replied Seth, remembering the bleak landscape he'd seen in his mind, a place cold and wet and foreboding. 'I couldn't reach them completely or get them to come to me, but that much I know. We will find them.'

28

THE HORSES STEPPED OUT of the air, as if an invisible door had opened from another world, and the Earth shuddered faintly with their presence.

It was dark and it was hammering down, as Seth had heard his dad say often enough. Now that description came into its own. The sound of the rain was as though sledgehammers were being thrown from a cliff to land in a dump truck.

The mountains around them were dark and brooding and seemed to lean in as though they would topple over to crush them like ants at any moment. The rain must have been coming down for hours as the sides of the mountains were scored with dozens of silvery rivulets, the water racing down, cutting fresh gullies into the ground like a

butcher's knife into fresh meat.

'I can see why people come here on holiday,' remarked Kelly. 'Must make such a nice change from all that sun you can get everywhere else at this time of year.'

Demetrius, though, didn't find it so funny.

'I'm freezing,' he said. 'I'm not exactly dressed for this.'

Seth hadn't really noticed what Demetrius was wearing, which made him realize just how wrapped up he was in what was going on. He always noticed things, didn't he? It was his job! Dem's point was a fair one; sandals, shorts and a T-shirt were a sure route to instant hypothermia in weather like this.

'We're close,' he said, shutting his eyes, remembering what he saw in the fog. First the jungle, which had brought him Demetrius, then this place of cold and rock and rain. 'They're here. I've seen it.'

'Where though?' shouted Lily, pushing soaking hair from her eyes as a thick boom of thunder rolled down the huge mountains that lay about them. 'I can't see anything anywhere round here!'

'What about that track?' asked Demetrius, his horse moving him forward towards it.

Just a few metres away, the track crossed directly in front of them and disappeared into a thick, dark forest like a needle into a pincushion.

Seth nodded. 'Has to be,' he said. 'You lead the way, Demetrius.'

The horses were unmoved by the weather and walked forwards to the track then turned right to face the forest.

Around them the forest closed in, shielding them at last if not from the rain, at least from the wind. And just when Seth was beginning to think that perhaps he had got it all wrong, a black shape ahead oozed out of the rain and shadow, an imposing house of dark stone, its windows staring out like mean eyes.

The door to the house fell open and a voice called out to them.

'Welcome, Riders . . .'

Seth recognized not just the voice but the smile.

They all did.

The man at the door surveyed them with the air of a king. But then, thought Seth, a person called The Protector was, if nothing else, the ruler. They'd all seen his grinning face before, knew it almost as well as their own, but in the flesh Seth thought how it was something altogether different. Whereas the picture displayed a smile that was all heart and warmth and concern, the one now before them was of stone; cold and unfeeling. And the photograph gave no indication as to the man's size. Not that it could ever have done, because he was not just tall, but imposing, as though to be the very mediator between mankind and God required a height advantage so as to hear the creator better. But it was The Protector's eyes which Seth was drawn to. They stared out into the night like searchlights, bright and piercing. This was no weak man of God, or church council member. This was a man with power that seeped from his body like water from a flooded well.

'He stares at us like a hawk sizing up its dinner,' Seth whispered.

'Then perhaps that is exactly what we are,' said Lily.

Seth fought the urge to take his bow and drop the man where he stood. He knew that if he did that, the twins might be put at even greater risk, assuming that they were still alive. So he held back. Just . . .

'Will you not dismount?' asked The Protector. 'I prefer to talk face-to-face. I have refreshments prepared.'

'Sounds like you've been expecting us,' said Seth.

'Of course,' The Protector replied. 'But then surely that is to be expected.'

Seth asked, 'Where are they?'

'Of whom do you ask?' The Protector called back.

Seth didn't like The Protector's tone. He'd heard him speak before, on television, on the radio, his voice all kindly and warm. That was not the case now. It had a superior air to it that reeked of arrogance. And an edge laced with a glacial coldness that could freeze air in a moment.

'Just tell me,' Seth replied, as the horses edged them closer to the house.

'I would ask that you speak with me first, Seth,' said The Protector. 'All of you.'

'You know my name,' said Seth, more as a simple observation than anything else. But hearing The Protector use it was deeply unnerving.

'I know all of your names,' said The Protector.

Seth was about to ask for the twins again, when Lily cried out, her voice making Seth's ears ring.

From the brooding darkness of the house behind The Protector walked a huge dog. After circling him once, it then sat down by his feet, its head cocked to one side, its tail wagging.

'I see that you recognize my dog,' said The Protector, reaching a hand down to stroke the animal. 'Talon was always a faithful pet. And I have missed him dearly.'

Seth heard a whimper from Lily then felt her head rest against the back of his neck, the dampness of her tears against his skin.

The sense of betrayal was thick in the air. That they'd thought the dog was dead was enough, killed with Saul before Seth had taken his revenge on the helicopter. But to find it here, with The Protector? It was the deepest of cuts. Seth found himself hating the dog as much as the man it was now standing with. And where was Saul? Because if it was here then—

'We can't trust him,' said Lily, interrupting Seth's thoughts, her voice still breaking on her tears. 'You know that.'

'This has nothing to do with trust,' said Seth. 'He knows

where the twins are. I've tried searching for them, but can't get through. If we do something stupid now, they're dead. That's what this is about.'

The Protector remained quiet, patiently waiting, and as still as a tree.

'Who is he?' asked Demetrius. 'And I'm still freezing, by the way. Can't feel my hands or my feet and I think my nose is about to fall off.'

The others stared at him, but none of them answered.

'We have no choice,' said Seth.

He didn't wait for an argument and pushed forwards toward the house.

At the steps leading up to the door, Seth realized that The Protector was clearly waiting for them to dismount. The door itself was huge. Not just wide, but high too. He'd have to duck, but . . .

'What are you doing?' asked The Protector, his calm broken by confusion as Seth guided his horse up the steps.

Seth thought how it would have been worth doing this on a normal horse, just to see the look of bemusement on The Protector's face. But on a horse like the one he had now, that cracked each and every step it rested a hoof on, and left behind a scorch mark that sizzled as rain struck it, well, that was something else. The Protector and his dog backed off from the horses as one by one they strode through the door and into the house, the place shuddering with the sound of hooves.

The hallway inside was clearly large but, with the three horses standing in it, the space had become cramped and dark and small. Oak panels lined the walls and a staircase swept dramatically left and right to an upstairs landing hidden in shadow.

'Follow me,' said The Protector, trying to regain his composure and carefully edging past the horses as his dog, bored now, slipped off into another part of the house. 'Through here, if you will.'

Another large, tall door led through to a room clearly designed for grand functions attended by the rich. The high vaulted ceiling was beautifully ornate and oil paintings hung on the wall, each no doubt worth a small fortune, thought Seth. At the end of the room was a large screen.

'I asked you where they were,' said Seth. 'So whatever you've brought us in here for—'

'It will not take long, I assure you,' replied The Protector.

Seth didn't like the way he said that at all and his senses heightened. Seth scanned the room for any hint of something awry. But it was just a room.

The screen sparked into life.

'The news?' said Seth, staring like the others at the screen. 'Look, we didn't come all this way for a—'

The Protector cut him off with one word. 'Saul!'

The door to the room clicked shut as footsteps echoed and Seth's earlier silent question was answered.

Seth's eyes narrowed to slits. And when Saul looked up at them, not a flicker of emotion or recognition betrayed itself on his face, his eyes hard.

'Saul has told me everything,' said The Protector as behind him channel after channel was added to the screen until they were staring at an animated chessboard, with each square another window to destruction and despair.

'Really, he had no choice, did he?' continued The Protector, like a smug detective who'd come to tell of how he had decided to arrest those before him. 'When he came to dispose of you and the rest of those Activists hiding away like stinking, diseased rats in that church, he didn't stand a chance. He could do nothing against your power.'

Seth went to say something but a stare from Lily shut his mouth tight.

'We did not expect you to become what you now are so quickly, but then, trying to halt a prophecy is not an exact science.'

'What else did he tell you?' asked Seth, his eyes now boring into the emotionless face of Saul, searching for anything that would give him away.

Nothing did.

'That you killed them,' The Protector continued. 'And that you used your power to manipulate him so that he would in turn help you. If anything, I'm amazed that you let him live. Though perhaps that was an error, yes, when you destroyed the car he was driving and the helicopter that had been sent to track him down?'

'Me too,' said Seth, bemused by what he was hearing because it wasn't making much sense, not compared to what he could remember happening. 'I must've been having an off-day.'

'I liked the touch of using the woman's pistol. Now, that really was particularly clever. It would make it look as though she had carried out the executions, not you.'

No, thought Seth, *Saul did it so you would never suspect him* . . . The Protector nodded at the screen.

'This is the world before you,' he said. 'It has always been a place of unrest, a place of pain, but look at it now, Rider. Look at it!'

And Seth did just that. Each channel was spilling hopelessness into the room. Natural disasters were fighting for attention against famine, social unrest against war. Not one screen seemed to show a species that could be saved. If he needed to see his destiny then it was all there in front of him. All he had to do was finish it.

'Is this what you want?' The Protector burst out, spit flying from his mouth like hot fat from a joint roasting over a fire. 'The Way has hunted you and your kind for centuries because of exactly what you see before you now. This is your doing! The cost of your life being allowed to continue is everything going to the dogs. The world chewed up and forgotten. Is that what you want? Is it?'

Seth wasn't listening. He was staring at the screen

and beyond it, into the stories and individual lives in front of the camera, into the suffering and pain that seemed to be mushrooming across the world. And the dark figure was back again, only this time, for the first time, he was talking.

Like a wounded animal, remember, Seth? That's all you need to do, and it's the kind thing to do, isn't it? Just let the power control you and everything will be over and the world can start again because it needs to, Seth, and you can see that, can't you?

The voice was soft, measured. It was the kind of voice a therapist would be proud of, or a hypnotist. And it was telling Seth what he had to do, leading him, making it all seem just fine.

That's all there is to it, Seth. Nothing to stop you now. Nothing at all. Wonderful, isn't it?

'No!' yelled Seth, and before he could stop himself had called the bow to his hand and aimed an arrow at The Protector's chest. The screen behind him gave way to a view of the earth, a wondrous picture of the blue planet, images streamed from a distant satellite.

The black figure was still talking, its voice honey-sweet and sticky, temptation in every word.

Come on, Seth! Don't you see how the world needs you? You're a surgeon, Seth, that's all. Just cutting out the pus that's destroyed the world. Once the wound's clean, things will be different. Just go with it, Seth. Give in to it!

The Protector was staring at the images as well.

'Beautiful, is it not?' he said, motioning to the screen. 'Yet you will destroy this, Rider. You all will . . . The seas will become as blood and boil away!'

It's what you're here for, Seth, what the world needs. Don't listen to him, listen to the Earth, to what it needs! Clean it, Seth, help it start afresh!

'The sun will die,' continued The Protector, 'and it will blacken to a lifeless rock and the moon turn red. All humanity will be wiped from existence, all life everywhere will be no more. And all because of you abominations here in this room!'

Seth wasn't listening to The Protector any more. Couldn't. All he could hear was the voice telling him to just let go, to give in to it and crush the world in the palm of his hand. And the more he heard it, the more he wanted to do what it said because it seemed to make so much sense, so much sense . . .

Just do it, Seth! Do it, and the others will follow! You'll be making history! Changing the world completely! The universe will thank you for it! Do it, Seth! Just do it!

Seth squeezed his eyes shut. Forced stars into them. Battled against the voice so that he could hear himself.

'You're wrong,' he muttered. 'It doesn't have to end unless we say so. Unless I say so.'

'Rubbish!' shouted The Protector. 'All that spews from your mouth is rubbish!'

See? They deserve it! Don't waste any more time, Seth! Release that power and sweep this planet clean once and for all!

'We're not here to destroy unless we judge it necessary,' said Seth, his mind aching with the agony of ignoring the voice inside. 'And that's what you fear, isn't it?'

Seth caught a flicker in The Protector's eyes and in that moment he was the Apocalypse Boy again, the stinging smell of stage make-up in his eyes, the worn cape on his back and his audience, his *congregation*, in the palm of his hand.

Do it, Seth! Bring this world to an end! It wants you to!

'You cannot judge!' The Protector snapped. 'It is not your role in this! I know. I have studied the text! And you must be stopped!'

A sound of sharply whispered words cut the air. Seth saw Kelly and Demetrius jolt as though struck. There, standing in the doorway, were four men. Though he had never seen them before in his life, a deeper darker part of him, like some scar on his soul, screamed out at their presence and his whole being wanted to shrink from them and run.

Their faces were hidden by rough leather masks and from their shoulders hung dirty brown cloaks brushing the floor like curtains round a crypt. They were each wearing breastplates and carrying swords at their sides. For the moment, though, they were all armed with crossbows. And there was nothing medieval about these weapons; they were sleek black things of metal and the strings were powered by a system of short thin limbs and wheels.

Demetrius was the first to topple from his horse. Seth caught Kelly's confused, hurt eyes before she followed soon after. Then the pain struck home and glancing down he saw a third crossbow bolt rammed deep into his side. Seth knew then that the figures at the door were The Calling. And that they had come for him.

'You must all die,' said The Protector. 'For the good of us all. You understand, yes?'

The four figures raised their crossbows once more when a shout rang out.

It was Saul – and his pistol was pinching The Protector's pale temple.

'I wouldn't do that if I were you,' he called out. 'Drop them!'

The figures remained unmoved.

'I mean it,' Saul said, and eased back the hammer. 'Drop them! Now!'

With electric speed, one of The Calling snatched their aim from Seth to Saul. The bolt sped out and thwacked into Saul's shoulder with enough force to send him spinning to the floor. His pistol fired and the bullet, though missing The Protector's head, tore instead through his left ear. The Protector screamed and collapsed to the floor, desperately trying to stem the flow of blood as it pooled around his head.

The only thing Seth was aware of was his own heartbeat. It throbbed in his head, thundering through him with a power he wanted to unleash. He glanced back at Lily, saw fear in her eyes, caught movement from The Calling as they switched their aim not back to him, but to her.

No! Not Lily . . .

Seth whipped his horse round, heard the muscles in the fingers of The Calling contract against the triggers. He spurred the horse on, heard the cables snick forward with such force that the four bolts were loosed at a rate of three hundred and fifty feet per second. And when they hit home, their target spun from the horse and across the floor.

The room was quiet of all but the sound of the breathing of horses. Until Lily's scream burst through it, ripping out of her chest to scream round the great room like a banshee.

'Get up!' Lily yelled, staring at the three fallen Riders on the floor, her brain crashing in on itself, pulling itself apart at the vision of everything ending in death at her feet. 'It can't end like this! You know it! You have to! Not after all this! NOT AFTER ALL THIS!'

On the floor, Kelly, Demetrius and Seth lay bleeding.

29

SETH'S WORLD WAS LITTLE more than a blurry image of the roof high above him. The pain of the crossbow bolts deep in his chest had already been replaced by the warmth of his own blood leaking his life away across the floor beneath him. Was this how it ended? But that didn't make sense. Wasn't he the first Rider? What the hell had happened?

Seth was acutely aware of the silence that was settling around him, as though he was at a funeral in a cathedral. His own.

Seth had to focus. The fact that The Way would've been able to kill him before he changed into what he'd become was still a raw, bleeding wound in his mind. But now it was different. He was the first Rider. A harbinger of doom.

The Doom Rider.

Seth saw the black figure again. Before, when he'd seen the figure, it had almost been playing with him, dancing in front of him and pointing out exactly what he should do with his power. Now it was cowering, hiding in the corner of his vision, afraid.

Seth heard movement. His eyes flickered and he saw The Calling walking towards him, Kelly and Demetrius. As they drew close, the one leading the others reached up to his breastplate to unclip two clasps pinned over his heart. Two stones fell out into his palm.

More movement. It was The Protector, now standing, blood staining his clothes as it gushed through the fingers of his hand hooked over his ruined ear. He walked over to Lily, whom Seth could see was still sitting on his horse.

'It is finished,' The Protector said, glancing at the downed riders, then up to Lily. 'Well, almost, dear little Lily.'

The figure with the stones held them aloft in his fist and muttered words only he could truly hear. He lowered his hand and opened it, stared at the stones, then nodded to the three others. As one, they swept back their cloaks, drew forth their swords and raised them high, their eyes now on The Protector, waiting for his sign to let the terrible blades fall.

Seth's vision burst apart like a smashed television screen, little jagged bits and pieces of pictures and visions and memories scattering in front of his eyes. It was the swords that had done it, cut him open like a surgeon's scalpel, and for the second time since all this had begun he saw not just who he was, but who he'd been so many times before. Hundreds, thousands of lifetimes cut down. Destroyed.

Seth searched the minds of those around him, delved deep to find something he could use. Lily was the easiest, her rage burning white-hot. Her voice, screaming inside her head, was clear in Seth's head, as if she was speaking to him.

Lily spoke. 'You have to stop this,' she said, wiping her eyes and trying to stop her voice breaking in pain, not really sure if she was speaking to The Calling or The Protector. 'There's no point to it. Not any more. There just can't be!'

'Oh, but there's every point, Lily,' said The Protector. 'By their deaths, and yours, humanity is saved!'

Lily sobbed. Seth turned his attention to Kelly and Demetrius, slipping into their minds, their very souls.

'There are others out there, Lily,' continued The Protector. 'Others like you. And when they have served their purpose, they too will be dealt with. It is how it has always been and how it must always be. If we are to survive at all.'

'The world will find out eventually,' said Lily. 'You can't murder children and keep it a secret.'

'When it does, it will understand the necessity,' argued The Protector. 'That through death humanity was saved.'

Seth flicked a switch in the minds of Kelly and Demetrius. *With me!* he whispered. *With me . . . Now . . .*

Then Seth found someone else in the room. Someone he could use to change the odds. Someone with a loaded pistol in his hand, its barrel still warm.

'You're not God!' Lily screamed, her voice tearing from her like a spray of shattered glass. 'No one is!'

'We do what is necessary to guide all to salvation,' replied The Protector, now sounding ever more composed. 'And to protect. You must understand that more than most, Lily.'

Lily didn't. Not in the slightest. And as she was trying to, something on the screen caught her attention. At first she couldn't work out what it was, but then she realized something; it was the view from the satellite. And the satellite was pointing away from the Earth.

'What's it looking for?' she asked, nodding at the screen, wiping her eyes dry. 'That satellite isn't looking at Earth. Why's it looking out into space?'

'As you well know,' said The Protector, 'we take all prophecies seriously, no matter how far-fetched.'

'What's that got to do with this?'

'We scan the skies, Lily,' The Protector explained. 'We watch the heavens, observe the constellations; was our Lord's arrival not itself witnessed by a star? Think what it would mean were something like that to happen again! Can you imagine?'

The cold echo of a gunshot bounced round the room uninvited. Lily jumped, half expecting to see a hole in her own body. Instead, she saw one in the chest of The Protector. At the same time she caught sight of Saul, still collapsed on the floor, his weapon raised, though barely.

Shock and pain lit The Protector's eyes as a stain of blood started to ooze across his belly.

'But . . .' was all he managed before collapsing to the floor, his last breath seeping out to cloud briefly in the cool air before disappearing completely.

The Protector was dead.

The Calling went into automatic pilot. They tensed to bring their weapons down on Seth, Kelly and Demetrius. Then another sound rode in on the back of Saul's killing gunshot. A note of such purity it was as though the very bells of heaven were ringing.

Lily saw Kelly climbing to her feet, her lips pursed in a whistle. Next to her, rising too like the undead, were Seth and Demetrius.

A clatter drew Lily's eyes and she saw The Calling's terrifying swords, glowing red, smoking and burning.

'I thought you were dead!' cried Lily, staring at Seth, her voice catching in her throat. 'I saw you fall. All of you!'

The Calling began to retreat, swinging from their backs the deadly crossbows.

Seth glanced up to Lily as he removed the crossbow bolts from his body one by one, dropping them to the floor that was wet with his own blood. Then he wiped his hands clean as Kelly and Demetrius did the same. The Protector's still body was at his feet, a look of bewilderment etched into his dead face. Seth knew he should feel some sorrow here, feel *something*, but he didn't.

'What happens when a people loses its king?' he asked.

'They find another,' said Lily.

'That's what worries me.'

The Calling had their crossbows raised, but something was stopping them loosing another murderous volley. Seth guessed it was because The Protector was gone. Without him, they were like headless chickens.

Something caught Seth's senses. It was weak, but it was there all right. A faint fog of decay seeping into the moment.

The Calling backed off and spread outwards.

'There's a secret here,' said Seth. 'Something no one knows about . . . I don't know what it is . . .'

'Do you mean the twins?' asked Lily. 'Is that it?'

Seth shook his head, glanced at The Calling, then at the screen. 'It's there,' he said, nodding at it. 'But I don't know what, Lily . . .'

A clattering, buzzing sound filled the air and the windows to the room darkened further as a billion insects covered them, their wings humming, beating against the glass with the sound of hail.

Seth glared at The Calling. 'You can't kill me,' he said. 'Not now. Not like a snared rabbit. You realize that, don't you?'

The Calling said nothing and made no movement.

'Don't . . .' said Lily, but only to herself as no one was listening to her now.

Seth recognized the latest incarnations of the sect that had murdered him a million times over. Though they were hidden behind their masks, he could still see behind them and stare into their souls. All men were weak. And like those in the café these too would do what he told them to, of that he had no doubt.

The crossbows clattered to the floor and, without any warning, The Calling fell into each other in rage: thousands of years of dedication to the cause lost in a moment to a brawl. Fists and feet flying, they thumped and kicked and headbutted each other, none of them giving ground. Soon they were battered and bruised, their faces a mess of swollen eyes, broken noses and smashed teeth, their fists cut and bleeding. Two had broken arms, one was on the floor with a broken leg, the last was flailing about desperately, blinded from a volley of blows to his face by the others.

Then Kelly was singing again and her sword was drawn. The Calling could do nothing to escape as the girl raised her weapon and took aim. When the sonic wave hit, The

Calling didn't even have time to yell out. For a moment, they were frozen in their last moments, a tableau of their very moment of death, then they were nothing but dust falling into dust on the floor.

30

D OWN HERE!'

Lily and the others snatched their heads round to see Saul against a far wall, nodding at a door. He didn't look well and was holding his shoulder, the crossbow bolt still jutting out from it like a tiny flagpole.

'The twins!' Saul shouted. 'This way! Quick!'

Seth was first to move, then Lily slipped from Kelly's horse to the floor to catch him up. She glanced up again at the big screen, which flickered slightly, as though the signal had been interrupted. Something about what it was showing them still bothered her.

Seth glared at Saul.

'Seems you're pretty good at disappearing,' he said. 'And betrayal. We thought you were dead.'

'So did I,' said Saul, his breath rattling in his throat. 'The helicopter had come for me as well as you. The Protector knew I'd betrayed The Way.'

Lily came over. Saying nothing, she backhanded Saul hard across his face, drawing blood from his lip.

'I was at a safe distance when they sent rockets into where we'd crashed,' he explained, not even bothering to wipe his mouth. 'I was about to make a run for it when you took out the helicopter. That saved me, Seth. I had enough time then to come up with a cover story and to give you a bit more time.'

Lily sneered. 'They found us,' she said. 'The Chosen came, but Seth wasn't there. They took me though, Saul. 'And they weren't exactly gentle.'

'I know,' Saul replied. 'I could do nothing about it. I found out too late. I'm sorry.'

Seth asked, 'So why are you here now, Saul? Haven't you seen enough?'

'The twins,' Saul said, pointing with his pistol at a small door sunk into the wall. 'Prophet, it seems, was more effective than any of us ever realized. It found them weeks ago and the Protector took them.'

'How did it find them?' asked Seth, anger boiling in his gut. 'I was the first Rider, Saul! If I hadn't turned thirteen and become *this*, then they would have never known any different! And why let them live?'

Kelly approached the door and sang. It gave way

immediately, shattering in slow motion, then fading to nothing. From behind it came the stench of death. Seth shuddered, not just the smell, but something else. At first he didn't know what was wrong but then he realized that what was down there made him afraid. And that was an emotion he hadn't expected at all.

'You've read *The Book*, Seth!' hissed Saul, coughing blood now. 'It's the fourth Rider the world is most in fear of! Somehow Prophet knew that and found them first.'

Seth tried to focus on what Saul was saying, but with the door now gone, and the darkness beyond it seeping out towards them, it was difficult to focus. It was all he could do to not back away. The presence down there wasn't simply of power, but of evil.

'That doesn't explain why they're still alive.'

'Bait,' said Saul. 'If The Chosen and The Calling failed, The Protector knew that holding on to the final Rider would draw the other three. That way, he would have you all in one place. And he was right, wasn't he?'

'A trap?' said Lily.

Saul just stared back in answer.

Seth turned from Saul and, narrowing his eyes, forced himself to stare down into the gloom beyond the door. At the bottom of a small flight of stone steps he could see two boys, lying unconscious on a mattress. The sight of them made his skin crawl. They were pale to the point of turning a faint blue. Racked by fever, their bodies were sweating horribly and shaking. The cellar was a grubby, wet, dirty place and had a fetid air to it. But it was the shadows that were even worse. It was as if the darkness was little more than a curtain behind which a million souls were waiting for the boys to awaken. Souls whose own hearts were shrivelled and calloused and sick.

Seth didn't want to head down into that room. He was powerful, and he'd known that from the moment his horse had arrived, but these boys were different. There was a weight to their presence. The weight of death. Hell even.

'Remember they've got SCID,' said Lily, her voice quiet yet still managing to be heard. 'Severe combined immunodeficiency. They were born without an immune system. And they won't stand a chance left here in a stinking, damp, germ-filled cellar! We need to get them out!'

Seth wasn't so sure. On the outside, yes, they certainly looked fragile, but it wasn't their bodies that had him on edge. It was what lay beneath it. With teeth gritted, and with every sinew in his body pulling him the other way, he edged down towards the twins. The others followed.

Lily moved towards the mattress, but as she did the boys, as one, sat up. They turned their eyes to meet hers and she gasped. Four black holes stared back. Kelly, Demetrius, Seth and Saul stayed where they were. The darkness, Seth was sure, stretched out towards them, as though whatever was behind it was trying to break through.

'Where are we? And who are you?'

They spoke in unison and their voices were like the final hymn at a funeral wake.

Seth said nothing as the boys slid to the end of the mattress and stood up. They looked even thinner now standing before him. There was no fear in their faces.

'It's our birthday,' the boys said, and such a simple, innocent statement sounded horrifying coming from their pale, thin mouths, because in it was the powerful momentum of what would follow them, burning with the heat of a thousand suns.

The boys stepped forwards and Lily stumbled back into Seth. Kelly and Demetrius remained still as statues.

'Talk to them!' she hissed, her eyes wide. 'You have to get through to them, like you did with Kelly and Dem, remember!'

All Seth wanted to do was stay out of their way. But *he* was the first Rider, the one the others would follow, and he should not have been afraid.

But he was.

The boys were fragile, like skeletons held together by the last remnants of a corpse's skin, yet with their every movement the world seemed almost to shrink away from them in fear, like a crowd watching as the hangman walks by.

'I . . . can't . . .'

The boys took another step forward as from behind

them, like a great dam collapsing, the darkness burst outwards. Seth shielded his eyes but it had no effect in protecting him.

The darkness swept over everyone in the room, blocking out all light as it drenched them in the absolute physical presence of agony, sorrow and loss, and an endless, harrowing loneliness. Drowning in it, fighting to keep their heads above the glimmering surface of the stuff that swilled around like an oil slick, they coughed and gagged as it splashed down their throats, blocked their ears, and blinded their eyes.

As quickly as it had arrived, the black swill was gone, and Seth and the others were on the ground struggling to breathe. Not only because of what had just happened, but because of a cloying humidity now in the air, an intense, burning closeness like the heat of a sauna.

It took everything he had, but eventually Seth dared to look. Lily was close by and coughing. The others he sensed but couldn't see. Blinking away the sweat that was beading on his forehead to drip into his eyes, wiping his forehead with the back of his hand, he was drawn to the sight of the twins standing in the centre of the room. He remembered the place being small and claustrophobic, the walls of roughly hewn stone standing silent around the ugly mattress the boys had been lying on. But the mattress was gone and in its place now lay a great hole, like the mouth of a broken well. Yet that wasn't the worst of it, not by a long way.

Where the walls had been was a vision of such awful desolation Seth wondered if the world was already finished, his work done without him even realizing it. They were no longer in a room beneath a house, but sat on an endless plain of earth scorched red, riven apart by great rifts and tears from which bled liquid rock, blood-red and steaming. Far off, mountains jutted upwards, their peaks hidden behind a thick blanket of bubbling, black smoke. Lightning danced in it, sometimes striking the ground below, blasting craters in the ground large enough to swallow London whole.

But even all this was not what made Seth want to tear his fingernails deep into his own flesh and to scream and scream and scream till all that he was had faded completely away.

No. It was the hole that did that.

Its edges were cracked, like lips worn by a harsh winter's wind, yet these cracks were wet and seeping. And the darkness it contained wasn't just an absence of light, but a presence, a thick syrupy thing that spat forth . . .

First came the hands. Millions of them clawing at each other, pulling and ripping to get out of the hole, some tumbling back only to be replaced by others just as desperate. And after the hands came the arms. Thin, grey things of leathery skin, stretched and flaking in the heat. And those hands and arms that managed to hold on pulled with them the for ever damned.

Then that voice came again, only this time it was cracked and broken and in pain, the sound of it like rusted knives down a chalkboard . . .

'When the Lamb opened the fourth seal, I heard the voice of the fourth living creature say, "Come and see!" I looked and there before me was a pale horse. Its rider was named Death, and Hades was following close behind him.'

31

THE TWINS SLIPPED PAST, towards the steps. The dead followed even though the pain of their every movement made them scream and yell and tear at their own frail bodies with hands that were more like claws.

A cold blast of air swept down from the hall above and the familiar sound of horse's hooves was wrapped up in it. Seth forced himself to his feet and grabbed Lily. Half pushing, half pulling, he forced her up the steps with him. Kelly and Demetrius followed, though their eyes were on the evil approaching.

In the large room above, the three waiting horses had become four. Seth's own, its white coat glistening, was at the front. When it saw him, it whinnied and scratched at the floor, scorching it with a thin line of fire, excitement in its eyes. By its side the horses of Kelly and Demetrius stood patiently, waiting for their own riders. But it was the fourth horse which drew Seth's stare.

It was thinner than the others, starved almost, its ribcage – indeed its whole skeleton – visible beneath its hideous coat, which was the colour of rotting flesh, putrid, pale and diseased. When Seth looked closer, he saw that in places the bones actually poked through the horse's flesh, which fluttered like curtains in a breeze with each breath the creature took.

For the briefest of moments time stalled, and Seth was aware of everything around him. Not just the people, the horses, the house, but the world beyond the building's walls. And it seemed to him as though every eye in every creature in every part of the world was staring at him in unimaginable horror. He climbed on to his immense horse and watched as silently, almost in slow motion, Kelly and Demetrius made their way to the centre of the hall. The horses met them halfway, bowing down to allow Kelly and Demetrius to swing themselves over on to the huge backs of the enormous animals. Kelly's horse rose first and Seth saw in her hand the sword. The awful thing was vibrating and the air around it shimmered. Demetrius followed. Outside, his own hideous weapon reached a crescendo, as the rattling of the insects against the windows reached a point of no return. The glass shattered inwards and the swarm flooded in, tumbling into the hall like an avalanche.

Lily screamed out but her voice was lost as the insects swirled and tumbled and finally came to rest, as a cloud draped over Demetrius, only pulsing and moving, and above the riders, as a hovering storm maelstrom just waiting . . . waiting . . .

Then, finally, came the twins. Like ghosts they glided over to their beast, the abomination from the room below crawling and stumbling after them. Their horse lowered itself to welcome them and they climbed on to its back, dead things on a dead horse that was pale as the moon when winter's cold hand has dragged all warmth from the world.

A light bright enough to take on the sun at its own game blasted through the room. Everyone shielded their eyes to try to hide from it, but there was no hiding. Then a voice entered that space unbidden save for the gathering of the four Riders. A voice that was of this world and none, of all space and time and existence. A voice that spoke not from without, but from within, from the very centre of everything that could have ever existed.

'For the great day of his wrath is come;
and who shall be able to stand?'

The figure in black was back, only this time Seth saw it running from him, racing away, but unable to escape. This was it; the four Riders together, bringing doom with them. It was the end of the world. And it was Seth who would start it. And it was he who would end it. Scorch the Earth to a blackened husk and at last give it a chance to rest, to heal.

Go on, Seth! Do it! This is why you are here, why you were born, why you are! Give in to it and do what is right, the only thing you can. Do it! DO IT!

The voice was no longer calm, but excited to the point of insane.

A hand grabbed Seth's shoulder and spun him round, snapping him out of the trance he was in, blocking out the voice. He opened his eyes. The bright light was gone and in front of him was Saul. Though pale, his bloodshot eyes were alive, and behind them Seth saw insanity taking its first dance. Something told him his own were not too dissimilar.

'Don't . . . touch . . . me . . .' Seth said. The fight inside him to maintain some control was being lost. He couldn't hold on for much longer. Wasn't sure that he wanted to. That voice was so tempting. And the power in his veins a drug.

'You can't stop it, you know that,' said Saul, a grin wrapped across his face, wild and hysterical. He was breathing hard, blood bubbling on his lips. He then dropped a hard finger into Seth's chest, right over his heart. 'It's in here, Seth. What you are. You have to listen to it. You have to! The world heard that voice, Seth. It knows you're coming. It's ready!'

Seth knocked Saul's hand away, his mind still trying to work out what it was that was racing towards them, and to ignore that which was crawling across the floor from the room that had contained the twins, filling the room with the reek of death and decay.

'What are you talking about?'

'You, Seth. All of you. What you are. And why it is that you're here.'

Listen to him, Seth! He's talking sense, you know he is. You can't fight this because you're not supposed to. Give in to it!

Seth shook his head, tried to dislodge the voice. But it did no good. It just went on repeating itself, over and over: *Give in to it! Give in to it! Give in to it! Give in to it!*

An explosion cracked the sky, lighting it up like oil burning on the sea. Those windows that hadn't collapsed under the weight of the locusts now swarming around Demetrius and above the others burst inwards, filling the air with tiny glass shards like an ice storm of razors.

As the air settled, a rumbling sound of aircraft and tracked vehicles rolled towards the house.

Seth knew that The Protector's trap had been sprung.

Saul spoke once again.

'It's time to clean up,' he said, stumbling back from Seth to get a better look at him. 'Do what you were sent to do. It's the way it's meant to be, Seth. Don't fight it.'

Seth tried to move his attention to whatever Saul was

saying, but it was like trying to listen to someone speaking underwater. He could see Saul's mouth move, hear sounds even, but it was all jumbled, messed up.

Other voices entered Seth's mind now, walking in as easily as if he'd left a door open to his soul.

We're ready now. We know why we are here. Lead us!

The eyes of Kelly, Demetrius and the twins burned into Seth. Their voices were clear and bright in his mind. Yes, they needed him, didn't they? He was the first Rider, the one to take them forth. Of course! And it would all be so good, so right!

Then Saul's words came back at Seth and his head spun like he was on a rollercoaster.

'I . . . don't understand, Saul,' Seth said. 'I have work to do. I . . . *we* must go now.'

'Exactly!' cheered Saul, his eyes lighting up with the fervour of a religious fanatic. 'The world deserves it, Seth! This is what I worked all my life to achieve. And the cause Colin died for! Hallelujah!'

Saul's words ripped a hole in Seth's mind. He was confused now. What was Saul saying? The man himself was staring up at him, his face wild, as though caught in rapture. A few steps away, Seth could see Demetrius, Kelly and the twins staring at him, waiting for his orders. And beneath them all the floor was moving. But it wasn't the floor, it was grey starved bodies sliding and crawling over each other to get to the twins. Some had already made it, and their horse, Death's own steed, was now knee deep in animated corpses.

'But you saved Lily from The Way,' Seth said, trying to focus on Saul just a little longer, to hold on to some faint notion of normality. Inside him, the voice was calling out to him again. *Do it, Seth! This is your moment! Become what you are! Become Conquest! Lead the others! Wipe the Earth clean!*

Seth shook his head, stared down at Saul. 'But you wanted to stop the killing, Saul, didn't you? You wanted to bring The Way to its knees and save a few lives in the process.'

Saul held up his hands and shook his head as the other Riders, unbidden by Seth, gathered with him to stand around Saul. Saul tried to back away but was soon at the centre of an ever-decreasing circle, a noose tightening round his neck. Locusts were gathering about him, landing on him, crawling through his hair, pushing into his mouth. The fingers of the dead were reaching for him, pulling at his legs, dragging him down towards them hungrily.

'The Way is only part of the problem,' said Saul, his eyes snatching desperately from one Rider to the next, his feet kicking out uselessly at the things grabbing for him, his hands trying to slap away the locusts in panic. 'It's the world, all of humanity, that needs bringing down. Can't you see? Surely you all understand that now?'

'You're lying!'

The words cut through like a welding torch and Seth spotted Lily, her face ravaged with the stress and strain of the past few days.

'You have to be, Saul! You have to be lying, because if you're not, then . . .'

Saul laughed as he registered the horror on Lily's face. It was a bitter sound. 'What, I'm an Activist? Is that the word you're so afraid to say?'

Lily said nothing in reply. Couldn't. Seth could see that much for sure.

'The Earth has suffered enough,' said Saul, a zeal in his eyes now that Seth had never seen in the man before. 'And it is humanity's doing. Punishment isn't enough. It must be brought to its knees. That's why you're here, all of you! And you'd only be doing what has been put off for too long!'

'We still have a choice in this,' said Seth, sitting back. But did he really believe that? Wasn't the voice inside him the one to listen to now? The one that made the most sense? All he had to do was say the word, and he could lead the Riders out together, set the world aflame, wipe the slate completely clean!

Just do it, Seth! Be the Rider! Do it!

'I am the Doom Rider . . .'

That's exactly who you are, Seth! Don't fight it. You're not giving in, you're accepting what you are. And what you are is the Earth's only true salvation!

'The Doom Rider . . .'

Lead them, Seth! Lead them!

'But it's my choice . . . I decide what I do . . . what I always believed . . .'

Saul laughed, knocking Seth from the battle he was having inside. 'No, you don't! You have no choice at all! Deal with it!'

'We always have a choice . . .'

Seth crunched his eyes shut, opened them fast to stare at Lily. She was shaking her head slowly, begging him, he knew, to not do what he could so easily do.

'You were sent by whatever power there is in the universe!' yelled Saul, clearly trying to keep Seth's attention. 'The power that created it in the first place! It's why you're here, Seth! You have to see that! You have to!'

'We . . . I . . . have a choice . . .' Seth repeated, like it was a mantra, something to help him keep a grip on reality, on his own sanity.

'You're the help, Seth, that's all! So don't go getting ideas above your station. You can't change what you are. None of you can!'

'. . . a choice . . .'

Seth's words died on his lips as he noticed other sounds. Not just aircraft, but weapons systems going online, missiles readying for launch, cannon being loaded. Whether he heard them he wasn't sure, but he sensed them, as if he was hardwired now into every single event occurring at that moment and for ever.

The voice came again.

This is it, Seth! What humanity has come to! Its very pinnacle of brilliance shining most brightly when destroying and killing! And it will go on doing it unless you stop it, Seth! You! Do it! Lead the Riders, Seth! Lead them!

No more, thought Seth. *No more . . .*

He leaned down then, and eyeballed Saul.

'You want an apocalypse?'

Saul stared back, unflinching, his faith as a rock.

'Then you can have one . . .'

32

IT WAS LILY WHO heard them first, filling the air with a great whooshing roar. She couldn't see them, but Seth and the others could; a sky filled with dozens of missiles, hundreds even, that would land in a moment, obliterating not just the house, but the land around it. And this would be but the first wave of many.

Lily saw Seth glance over at her, his head cocked to one side like a dog trying to work out what it was going to do next. She saw immediately that his eyes were gone again to that blackness, snatched away by the shadows and the night, and that was sign enough for her things had gone from bad to worse to end of the world. Hopelessness threatened to swamp her and she tried to hold Seth's stare, to get through to him somehow, but then, almost as though he'd lost interest, Seth turned away and stared at Saul.

Lily could do nothing as Seth looked down with little pity on the man whom she had always believed had saved her from herself. Saul's face was pulled from emotion to emotion as fear and terror and wonder and excitement all jostled for position. Then Seth raised his eyes to the twins, Saul shrieked, kicked out, beat down with his fists, twisted to get away, but the dead hands that had been pulling at his legs sank into them like metal claws, ripping cloth and tearing flesh. Saul fought for his life, but it was pointless and the last thing Lily saw of her old friend and betrayer was an outstretched hand. Then he was gone.

Lily collapsed back against a wall. The cold of it shocked her, like nails piercing her back, but it did nothing to wake her from the nightmare she was living. She knew truly that nothing ever would.

Another explosion smashed the night apart and bits of it flew to the horizon, scattered among the flames and the smoke and the stars.

But Lily hadn't given up yet. She didn't care how hopeless it was, she wasn't going to stop fighting until her last breath. She had to get through to Seth, knew it was down to her now to at least try. And what choice did she really have anyway?

'You have to stop this, Seth!' she yelled, her voice breaking on the words as the echo of the blast rolled through the mountains. 'Free will, remember? That's what you're so big on, isn't it? Well, this isn't free choice, is it? You've given in, Seth! Given in! You're weak!'

Seth ignored her as Kelly moved her horse to stand in front of the wall that faced the way they'd approached the house. Through the splintered remains of the windows they could all see a shadow approaching along the track they'd followed. It was formed of men and vehicles and weapons all with one purpose; to stop the Riders.

Seth reached into Kelly and called her forward without a word spoken. Calmly, as though nothing about what was happening around her was anything other than normal, she whistled the purest of notes, which itself seemed to sing from the very stonework of the building. Then she swept her sword from left to right, cutting the air in front of her with its blade. The wall ruptured as the keen edge passed by, then rubble and glass and wood burst outwards.

The wall gone, Seth led the four Riders through the dust and splinters and rubble, out from the house, and into the night.

Lily chased after them, tripping over and on to her knees, lacerating her hands on shattered glass as she heaved herself back to her feet, yelling out for Seth, desperate for him to listen. But there was no response.

Seth heard a voice, but now it seemed unimportant. A distant memory perhaps? He wasn't sure. It didn't matter.

No, it did! It was Lily! Remember her, the girl who saved your life?

No . . . Not enough, anyway.

Beth! The name appeared like a shooting star in his mind, familiar. And dead. Like his parents. Like the world soon would be. This was what mattered now; the horse and the bow and the crown and the Riders. Inside his mind, Seth tried to see the black figure, but it had gone for good. Now it was just him and the voice and they would dance together on the bones of the world. And it would all begin here.

The air thrummed to the tune of fighter jets and missiles, bombers and attack helicopters and tanks.

Now the Riders went to war.

Demetrius, walking his black horse forwards, raised a hand. Around it a tornado of locusts stretched upwards, towering above them to split the sky, a ferocious storm of insects swirling and massing and heading out to meet the missiles head on. And when they did, the sky split open and fire scarred the night. But the missiles were not enough for the swarm's appetite and it headed then for the men and the machines. Screams of abject horror fought for space in a world bursting at the seams with violence. Men collapsed under the weight of the swarm and could do nothing to stop it gnawing at their eyes to blind them, crawling down their throats to suffocate them.

When the second wave came, Kelly crushed it with such

ease, her whistle, and then her voice, shattering anything that humanity could throw at them, that Seth wondered if a third wave or a fourth would be bothered with at all. When it was, he almost gave into a sense of sorrow at humanity's helplessness. It was admirable, he supposed, but ultimately pathetic. What chance did it stand against them? What chance did anything stand? And would it fight to the bitter end? Seth hoped so. It would be more fun that way, seem more worthwhile if at least a little resistance was encountered.

Fighter jets fell from the sky to explode in fireballs down the dark valley. Helicopters spun out of control and slammed into each other like death-wish dragonflies. Missiles, their engines dead, either exploded in mid-air or crashed down in the forest.

Seth looked on and saw that it was good. Yes, this was how it was meant to be, what his destiny had given him to do! It was obvious now, and the destruction was wonderful to behold, beautiful even! He could almost sense the Earth sighing in relief that it would soon all be over.

Something caught his eye. Seth moved his head just enough to see what it was and his soul shuddered and shrank back. The greatest horror of them all was now amongst them, edging forwards on a pale horse. The twins were joining the battle, and with them the atrocity that hell itself had vomited out. They made Kelly and Demetrius look like the warm-up act to the main event.

Slowly the twins moved away from the others towards the oncoming column of awesome and murderous firepower. As their horse advanced, around its feet the dead jostled for position and the creature looked as though it was walking on a sea of death. On contact with the twins, and with the gnashing, screaming, screeching darkness that followed them and swam around their feet, anything living faded immediately to a dull, listless grey, as the shadow of death flowed from them and stretched outwards.

The forest and all it contained died where it stood. Trees blackened and fell, twisting in on themselves like shrivelled, dried corpses. The grass turned to dust. Birds fell from the sky, a hail of dead feathers to clothe the earth. Deer and rabbit and fox, mouse and stoat and squirrel raced to escape but slumped to the ground their heartbeats stolen. And this was only the beginning. When the twins reached the advancing forces, there was nothing any of the soldiers could have done to stop them. But they tried, with rifle and mortar and grenade. And when the ammunition was spent, the twins moved on, the shadow of death advancing quickly, sweeping hungrily over everything before it, silencing engines, stilling hearts. The war was over before it had even begun.

Lily ran out, barely able to keep herself from stumbling and tripping to the ground. The air was thick with the sweet, nauseating smell of decay and it turned her stomach. Around her the forest was black and dead. She saw the corpses of animals littering the ground, flocks of birds lying lifeless like gravel thrown on a path.

'Look what you've done!' she yelled at Seth. 'Look at it! Is this what you wanted?'

Seth was listening only to the inner voice. The destruction was so beautiful, and he wanted to see so much more, just like it promised.

This is just the beginning, Seth! Think what you can do to the rest of the world! Imagine the cities you will crush, the civilizations you will rip apart! This is nothing compared to what comes, nothing at all!

Lily tried one last time. 'Seth! You have to listen to me! SETH!'

It wasn't Seth who approached her then and when she saw who did, it was as though her soul was shrivelling up into a dried husk.

'You stay away from me!' Lily yelled as the twins walked towards her from out of the dead forest.

The twins did not alter their course.

'Not like this!' she said, wiping tears from her eyes, the land between her and the twins turning even blacker and more scorched and dead. 'Not like this! I'm worth more than this! Seth, you have to hear me! SETH!'

At last, the twins stopped. Lily backed away, tripped, landed badly and cried out. When she tried to move it was too painful; her ankle had clearly twisted badly in the fall. And now she was at the bottom of a deep hole, its sides muddy and sticky, and the bottom slowly filling with icy water. She was going nowhere, and she knew it.

A deathly silence fell around. It was an unreal quiet, as though the world had been snuffed out like a candle.

Movement. Lily narrowed her eyes to get a better look. She soon wished she hadn't. The twins, sitting astride their skeletal horse, were staring down at her. And between them and Lily, at the top of the hole she was now trapped in, shapes were forming. Evil, twisted shapes spewed out by Hades, clawing after the twins, following their every move, obeying. Death was circling Lily, its eyes wide with lust, its tongues licking its lips in anticipation of the feed just below.

'Seth!' Lily cried out. 'Seth! Don't let this be it! Do something!'

One of the creatures toppled forwards and slipped into the hole. It lunged at Lily, but she caught it with her foot, kicking it hard, sending it sprawling. It came at her again, only to be met once more by a well-aimed foot. It hissed at Lily, who was readying herself for the next attack, doing anything to stay alive just a few more seconds, just a few more.

The creature pounced. Lily caught it round the neck, slammed it into the puddle at the bottom of the hole. It sank under the water, deep into the mud beneath, its face disappearing. It struggled, lashed out, but Lily held it there. Lily had no idea if it was possible to drown such a

thing, but she was going to try.

The creature pushed itself out of the puddle, snarled and caught Lily around the head with a sharp, bony slap. The shock of it smacked Lily into the ground.

The creature leaped again, only this time Lily was ready for it. She caught it again, brought it to the ground, punched it hard. The creature snarled as Lily struck it again.

'Seth!'

Another punch . . .

'Seth! You have to help me! Please!'

Reaching for a rock . . .

'Please, Seth! Remember Beth! Remember your family! Don't let it end like this! You can't!'

Bringing the rock down with skull-crushing force . . .

The creature rolled out of Lily's hand, unmoving. She was exhausted. As close to death as she'd ever been. And judging by the eyes staring at her, she knew she was only moments away from getting even closer.

The dead parted as the Riders edged forward to peer down into the hole at Lily.

'Can none of you hear me? Can none of you see any sense?'

Nothing. No response.

'Is death and destruction so addictive?'

Lily knew the answer to that and, in desperation, she pulled something from a pocket in her jeans and with her

eyes fixed on Seth threw it hard at his head.

'Remember Beth!' Lily yelled as the silver necklace struck home. 'Remember your family! Don't let it end like this! You can't! You just can't! You hear me? You have to! Seth!'

As Seth held the necklace in his hand the whole world shuddered, as if something had crashed into it. Lily was knocked from off her feet and landed hard on her back in the puddle at the bottom of the hole, winding her momentarily, the foul water splashing up and into her mouth, causing her to splutter and cough.

Lily gasped for breath, the creeping cold of the puddle's water seeping through her flesh and into her bones, and watched the sky split and tear as hideous ribbons of flame shot through it to taste the world below, fires starting instantaneously.

Lily wanted to crawl away and hide but there was no hiding from this. Then, just as she thought all hope was lost, she remembered what she had seen on the screen in the house, the odd angle of the satellite, as if it was looking for something, then that strange shadow had fallen across the stars before finally transmission had been lost.

'Planet X,' she breathed. 'Naribu . . .'

Seth wasn't listening. He was staring at the little shell in the palm of his hand. It had meant something to him once, hadn't it? But why? A face slipped across his mind and he had to run to catch up with it. Beth?

Like a tidal wave, memories crashed down on Seth, almost knocking him from his horse. He screamed as they flooded his mind as though they wanted him to drown. He saw himself learning to walk and following his father, copying him, then helping him on stage, then eventually performing as the Apocalypse Boy. He saw his mum caring for him, playing with him, looking after both him and his sister Beth. And he saw Beth staring back at him, love in her eyes, and jealousy too.

Another scream came, ripping itself out of Seth's throat to send a shockwave out from him that flattened the now dead forest to the ground, snapping trunks like matchsticks.

Silence.

Seth looked down at his hand again. The silver shell was covered in his blood from where he'd gripped it so tightly and it had cut into his palm.

'Seth!'

He knew that voice, too. Trusted it. Looked down into the hole at the figure below, barely visible beneath the mud and blood and grime.

'Lily!'

Lily snapped her head up to find Seth staring down at her. His eyes were his again, piercing and keen, not empty and black and disturbed.

The sky shook again, and they both looked up to see the impossible. The other Riders, too, were staring. Whether it was another planet or a meteorite, Seth had no idea, but that it was there at all was enough. It was larger than the moon, perhaps five times its size, and its black surface was laced with ribbons of red that spat fire and lava into space to burn up in the Earth's atmosphere. Where it had come from he couldn't guess. Didn't want to know.

Lily remembered what she had read about the mysterious planet, but none of that mattered here facing it, because now it seemed all that was left was to abandon all hope.

The world was lost.

All would die.

Seth called out to Lily as a memory sparked in his mind. 'I've seen this! When you touched me that first time, Remember?' He pointed at the approaching planet. 'Except I was up there instead of it, or perhaps I was a part of it or something, and I was crashing to Earth!'

'So what?' Lily replied, her voice all but gone, her whole being still wary of the dead eyes staring down at her, and the Riders themselves. 'How does that help us now?'

'It's here because we're here,' Seth said, his mind becoming clearer by the second. 'Our arrival summoned it.'

Seth snatched his eyes round to the others. They were all staring to the heavens, as though waiting for the inevitable.

Then Death's twins spoke, their voices as one. And to Seth they sounded almost excited.

'It comes,' they said.

33

'YOU HAVE TO STOP it, Seth!' Lily called out. 'You have to stop it, all of you!'

No answer came, no response. Just silence.

'Didn't you hear me? I said we have to stop it! Before the very thing we don't want to happen actually does!'

'It's beautiful . . .' said Kelly. 'The colours . . .'

Demetrius was just staring.

The twins had turned from Lily and were also facing the burning, ruined sky.

Lily found a pebble at her feet and launched it at Seth. It caught him on the back of his head.

'Do something!' Lily cried out. 'Now! Before it's too late to even try!'

Seth, head smarting from the stone Lily had just cast,

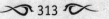

was still gripping tightly Beth's silver shell. Right then, he'd have given anything to go back to his old life in the caravan, to being the Apocalypse Boy, arguing with his parents, getting annoyed with Beth, heading out on stage for another of his shows.

'I don't know how . . .'

'Then think of something!' answered Lily. 'You have to!'

Seth turned his attention from whatever it was heading on a collision course for Earth to the other Riders. He focused, pushed his mind into theirs.

You have to listen to me! Now!

No response. The Riders just kept on staring, as though what was happening was something they didn't want to forget.

I'm speaking to you! Listen! Listen to me!

Still nothing. Seth was growing desperate. The next time he went into their minds, he wasn't so tactful and instead barged in like he was going to try and smash his way out through the other side of their skulls.

Listen! To! Me!

Kelly yelled out in agony and Demetrius screamed. The twins both grabbed their heads and only just managed to stop themselves toppling from the back of their horse.

We have to stop it!

Lily, with the Dead having retreated from the lip of the hole she was in, scrambled to the top. The twins, Kelly and Demetrius were lined up together in a semicircle facing Seth.

'Seth? What's going on?'

Facing the four other Riders, Seth didn't quite know how to answer Lily's question.

'Just stay down,' he answered. 'Please . . .'

He saw Lily slip back into the hole as in front of him the three Riders turned their back on him and started to walk away.

'Hey!'

The Riders kept going, their pace slow and steady and filled with the weight of deadly purpose.

Seth shouted for them all by name. Got nothing back. Then reached out for their minds, casting himself out to them like a hook on the end of a fisherman's line. When that didn't work, all he had left was his bow.

Seth pulled an arrow from the quiver on his back, clipping it to the bowstring. He wasn't going to knock them from their horses, but he did want to scare them into stopping so that he could talk to them.

Lifting the bow to his cheekbone, Seth took aim, let the arrow fly. It sang through the silent night air, which still hung heavy with the blackened, smouldering smell of battle and death, sped between the Riders and, just ahead of them, ruptured the earth with a wall of flame and heat.

The Riders stopped, turned, faced Seth.

'Got your attention,' Seth said.

Kelly trotted forwards.

'This is who we are, Seth. We can't go back. Not now. There's nothing to go back to.'

'You can and we have to,' Seth replied. 'You can see that, can't you, Kelly?'

'What if we don't want to go back?' Demetrius called out. 'This is the way it's meant to be, Seth. Fighting it is futile.'

'No, it isn't!' answered Seth. 'We always have a—'

His words were cut short as Kelly swung her sword, slicing the air between them, and sending a shockwave towards Seth that hammered into him with all the tact of a runaway train. The force of it launched Seth from the back of his horse, high into the air, to land in a pile of ash and wood and bone.

'We have no choice in this!' Demetrius called out as Seth rose to his feet, amazed his back wasn't broken.

Seth wasn't about to give up and let loose another arrow. This time, though, the twins raised a hand and the arrow dropped from the sky like a bird shot dead.

'You can't fight us,' Kelly called out to Seth.

Seth drew an arrow back once more, only this time when he let it loose, it was swamped by a thick cloud of insects. When the swarm returned to cloud around Demetrius, all that remained of the arrow was its evil-looking, razor-sharp head, still on the ground.

'You'll have to kill us to stop us,' Demetrius shouted out.

Seth released another arrow. This one sped towards the other Riders, only it was aimed directly at Kelly. With lightning reactions she swatted the thing from the air, but she had been so focused on the one arrow, she hadn't spotted the other so quickly sent by Seth to follow the first.

The second arrow thunked hard into Kelly's shoulder, spinning her from her horse. She fell hard to the ground, yelling out.

'Don't call my bluff!' Seth shouted out. 'Now we speak!'

As he'd suspected, seeing Kelly fall had weakened the minds of Demetrius and the twins. Entering this time was easier than he could have imagined. And in moments he'd found just the memories he needed to get them to see his point of view. Not knowing how he was doing it, but doing it none the less, Seth pulled those memories free, forced them to the front of their minds. Images of family, of friends. Moments of shared happiness, love, laughter. Moments of hope. And in those seconds of weakness, Seth pulled them back to him.

'Seth . . .'

It was Kelly. Her hair was lank, her clothes in ruins, and her eyes were sunk into the back her skull behind dark rings of exhaustion. 'You . . . shot me . . .'

'I had to get your attention,' Seth apologized. 'We have to stop this. All of it. It's our choice!'

'Too hard,' said Demetrius, shaking his head as though

trying to knock something loose. 'I can't . . .'

'We have to and we must!' said Seth. 'We're all the hope that's left.'

The twins pointed towards the approaching ball of fire. 'There is no hope in the face of that. No hope at all.'

'You're wrong,' said Seth, shaking his head, pursing his lips. 'We were sent to destroy a planet, right? Well, who's to say which planet we decide to destroy?'

Realization cast itself across the others like a net thrown on to water.

'But we're here, not there,' said Demetrius. 'We can't . . .'

Seth gripped his hand harder so that Beth's shell bit into his skin once more, again drawing blood.

'Not alone, but together,' he said. 'We have to at least try!'

The sky shook once more and the ground beneath them cracked. The horses, unconcerned, simply dodged out of its way. Kelly, despite the arrow jutting out of her shoulder, climbed back on to her own horse.

Seth placed an arrow to his bow and made to take aim.

'It's not like we've anything to lose, is it?' he said, then let the bow string loose and the arrow fly.

The arrow turned to flame and raced up and up. But no sooner had it been released than Seth had another strung, then another and another, until his hand was little more than a blur and the sky between him and the approaching doom lit with a deadly fire. And to it was joined Kelly's voice, which sung out high and pure and sharp, then wrenched itself down the blade of her sword to not just chase after Seth's arrows but mingle with them, twisting them into a maelstrom of awful burning destruction. Yet still it was not enough as Demetrius called forth a vast cloud, a billion insects whipped and pulled skywards, their colossal weight growing and growing as more and more joined in, their armour welding together and soon forming an impenetrable core at the centre of the spinning vortex created by Seth and Holly. Then finally, quietly, the twins joined in and from them the thick, suffocating shadow of death reached out its fingers. When it finally grabbed hold of the vortex, it was as though cloth had been caught in a spinning wheel, and it ripped from them at an awful speed, wrapping itself round the stream of destruction flowing out from the other Riders like liquid fire from a flame-thrower.

Lily could not draw her eyes away as she watched, not until the moment of impact. And then she had no choice.

The sky exploded. A light so bright and vast it smashed its way around the world, ripping through and into everything, and it was then that Lily turned away, throwing herself to the ground, diving beneath the cold, mucky water at her feet, shielding herself from the blinding flash that seemed capable of deleting all colour from existence.

Then it faded, like the sun dipping over the horizon, and a stillness returned to the world.

Breathing . . .

It was the first thing that Seth noticed. Not just that he was, but that he could hear others doing it close by. Opening his eyes, he discovered that he was no longer astride his horse, but lying prone on the ground which was steaming and in places aflame. Everywhere was black or grey, as if the world had been recreated as a picture drawn simply of charcoal on white paper. The sky was hidden behind drifting veils of smoke and ash.

A name came to him.

Lily . . .

Movement, just away to his left, and a head with cropped black hair raised itself and smiled. It was smeared with mud, almost unrecognizable.

Seth waved weakly.

'You OK?'

'I'm not sure I'll be able to use that word to describe how I feel ever again,' said Lily, sitting up now and vainly attempting to clean herself down.

Seth caught other movement then and saw Kelly, Demetrius and the twins rising on to their elbows, pushing themselves up from the ground to sit and stare, bewildered, at all that lay around them. Seth's arrow was still rammed through Kelly's shoulder, her clothes stained with blood.

'You're going to need to see a doctor about that,' said Seth.

'I don't really remember it happening,' said Kelly, wincing in pain. 'It's like a dream.'

'Probably best it stays that way,' said Demetrius, holding his head as though he was expecting it to explode into a thousand pieces at any moment.

The twins, without a word, stood up, and, like statues, stared out towards the hidden sky side by side. Silent.

Seth was aware of the grimy darkness around them and he joined the twins staring up through the drifting smoke to catch a glimpse of the night's blackness he knew lay somewhere above. It was as though, were he able to glimpse the night again, it would be a sign of something. Whether it was hope or just relief he wasn't sure, but he kept on staring for a while longer.

With the smoke still hanging about them like a death shroud over the Earth, Seth drew his eyes away and sat himself up. Every movement felt as though each bone in his body had been snapped in two. But it wasn't just his body, but his mind that had suffered. The visions, the destruction, the death, it was all still there, staining his memory like old blood. And the sorrow at the loss of his family pushed its way to the front of his mind, causing him to choke back a cry. It wasn't something he could ignore and he knew that if he tried to it would jump out on him like a devil hiding in the dark.

Lily crawled over slowly and reached out to squeeze his hand to get his attention. Kelly and Demetrius stood and walked over, slumping down next to them, exhausted. Still the twins stood apart and alone.

'The Protector's dead,' said Kelly. 'That much I do remember clearly.'

'Everything's changed,' said Lily. 'It's not as though everyone can just go back and pretend everything's normal, is it? That's just impossible. The world went crazy. Nearly came to an end.'

'Because of us,' said Seth.

Everyone fell quiet for a moment, as though the enormity of what could have been had killed all possibility of further discussion.

Eventually, Seth found the strength to speak again. 'So, what now?' he said, forcing himself to ignore the horrors desperate to claw at him and send him mad. He repeated Lily's question, almost as though he was using it to nail him to the moment, to stop himself falling back into everything that had happened these past few days.

Lily didn't respond, just waited.

'Well, I guess it's up to us, isn't it?' Seth said finally.

'Free will?' said Lily.

Seth nodded.

'Maybe people will start to think again, now that The Protector's not breathing down their necks,' said Lily. 'Maybe.'

'Or maybe they'll just go back to their old ways?' said Kelly. 'Slip back because it's easy.'

The others stared at her and she held up her hands in defence.

'I'm just saying, that's all,' she said. 'It's not like humanity's got a reputation for doing the right thing, has it? We see an easy path, we take it.'

'There's a third option,' said Demetrius. 'One none of us has considered yet.'

Seth leaned in. 'What?'

'That this is just the beginning,' said Demetrius, casting a hand at the ruined world around them.

At that moment, the thick, acrid smog shifted, twisting and swirling like oil on water, and a gap opened above them, clearing swiftly to reveal a window to the sky above. Seth stared. The pitch-black night, so stark against the grey fog, was filled with the distant twinkle of diamonds, the blinking eyes of planets light years away staring down at a world that had survived against all the odds. Seth wondered for a moment if they were glaring, rather than staring, annoyed to see that the Earth had scraped through something they all thought it fully deserved, had perhaps even wished down upon it somehow.

'It's a clear sky,' said Seth and became aware of something in hand. 'No clouds. Nothing. Just stars. Millions of them.'

The others looked up to the sky as Seth opened his hand to see Beth's silver shell.

Without a word, Lily lifted it from his palm and

slipped it round his neck.

'Suits you,' she said.

Seth was about to say something when his pocket buzzed. Reaching round he pulled out his phone and punched a button to light up the screen. With a disbelieving smile, he shook his head.

'What is it?' asked Lily, half amazed that Seth's phone not only still had charge, but was able to get any signal in the first place. 'What does it say?'

Seth looked at the screen and Demetrius and Kelly listened in. Even the twins turned an ear.

When Seth next spoke, a faint smile slowly smoothing away the lines of stress across his face, his voice was calm and at peace.

'*Then I saw a new heaven and a new Earth, for the first heaven and the first Earth had passed away.*'

Above them, the stars shone ever brighter.

AUTHOR NOTE

The first ever mention of *Doom Rider* was in an email I sent through to my editor, the quite brilliant Naomi, in January 2011. It was little more than an aside to something else I was developing, and went like this: 'I've also been dreaming up something about a boy who discovers he's one of the four riders of the apocalypse . . . And he's lived a 1000 lifetimes and been killed before reaching his 13th birthday in each one. But now . . .' Two months later, with my original idea ditched, *Doom Rider* took over.

I've always been fascinated by the imagery associated with the four riders of the apocalypse, and I have no doubt that growing up in the church has something to do with that. Not that my dad was all hellfire and brimstone, but the Bible really is jam-packed with astonishing, and sometimes exceptionally dark, imagery.

I knew from the start that I didn't want it to be a humorous story. For it to work, and for me to enjoy writing it, it had to be a dark book that dealt with religion, by which I mean not just the big four, but belief in all its possible incantations, as well as the notion of destiny, and how freedom and free choice would clash with it. After all, in many ways a teenager is the very essence of wanting to be free. And I figured that, if my lead character discovered his future had already been chosen, he might be a little bit miffed.

I decided not to use the generally accepted interpretation of the four riders of the apocalypse: War, Famine, Pestilence and Death. Instead, I went with a more literal translation of the biblical text: Conquest, Strife, Famine and (obviously) Death. This gave me something new to play with, as well as a fair few headaches. It also enabled me to provide you, the reader, with something a little bit different in the reading. That, above all, was my aim. And I hope, in the end, that I in some small way achieved it.